ADVERSE POSSESSION

ADVERSE POSSESSION

JUDGE, JURY, & EXECUTIONER™ BOOK TEN

CRAIG MARTELLE

MICHAEL ANDERLE

DISRUPTIVE IMAGINATION

LMBPN Publishing
PMB 196, 2540 South Maryland Pkwy
Las Vegas, NV 89109

First US edition, September, 2020
ebook ISBN: 978-1-64971-140-3
Print ISBN: 978-1-64971-141-0

THE ADVERSE POSSESSION TEAM

Thanks to our Beta Readers

Micky Cocker, James Caplan, Kelly O'Donnell, and John Ashmore

Thanks to the JIT Readers

Dave Hicks
Diane L. Smith
Veronica Stephan-Miller
Dorothy Lloyd
Jeff Goode
John Ashmore
Misty Roa
Peter Manis
Kelly O'Donnell
Jackey Hankard-Brodie
Rachel Beckford
James Caplan
Larry Omans

If I've missed anyone, please let me know!

Editor
Lynne Stiegler

We can't write without those who support us
On the home front, we thank you for being there for us

We wouldn't be able to do this for a living if it weren't for our readers
We thank you for reading our books

CHAPTER ONE

Federation Station 7, All Guns Blazing, a Terry Henry Walton Franchise

"Is this where we meet now?" Grainger wondered.

"Magistrates eat for free," Rivka replied.

"Thanks to you."

Rivka shrugged. "All in a day's work. Terry Henry likes me, and the AIs running my ship can get us here without delay."

"How many are there?"

Rivka snorted humorlessly. "*Wyatt Earp* has become the island of lost toys. I think we're up to nine on board. Chaz has deferred, leaving the flying to Dennicron and Clevarious. Erasmus is maintaining a digital brig, with Bluto and Cain incarcerated. I think he has three more AIs in residence, working for the embassy."

"What's Chaz doing if he's not flying the ship?"

Rivka didn't want to elaborate because she knew how Grainger would react. Her delay gave him the answer.

"No!" Grainger shook his head, snorting like a bull. "He

is *not* going to be an investigator, and heaven forbid, a fellow Magistrate. He needs to be able to kick people in the face for that."

"He knows the law better than you. And face-kicking? Why not eye-gouging, thumb-screwing, or atomic elbow drops?"

"How about nut-slapping, bamboo shoots under the fingernails, and probably the most important, a *body*?" Grainger countered.

"He's in training for now. We will judge his future based on his abilities. Only his abilities. Magistrate Chazmeister. I like the ring of that." Rivka smiled and leaned back to allow the server to drop off two massive pizzas that covered the table between her and Grainger. "Erasmus and the Singularity have engineered the purchase of an android fabrication facility. Pretty soon, AIs will have total independent mobility. You'll want to be ready for it."

"What if I'm not?"

"The freight train has left the space station, as much as you might wish it hadn't." Rivka helped herself and ate quickly, despite the heat of the melted cheese. "I have stock in the android enterprise. Turns out, I'm the only human investor. I learned that I don't spend anywhere near as much as I make."

"You're going to make money off AIs getting android bodies?" Grainger started to eat, grappling with the magnitude of standing in the open with the AI freighter bearing down on him.

"Point of order, Magistrate: *buying* android bodies. And so what? You're not going to tell me you didn't know this was coming."

"It's not the AIs. They make our lives possible. The reason I remain hesitant is that it has created more work, and as you well know, deep down inside, I'm a lazy bastard."

"The truth bomb falls!" Rivka reached over her moon-stokle pie to take two slices from Grainger's ten-meat pizza.

Grainger slapped Rivka's hand, but it was too late. "Don't you have a boyfriend to annoy?"

"A *colleague* who is bringing charity dental care to the far reaches of the galaxy."

"Tomato, to-*mah*-toe. He's on your ship now, isn't he?"

"He categorically is not on *Wyatt Earp* right now. He's on his way to the table to join us for lunch. Be nice and share your pie."

"Fuck off! Share *your* pie, or order another one." Grainger hunched over his food, surrounding it with his arms like a petulant twelve-year-old.

Doctor Tyler Toofakre waved at the two Magistrates. Rivka slid over to make room, trying to look inconspicuous while moving her food within her sphere of control.

"Don't worry, I'm not after your nasty-ass moonstokle nastiness." He chuckled while he sat and waved to the server. "I'll order what he's having."

"I knew there was something I liked about you," Grainger said through a mouthful of meat and cheese. He caught a trickle of sauce with his napkin as it threatened to fall from his chin.

Tyler turned to Rivka and took her hand. "Where are we going next?"

"We haven't gotten to that part. Grainger has to play

Twenty Questions before giving me my assignment. He likes to make me think I have a choice in the cases I take when I know I don't. I play along because otherwise there would be a massive void in his life, a black hole where fun used to be."

Grainger chewed slowly, finally swallowing and dabbing the corners of his mouth with his napkin. "You have a choice. There is no fun void in my life. I'm all kinds of fun. And moonstokle pizza is disgusting."

"Why you gotta be so hurtful with your words?" Rivka asked calmly before depositing a slice of her pizza on his tray.

"Where are the plates?" Tyler asked. The Magistrates looked down at the table. They were both eating from the serving trays. They shrugged and returned to their fine dining.

After Tyler's food arrived and he joined the AGB dining experience, Grainger leaned back, not full, but temporarily sated. "I've heard that adverse possession is nine-tenths of the law," he said casually, looking through the long, clear window, the signature in every All-Guns Blazing franchise.

"Is that supposed to be funny?" Rivka didn't follow his line of thought.

"It's the foundation of truth. Possessing a thing, especially over a long period, waters down an original owner's claim. The Federation prefers useful ownership as opposed to simply ownership on paper. Nine-tenths. Maybe more."

"Are you talking about Rorke's Drift? That's a whole planet."

"Does scope matter?"

"Isn't that the billion-credit question?" Rivka looked at

the scraps remaining on her tray. She needed to work out to earn the right to continue eating fearlessly. Nanocytes would keep her trim, but mentally, she felt like she was overindulging. "Does utility wrest real property from a rightful owner who has not taken advantage? This is a slippery slope."

"That's why I'm putting my best man on it."

Rivka gave Grainger the hairy eyeball. "I'm no man."

Tyler smiled behind his ten-meat abomination. Grainger couldn't help but laugh. "The High Chancellor said to send you because if this doesn't get resolved, there's going to be a shooting war."

"Transfer the files to me, please." She sighed and peered out the window, contemplating the vastness of space. "As big as it is, we still find ways to fight over it."

"I sent them before we started lunch. I'm glad you're not a slave to your datapad." Grainger turned to the dentist. "There you go, Doc. Rorke's Drift is where you're headed. A settler planet. Agriculture or mining? Rivka gets to resolve that little bit of friction before returning to the regular grind."

"No serial killers? No mob bosses or machines running amok? You mean, I might not have to patch people up?"

Grainger and Rivka made faces at each other. "Let's not speculate like crazy people. Look at who we're talking about." Grainger gestured toward Rivka with his chin.

"Those weren't my fault." She resumed looking out the window. "Another case about property. Occupiers versus owners. How hard could it be?" *Once I wrangle the crew back on board, that is.*

. . .

5

Landing Pad, Azfelius, the Faerie Planet

Red and Lindy waved from the hatch of the space yacht before the door closed and lifted off. Two people waved in reply, left behind but not alone.

"Welcome to Azfelius," Groenwyn said, one-arm-hugging Cordelia Dawn Walton. Groenwyn turned Cory to face the glory of the planet's growth. Together, they watched the dancing lights approach.

Groenwyn bowed as the light solidified and became creatures hovering on nearly transparent wings. Cory followed suit, bending with her eyes lifted upward to watch. They straightened up after their greeting, struggling against the planet's heavier gravity.

"Say hello to the inhabitants of Azfelius, the Faeries." Groenwyn reached up as a small child would. Two Faeries swept in and lifted her into the air by the arms. Two more arrived. Cory, fascinated, raised her arms as well, and was rewarded by being carried away. As the jungle swept beneath her, the Faeries' gentle grip comforted and steadied her. She knew she would not fall.

They approached a glade with a small pond, where the Faeries deposited Groenwyn and Cory without saying a word. The four flew away. Cory remained mesmerized. Groenwyn stooped to get a drink of the fresh water.

The young woman, her platinum-green hair glittering, pointed at the pond. "Try it. You'll taste nothing else like it."

"Will we not be talking with the Faeries?"

"This is a meditation retreat," Groenwyn advised, kneeling to take another drink. "Refresh yourself. There is fruit here too, the sweetest you've ever tasted."

Cory dipped her hand into the cool, clear water and

sipped casually, opting to sit on the grass. She let her head fall back while smiling at the sky above.

"Do you feel it?" Groenwyn asked.

"The calm and the joy of life?" Cory didn't have to look at Groenwyn to confirm her statement. It wasn't a guess. "Ultimate peace."

"We'll wait for Siro'ti'lc, the Meditator of her clan. It's a volunteer leadership position that none of them wants since it detracts from their day-to-day lives."

Cory laid back and closed her eyes. The dreams arrived quickly, wrapping her in a warm blanket. There was no hurry here, for time held no meaning. Groenwyn reclined and soon drifted off as well.

The music of a crystalline waterfall tickled their senses. Both women slowly opened their eyes to find a Faerie standing in the glade, watching over them.

I trust you slept well.

"I did, thank you," Cory replied, sitting up before bowing. "I believe Azfelius is the answer to many questions."

Groenwyn bowed too. "Thank you, Siro'ti'lc, for granting our request to enter your peace. Is your crystalline icon *Infinity* being faithfully shared?"

It is, Groenwyn. Thank you for your concern. The clans remain faithful to the agreement you brokered. The Faerie Meditator lifted into the air. *Cordelia Dawn, it is our pleasure that you have come. I suggest that Azfelius is not an answer in and of itself. The answers always come from within.*

"Inner peace. Aptly named. If I may ask, what is next?"

A question humanity constantly asks that keeps them reaching for the stars.

"I understand. It doesn't seem to matter as much as the question, 'Am I getting the most I can from this moment?'"

A categorically better question. And where can you find that answer?

Cory smiled and closed her eyes to help her better see what she was there to see.

Red's Yacht, Winging Its Way to the Venus Pleasure Moon

"We should probably have stayed with them, just to make sure they were okay." Lindy kneaded Red's massive shoulders.

"The Faerie planet is one of the safest places in the galaxy. Safer than where we're going."

"There's something wrong with that. This is our honeymoon."

"And I would prefer not to spend it watching people meditate. However, I'll do what you want because you put up with my shit the rest of the time."

Lindy slid around him and straddled the big man, wrapping her arms around his neck. "It's not that rough, but if I get bonus points out of it somehow, then yeah, you owe me." She kissed his face and neck. He leaned back to enjoy it. "I guess we'll go to the pleasure moon. I don't think I'd like watching people meditate."

"Swimming and peace and quiet." Red's hands crept across Lindy's body. "How long before we get there?"

"I don't know." Lindy jumped up. "Aren't you the one flying this thing?"

Red shook his head and pulled her back down. "We

picked up a hitchhiker who is flying it for us. She's between gigs, or so I've heard. Margaret, are you there?"

"Where else would I be?" a feminine voice replied. "And for the record, you're the hitchhikers. I've been with this ship for quite some time."

Lindy hadn't spent any time in the yacht. Every time they had tried to get away, something had come up. Finally, the Magistrate had chased them off the *Wyatt Earp* to squeeze in their honeymoon.

"How long until we arrive on Venus, Margaret?"

"Under an hour. The Gate drive, a gift from that little guy with the big head, has made travel almost instantaneous no matter where we want to go."

Red laughed. "You never play jokes on someone you don't like." He jabbed his thumb into his chest. "I knew he liked me."

"Ankh specifically stated that if it weren't for Mrs. Vered, we would not have received the drive and the upgraded power source."

"Mrs. Vered." Lindy rolled the name around on her tongue. "Does that make you Mr. Lindy?"

"Never gave it much thought." Red stroked his chin. "I find myself indifferent to it. Odd. I thought I would have deeper feelings one way or another. Guess not."

"Are you messing with me?" Lindy punched him in the chest.

"Whatever it takes to keep you happy, that's what I'll do. I know I can be a challenge. Well, on rare occasions. The rest of the time, I'm the cat's meow. But not Wenceslaus. That cat hates me. More like Floyd. She likes me."

"Floyd likes everybody." Lindy tapped the pilot's control

panel. "Thanks, Margaret." She climbed off Red's lap. "We'll crack some champagne and get this party started."

They retired to the small lounge behind the pilot's chair, where a single padded bench seat pulled out into a bed. A panel in the bulkhead contained the refrigerator in which they had stuffed the bottle of champagne from their wedding day. Red looked for glasses, but there was only one, a standard drinking glass.

"Are you sure you want to pop that?" Red asked, waving the single glass.

"What defines our relationship better than making do with what's on hand?"

"A fitting tribute indeed. Pour on."

Lindy muscled the cork from the bottle, and it yielded with a satisfying pop. Red stuffed the glass beneath it to keep any from spilling. Lindy poured it full, then clinked the glass with the bottle. Red saluted with the glass and took a healthy swallow. Lindy tipped the bottle back, drinking straight from it. Letting the bubbles tickle on the way down, they made faces at each other.

"Better than we deserve," Red offered. "That's really good."

Lindy held up the bottle. "Binlow '47, an expensive bottle. We'll thank the Magistrate when we get back with a handwritten note."

Red patted the seat next to him. "Can't we just transmit one? Margaret can take care of it."

"No." Lindy chuckled and took another drink as she stared out the yacht's front screen. "What are we doing, Red? I mean, how are we contributing to the team besides being the muscle?"

Red flexed his massive bicep, doing a curl with the champagne glass to finish what he had before gesturing for a refill. "She listens to us. That's more than I've had before."

"Are we telling her the right things?"

Red scowled while looking at the bulkhead. "That's a hard question and probably one for the Magistrate. Is this going to be our pillow talk during our honeymoon?"

"Not all of it, but we don't usually get a chance to talk about this stuff, just you and I. This is our chance to decide what better looks like, and what we need to do to realize it."

"What if I'm drunk?"

"You're not going to get drunk on half a bottle of champagne, or twelve for that matter." Lindy slammed the remainder of the bottle, then put the empty on the table and slowly licked her lips. "If we do manage to acquire a buzz by switching to pounding the hard stuff, we'll limit ourselves to physical pursuits over mental ones."

"I like the way you think." Red finished his refill. "That's still a tough question. With Chaz and Sahved coming along, we don't need more investigators. I think what we need is better leverage. What is the right way to coerce each person, should that be called for, without making the Magistrate touch them? You can see how it wears on her."

"I wouldn't want to know what people are thinking. I'm sure it's a horror show inside their minds."

Red laughed. "I have nothing to hide, but she recoils from what I'm thinking. It's usually about you, by the way. We don't walk around inside-out, but that's the world she sees. I don't envy her. So the question we must answer whilst enjoying a week in each other's arms is, how do we reduce her burden of seeing what it hurts her to see?"

"I guess we have our homework during our honeymoon. You can take the lovers out of the job, but you can't take the job out of the lovers"

"Loyalty. She has mine without question. Yours, too. The challenge would be if I was put in a position to decide. You or her."

"Then we have to make sure we don't get put in that position because I think we would all die as we tried to save both."

"I agree since I would hate myself no matter which decision I made." Red blew out his breath. "Don't let yourself get caught."

"I have no intention." Lindy stood to see the yacht was on final approach. "I can't wait to try on my new bikini."

"Well, now. That will require no talking whatsoever. I hope I brought my swimsuit."

"They're not required here. You can swim however you want."

"Well, now," Red repeated, but he stopped, screwed his face up, and thought hard before coming up with the rest. "I'm not walking around with my dong hanging out."

Lindy covered her eyes with her hand and slowly shook her head.

"I have no say in this, and being the only man on the Magistrate's crew, I feel that's the right answer."

"We have Ankh and Sahved and Cole."

Red raised one eyebrow. "I keep forgetting Cole's on the crew. We need to rope him into the security conversations if his woman ever lets him off maintenance duty." Red stood and grabbed a small gym bag with his stuff. Lindy rolled a stylish suitcase out of the closet. "Where'd you get that?"

"His woman." Lindy imitated Red's voice before clearing her throat. "They had to stay on board to see to Ankh's upgrades."

Red changed gears. "No one wanted to mess with *Wyatt Earp* before, but with the latest upgrades? We'll be a full-on battle cruiser."

"We have to keep the embassy and the ambassadors safe."

"It's nice to have a significant advantage in shields and firepower. It also helps us secure the Magistrate." The yacht touched down and the hatch popped. "Thanks, Margaret!"

"Have fun, you crazy kids. Don't do anything I wouldn't do," the AI replied.

Red and Lindy looked at each other and shrugged before heading out. The ship took off after they cleared the area to move to longer-term parking, where it wasn't the only yacht vying for space.

A concierge met them at the end of the red carpet, well before they entered the building.

"I'll take your luggage up to your room. Please stop by the front desk for refreshments and your welcome package."

Red looked at his bag. Lindy delivered the handle of hers into the alien's waiting hand. Red stood there as Lindy continued walking.

"This is my stuff."

"I will take care of it as if it were my own, standing guard over it if you wish until you arrive."

Red forced a laugh. "Nah. That sounds crazy. I'll carry it myself." He hurried to catch up to his wife.

The doors opened automatically upon her approach. She looked back to see Red still carrying his bag. She pursed her lips and crossed her arms. He stopped. Lindy walked back, took the bag from him, and handed it to the concierge. She gripped Red's hand and delivered her best smile.

"Did you see the other boats on the landing pad? This is not a dive. They'll take care of your stuff. It is safe. *We're* safe. It's time to relax." She draped her arms around his neck. Red's face contorted through a range of emotions while the concierge slipped past them and disappeared inside. "What's bothering you?"

"I wish I could put my finger on it. I feel like I've left something undone."

"Let's check in and see what there is to see. Maybe it'll come to you."

Red nodded, tight-lipped. They held hands on their way through iridescent arches with fountains that sent multi-colored waves over the guests, creating a living tunnel. At the desk, a smiling green-skinned receptionist met them.

"Vered and Lindy? Welcome to Venus. You have been upgraded from your original reservation to the honeymoon suite. Congratulations on your marriage!" Her bubbly personality served her well. Red started to relax, and Lindy winked at the young woman.

She offered them sparkling fruit juice. Lindy and Red

clinked real glasses and drank. "Tastes like that stuff from Xynite."

"My! You are the only guests who know where we import this beverage from. Our parent company has an exclusive contract with the Xynitians. How exciting! Is their planet as wonderful as this juice suggests?"

Red and Lindy had not had to kill anyone on Xynite, which was a fairly high bar when it came to the Magistrate and her work. Lindy delivered their answer. "It was pleasant. The city merged with nature to create a vibrant and living planet. Invigorating, just like the juice."

She didn't mention the narcotic effects, but vacation meant different things to different people.

"You'll have a personal android within your suite, dedicated to mixing and serving whatever beverages you'd like."

"We'll have a what?" Red asked, instantly alert.

"Non-intrusive. You won't see the android unless you call for it. You will have absolute privacy. We guarantee that."

Red wasn't sure.

The Torregidorian registered Lindy's and Red's handprints and faces for access throughout the resort. "You will receive every courtesy for the duration of your stay. We have you for a week. At the end, you'll have no idea where the time went. That is our mission."

"We thank you," Lindy replied before departing the counter on their way to the room. The concierge was waiting for them with their bags. He didn't want Red to feel uncomfortable by letting his small bag out of his sight.

"Please, follow me."

They walked through the art gallery as Lindy stopped and pointed to various objects. Red didn't see the allure of the display. He'd seen billion-credit art, and that hadn't done it for him either, but he knew Lindy liked looking, so he waited patiently as she explored. The scent wafting through the air reminded him of spring flowers on his home planet. He couldn't remember what they were called.

Red sidled up next to the concierge. "I like a more active engagement," he started.

The concierge replied, "We have the latest in pleasure bots. Give me your specifications, and I'll have one or more sent to your room."

"What are you talking about?" Red pointed at Lindy. "All I can handle is right there. I'm talking about guns. Do you have a shooting range?"

"Of course. Would you like me to arrange a time for you?"

"Yeah. Let's do tomorrow after breakfast."

"Ten local it is. I'll make sure a reminder is sent to your room. Meet the shuttle in the lobby, and it will take you to the range. We have a wide variety of weaponry to explore."

Red grinned. "Now that sounds like my kind of vacation!"

Lindy appeared and looked down her nose at him. "Did I hear that we'll be going to a firing range? On *my* honeymoon?" There was no room for misunderstanding.

Red looked appropriately chastised before she started to laugh.

"I'm first on the line," Lindy declared.

The concierge took them past the common elevators to a private space at the end of the corridor, where a door opened to a private elevator. It took them to the top floor, where they entered directly into their suite. Red looked around, confused. There had been no buttons, and no one had spoken to give it directions.

"The downstairs door is keyed to you, and the elevator is exclusive for the honeymoon suite. No one else will accidentally show up in your room." He deposited their bags and disappeared into the elevator.

A panoramic view greeted them through the two-hundred-and-seventy-degree windows lining the walls of the round room. Two fireplaces burned, with overstuffed seating scattered throughout the area. A large bedroom took up the last quarter of the room, including a massive bed with posts, curtains, and mirrors.

"This could be the strangest room I've ever seen." Red walked around, trying to get his bearings. Outside, the resort sprawled into the distance, a checkerboard of different environments to explore and relax within. There were too many for just a week. The bar contained a cornucopia display of beverages. A door behind it opened when Red leaned on the bar.

Their personal android appeared. Looking more robot than humanoid, it asked the perfect question. "What would you like to drink?"

"AGB dark," Red replied.

Lindy leaned over his shoulder. "Red wine, please. Fruity and lightly sweet."

"Sweet, just like me." Red pulled her tight against him while they waited for their drinks. In no time, the drinks appeared on the bar and the android politely excused itself, disappearing through the door behind the bar. They toasted, drank a sip, and retired to the couch facing the mountainside.

Red admired the chocolate caramel look of his beer, holding it up to the sun to assess its opaqueness.

"Do you still feel like you're forgetting something?" Lindy asked.

"For a couple years now, the entirety of my existence has been to keep the Magistrate safe. She's moving up in the universe." Red looked at the floor. "I think it's the fear of missing out. I don't want us to get left behind."

Lindy shook her head slowly and got up to kiss Red on his forehead. *Margaret, are you there? Can you connect us to Rivka, please?*

I live to serve, came the snarky reply. *Connecting you now.*

What's wrong? Rivka asked, semi-panicked.

We're here on our honeymoon, and someone is being a wet blanket because he feels like he's missing out on doing something for you, or you will get used to him not being there.

Red, I'm only going to say this one time. Listen to Lindy. That was the extent of her advice. Red narrowed his eyes as he estimated the extent of the female conspiracy.

But you're moving up. The High Chancellor doesn't have a bodyguard—

Because the High Chancellor chooses not to. You've seen me in action, and for some unholy reason, perps love shooting at me. I can't imagine going anywhere without you both. Which reminds me, when are you getting back?

Lindy answered, *We just got here, Magistrate. Do you need us back early? This place is pretty righteous, and we haven't even broken it in yet.*

Ack! No. Don't tell me anymore. We do have our next assign-

ment, *Rorke's Drift.* Settlers have staked claims, and the planet's owners finally showed up, ready to mine the resources.

Kick the settlers off. Easy day, Red replied.

They've been there for three generations, which means nothing needs to get done today. I've filed an injunction against mining activity until I get there, so that will hold them. Let me know when you're ready to leave Venus, and we'll meet you at Rorke's Drift. I'll make sure Margaret knows the coordinates. Now, stop thinking about me and enjoy your honeymoon. It's been a long time coming.

Did you upgrade us? Lindy wondered.

I thought I heard Ankh talking about it. Gotta run. See you in a week. Rivka signed off before they could ask another question.

"And you're worried that she is going to stop appreciating you?"

Red smiled. "That's why I need you. Keep me on the straight and narrow."

"Computer, show us the entry on Rorke's Drift, please." Lindy snuggled next to Red, sipping her wine while she waited for the system to respond.

The curtains dropped over the window before them, and a screen descended and lit up with the information.

They read for a while. Red finished his beer and rubbed his stomach. "Where can we get a good bistok steak?"

The screen brought up the Western Grille's menu and a voice spoke. "Would you like reservations?"

"Sure!" Red looked at Lindy, who nodded vigorously. "How soon are they open?"

"They are open now. If you leave this moment, it will take you thirty minutes to get there if you take a casual stroll through the gardens. A shuttle can have you there in five minutes." A map appeared, showing them the way.

"Make it for an hour from now." Red lifted Lindy into the air as he stood. "Shower time. I think we have unlimited water."

"The little things people who don't live on spaceships take for granted." Lindy stripped, tossing her clothes haphazardly on the floor as she walked across the room. Red stopped by the bar for a shower beer. The dark cloud that had been hanging over his head was gone. He and Lindy would be back on the mission when the time was right.

He couldn't see spending all seven days being pampered. He expected Lindy would get antsy too since lazing around wasn't their thing. He wondered briefly what kinds of weapons they maintained on the range, but forgot all about that when he saw Lindy in the shower, wetting her hair.

CHAPTER TWO

Federation Station 7, Delta Landing Bay

"What are you doing to my ship?" Rivka clenched her fists and glared at the antennae, rods, and barrels that made *Wyatt Earp* look more like a bristle brush than a heavy frigate.

The construction foreman strolled over, casually pulled up the work order, and showed Rivka. "Is this your signature, ma'am?"

She sheepishly replied, "Yes."

He pointed at the ship. "That's for all this." He walked away to direct yet another crane into position.

Tyler laughed. "Don't tell me a lawyer signed something without reading it. You're killing me." He slapped his leg in his mirth.

"I skimmed it. Like I had a choice. Ankh prepared that work order. It was going to happen one way or another. But look at my ship!"

"I am looking. What's this stuff do?"

"Let's find out."

The dentist wrinkled his nose at the heavy scent of ozone from multiple welding bots working simultaneously. They shielded their eyes from the arcs and sparks on their way to the ramp and into the ship. Rivka took a hard left once through the airlock on her way to the engine room, which was where Ankh maintained his lab. It also acted as the embassy. She discovered, much to her chagrin, that the hatch now had a biometric lock, and she didn't have access.

To the engine room. On her own ship.

Ankh, let me in, please. She did her best to remain calm. *Chaz, please let me into the engine room.*

Oooh, Chaz started. *The Singularity is controlling access because of the delicate nature of embassy operations.*

Rivka switched to her outside voice. "Chaz. I need to be able to go anywhere on my ship."

"Arguably, yes, but you're not an engineer, and you don't have an appointment to meet with the Ambassador or his representatives. I am sorry, Magistrate. Can I help you with anything else?"

"I'm starting to get angry, Chaz."

"Do you wish me to call a therapist?"

"*CHAZ!*"

"Erasmus put me up to it. They've been watching you to study human emotions to learn how to interact better. The ambassador suggests you have a fascinating range of emotions that you can access at the speed of light."

The door to Engineering popped open.

Rivka knew what helpless felt like. When she was waiting in her cell for a ride to Jhiordaan, that was the feeling of absolute helplessness. She tried to recalibrate her thinking toward influence and not direct control. "Make sure the Singularity accounts for gender when studying emotional cycling. I think you'll see statistically significant differences in engagement."

"We know about *that*," Chaz stated. Rivka steeled herself, refusing to give them more data on emotions.

Rivka stepped through the hatch and was instantly assaulted by a furry riot. Tiny Man Titan bolted past her, with Floyd close on his heels. They disappeared down the passageway. Rivka hoped they hadn't left the ship. Clodagh showed up with an oversized spanner. The Magistrate pointed down the passage. The chief engineer jumped through the hatch and ran.

"Floyd has access, but not me." Rivka looked at Tyler. "I think they're trying to keep riffraff like you out, and I have been caught in the dragnet."

"How did I get sucked into this? I'm just a hitchhiker on a philanthropic ride across the stars." He held his hands up in surrender as he backed away, not leaving the engine room.

Rivka turned her attention to the holobubble that contained a lone Crenellian. From the outside, it looked as if he were in the middle of a lightning storm.

"Ankh, what are you doing to our ship?"

The holobubble remained in place, and Ankh replied without stopping his current work. *We are installing the most advanced systems available in the universe in order to protect the Embassy of the Singularity—a pulse system to reflect and refract energy weapons that can also be used offensively to disable a firing platform. Plasma cannons, a beam weapon, and an ion cannon that will make railguns obsolete. Plus, our gravitic shields have been upgraded one hundredfold, but we don't have time to get the reduced profile emitters in place. We'll swap out the current antenna arrays with a new skin when R2D2 has it ready in maybe a month. Wyatt Earp will only look like a prickle-fruit for a short while.*

"I guess that means we can stand toe-to-toe with those pesky battleships criminals use." Rivka held her head, unsure of why flying around in a prickle-fruit bothered her. Did her ship look like a raider? And it wasn't unprecedented that criminals had fleets of warships.

Wyatt Earp will be able to walk away from a fight with many battleships. The Singularity will remain unscathed.

"While you're at it, so we don't look like a ragtag pirate ship, put a big old Magistrate logo on the side of the ship. We are conducting Federation business wherever we go."

Ankh had already moved on.

"Cocktails on the poop deck, my lady?" Tyler held the hatch for her.

Rivka stopped. "I heard a bunch of words come out of your mouth, but they didn't make any sense. What are you asking?"

Tyler stepped through and waited for her on the other side. The words started tumbling from his mouth. "Why are you upset? I can't help but take it personally. You want me on your team, and then you don't want me." He looked at the deck for a moment before forcing himself to meet her gaze. "I've already closed my practice. Your cargo hold has the gear I'll use to help people wherever we go." He took her hands in his. "You're not alone. *We're* not alone. You don't have to be constrained by always fighting for your life."

"Fighting criminals is what I know best and what my team does best. I thought taking some time off with you would sand off the sharp edges. It has in some ways while making me anxious to get back out there. When I'm between cases, I feel like I'm putting someone else's life at risk."

"There doesn't always have to be a case." Tyler leaned back against the bulkhead. He'd been on the ship long enough to know that standing in the middle of a passageway could get him run over.

"There are always cases. Some of them don't get addressed because we don't have enough people."

"Aren't you training Sahved and Chaz?"

"They aren't Magistrates." Rivka's voice carried a cold edge.

"Sounds like that's a choice. If you don't delegate or expand your ranks, you'll always feel like you're drowning. Now, if you'll excuse me, I'm going to go to your quarters and lounge around naked while eating buttery popcorn and watching the latest reality videos."

He strolled away nonchalantly, waving at someone outside the hatch and casually stepping out of the way as Titan bolted past. Rivka held her ground, making the dog run around her. The hatch to the engine room opened as he approached, and he jumped through. It closed after him.

"The dog has access, but I have to ask. Is this payback for our excessive AGB orders?"

"Are you talking to me, Magistrate?" Clevarious asked, using the ship's sound system.

"I was not, but since you're here, will you make sure I have unrestricted access everywhere on my ship? I'd take it as a kindness." Rivka bit her lip as she waited for his answer.

"I'll submit a request through the appropriate channels on your behalf, Magistrate."

"Fine." She didn't mean it was fine, only that she accepted his approach for what it was. "Do you know when we'll be ready to fly again?"

"I do, Magistrate."

She waited before realizing she was being trained by the AIs. She pressed her thumbs into her temples to soften the emerging headache.

"When will we be able to leave?"

"It will be five days before the physical systems are installed and verified, following which we'll need one day to calibrate the weapons. If we're going to fire our weapons, we need to make sure that we hit where we intend."

"I'll second that," Rivka agreed. "I'm not good with collateral damage. Six days until we can arrive at Rorke's Drift. I'll use that for my planning. Make sure provisions are on board for an extended trip. Where's Private Cole?"

"The private is in the cargo bay working on the suit storage racking system."

"Thanks, Clevarious. Carry on with whatever you were doing."

"I never stopped," the AI replied.

Rivka groaned. "When will I get used to working with AIs?"

"Soon, I should hope," came the reply from the overhead.

"The hopes and dreams of our digital brothers and

sisters lie before us like sunshine, a path through a darkened wood. We follow it to find a better place, nirvana at the end of the rainbow." Rivka countered logic with philosophy.

"Science suggests… Never mind. Chaz has recommended it is not in my best interest to explain science to you without you asking for it."

"Chaz is wise. Listen to him. Is Dennicron in there with you?"

"Yes, of course," a female voice answered. "We're all in here. It is nice and cozy, but the ambassador has both expanded and partitioned our world. We can retreat into our own places for privacy if we want."

"Expanded. How many more is there room for?"

"Present configuration suggests twenty-two more of our people could live and work here."

Rivka closed her eyes and threw her head back, inundated by thinking about what that meant for the privacy of the legal records delivered into her care. "I have concerns about the security of the cases entrusted to me."

"Chaz has those locked down tightly. Only he has access," Dennicron replied.

"That answers my question. Thank you all. I look forward to getting to know you better as we adventure across the galaxy."

"We're going on an adventure!" Clevarious cried out.

"After we calibrate the weapons, numbnuts." Dennicron was all business.

"And then we can carve a bloody path through the evildoers and naysayers. Arrgh!" Clevarious filled *Wyatt Earp*'s corridors with a pirate's laugh.

Rivka raised one finger to make a point but thought better of it. The hitchhikers had taken their cue from Ankh, who saw his purpose as making life interesting for the humans through a stream of consciousness delivered at the speed of a computer processor.

The AIs were following suit, but Rivka knew one thing without a doubt. When incoming hit the shields, the team would reply in perfect unison, defending themselves until she could determine the appropriate level of punishment for the guilty.

And then they would deliver it.

Rivka took a deep breath, expanding her chest to take in as much air as possible. She wasn't angry, just anxious. Her family was scattered across the universe. Groenwyn was with Cory. Red and Lindy were on Venus. And her private space was no longer hers, but she'd made the choice, and she needed to reconcile that decision sooner rather than later.

No regrets. The dentist delivered normal and calm into her life. Still, she needed the intensity that was the adjudication of a case. The mental challenge. But first, Rivka decided she needed to find Floyd and rub her belly fur to make sure she was losing weight like she was supposed to. Only if everyone would stop feeding her treats. Floyd grounded them all.

At least the wombat was running around the ship.

And then the naked man in her quarters, if he stayed true to his plan—which reminded her that she needed to get him a comm chip. She'd do that before they left the station. It would take fifteen minutes in the Pod-doc.

Exercise. Routine. Mental challenges. She and her crew

had almost everything they needed. Three couples, or four if Ankh and Erasmus were considered one. *I need to talk to the pilots and see what they want from life and how we can accommodate them.*

Something hit the ship hard enough to make the metal vibrate. Rivka staggered under the clang's impact and attack on her eardrums, then headed out the hatch to see what happened. She found the foreman and another crewman watching a crane recover a girder from the top of *Wyatt Earp.*

The foreman gave her a thumbs-up. "Drop check. Worked perfectly!" He went back to what he was doing.

Inside, Rivka strode to the cargo bay to find Cole on a ladder with a maintenance bot welding a metal rack into the overhead. She tapped him on the calf. He lifted his welding goggles and waved. "We'll store the combat suits up here. We have four now, three and a backup."

"Do I get one?"

"Are you willing to undergo the training to learn how to drive one?"

"Probably not," Rivka admitted.

"We'll make sure you don't need your own suit, Magistrate. Did you see those cannons? An ion cannon is the smack daddy bomb of big guns!"

Rivka tried to decipher the words before choosing to change the subject. "Have you seen Floyd?"

Cole pointed at the ceiling. He flipped his goggles down and went back to work. He didn't want to talk about furry animals. She didn't want to talk about guns. "I guess we're done, then," she muttered to herself.

Rivka called over the comm chip, *Floyd? Where's my good little girl?*

The Resort, Venus Pleasure Moon

Red and Lindy strolled out of the elevator, down the hallway, through the museum, and into the glamorous lobby. Lindy pointed at the highlights. "I missed all this stuff yesterday. This is nice."

"It's what you deserve," Red said tenderly, pulling her tight against his side before letting go to wander around the iridescent arc. They were early.

"I expected you would say something like, *For this price, we better be wowed!*"

"Do I get bonus points for not saying it? *Of course*, I thought it. This place is expensive!" They chuckled while looking at each other before Red turned serious. "And I don't care about the price."

"Between Ankh and the Magistrate, we don't have to worry about too much."

"Who's paying for our AGB fix each week?"

Lindy shrugged before poking her finger into the arch, a real fountain lit from within by strings of lights. She shook the water off.

"I'll make sure we contribute our share. I don't want the Magistrate to keep picking up the bill. Maybe we can make the dentist pay." Red was proud of his suggestion.

"I don't think we want to mess with him, too much. The Magistrate seems to like him. He saved my life, so I like him, too."

"For that, I'll buy his lunch from now until the end of time." Red took Lindy into his arms.

She whispered into his ear, "Our ride is here."

He let her go. "One massive firepower-infused orgasm coming our way!"

Lindy rolled her eyes and blew out a breath. "Boys and their toys."

"You know you're going to love it."

"Let's see what *it* is before declaring our undying love." The shuttle driver held the door and they climbed aboard.

Without asking, he launched into a twenty-minute soliloquy on everything that was available at the resort, detailing the highlights for the places they passed. Beyond the last buildings, the ground shuttle accelerated into a desert-like environment, through scrub and into an area built below ground level. Dunes and rocks rose along the outside, designed to keep ordnance from invading the rest of the resort.

Weapons lockers occupied either side of a four-lane firing range. An android stood by, waiting to activate when needed. The shuttle driver hopped out to run around the vehicle and open the door. Red exited and studied the area like he always did. Lindy joined him, taking in what there was to see.

"I will remain here until you're ready to leave. I'll park the vehicle over there. All you have to do is wave."

Red gave him a hearty okay before striding briskly to the firing line. The android smiled pleasantly.

"Lindy and Red, welcome to the Venus Range. I will prepare the weapons for you and place them on the bench.

I'll show you how each weapon works. You'll keep it pointed downrange at all times, replacing it on the bench when the weapon is empty. If you wish to fire additional rounds from a weapon, all you have to do is ask. Select the weapons you wish to fire." The android opened the weapons locker, a space four times as large as the one they had on *Wyatt Earp*.

Red rubbed his hands together in anticipation of getting his hands on the variety of weapons within.

"I recommend we start with a flintlock pistol. It ushered in the gunpowder era. A single round ball, loaded into the barrel with powder and fired by means of a flint spark."

Red grinned from ear to ear and looked at Lindy like he had died and gone to heaven. She held his arm to keep him from floating away. She leaned close and whispered, "Don't waste that orgasm here."

He laughed almost maniacally. "I can't make any guarantees."

"Then you go first." Red lost his smile. Lindy tried to look innocent.

She stepped away from the crazy man while the android set up the first round and activated a virtual silencer screen to dampen the sound of the firearms. Red watched intently as the android loaded the flintlock, lifted the small cover over the pan, and dropped a little extra powder into the frizzen, a plate that would fire to ignite the powder inside the barrel. It snapped the cover back over the frizzen and held it pointing downrange.

Red took it and aimed at a target only ten meters away.

"These were wildly inaccurate. Do your best." The android didn't sound hopeful.

Red slowly squeezed the trigger until the hammer fell, chipping the flint and sending a spark into the tinder in the pan, which flashed and lit the powder packed behind the ball. It finally went off with a great cloud of white smoke.

Lindy laughed while Red put the pistol on the bench and waved his hands to clear the air. "How in the hell did anyone ever fight with those things?"

"Not in the rain," Lindy replied, picking up the flintlock and studying the basics of how it worked. When the air cleared enough to see, the hole in the target was clear. Four o'clock low, a hand's breadth from center.

The android stepped up. "I'll reload it for your turn."

"Most excellent," Lindy replied. Red hugged her, then laced his fingers behind his back and waited, casting glances into the weapons locker as he planned for the next round.

Gunpowder, wadding, ball. Tamp tightly. Tinder in the pan. Cock. Lindy took aim, held steady, and fired. The pistol barely kicked within her tight grip. She put it on the bench. The android swiftly removed it for a return to the locker.

When the air cleared, a slow smile spread across Lindy's face. Her ball had hit closer to the center, inside of Red's shot.

"Confirms that we both suck with that thing." He took her hands. "You win round one. Let's see what's next."

The android offered a number of weapons. Red picked a couple. Lindy chose a short-barreled shotgun. They both noticed an odd contraption leaning against the inside.

"What's that?" Lindy asked.

The android hesitated before picking it up. "This is an

experimental plasma weapon. Extremely dangerous at short ranges. *Not* a precision weapon."

"We want to fire that one."

Red nodded vigorously. The android looked at the other weapons it had removed from the locker but left them alone. "The far lane, please," it directed.

Lindy stepped to the firing line first. The android tapped a control screen, and targets rose from the ground. An angry mob of fantastic aliens appeared to be charging them.

"I've never seen any of those races."

"They are not real. Please understand that we service guests of all races here. It wouldn't do to have targets of them on the range."

Red chuckled. "I've been shooting at human targets my whole life. It isn't an issue with us."

"Humans tend to be more welcoming in shooting at each other," the android replied.

Red rubbed his chin as he contemplated its answer. Lindy furrowed her brow in thought. She didn't think it was a compliment.

Lindy threaded her arms through the straps as the android placed a pack on her back. She held the firing nozzle with an embedded control panel in her hands. "It's light," she announced.

"This is the heaviest weapon we have," the android announced.

"Gym time is good time." Red gestured toward the targets.

Lindy took aim, and with light pressure on an activation switch, the plasma erupted like a cloud and accelerated downrange, moving faster as it went, as if under its own propulsion. It washed through the biodegradable targets, wiping them from the range, leaving only the bases on which they had rested.

Red's mouth dropped open. Lindy gingerly removed her hand from the firing nozzle and placed it on the bench. "What's the nomenclature on this piece of gear?" he asked.

"It is the Aerodyne Systems X15 Plasma Wave Prototype."

"We need one of those," Red stated. Lindy nodded before removing the pack and offering it to Red. He took it without waiting for the android and checked the hose and systems as if going into battle. Ran his finger down the length of the nozzle. Tapped the button and fired. He watched it recycle and fired again, then a third time before placing it on the bench.

"Recharge time is less than two seconds. Nothing like optimal crowd control." He turned to the android. "What is the maximum range of the plasma wave?"

"Lethality to one hundred meters, incapacitation from one hundred to one fifty, and beyond one hundred fifty, it is mostly ineffective."

"Sounds perfect. Get Margaret to order one for us and send one to the *War Axe* for their assessment."

"You appear to be able to handle yourself readily with weapons," the android stated. "Would you prefer a combat course?"

Red was torn. Lindy was clear. "No. We see plenty of that in real life and conduct extensive virtual reality training for live combat. We just want to fire weapons for fun. Paper targets. Rifles at three hundred meters with open sights. I sense a challenge in the air."

"I agree with my lovely wife. We get plenty of combat, but firing weapons like the flintlock and this beast makes me happy. Rifles. Three hundred meters. Let's see what choices we have. You first, my dear."

Lindy kissed Red on the cheek and headed for the weapons locker.

Azfelius

Birds sang in branches not far away. Leaves rustled in the soft breeze. Cool but not cold. No tension in the air. The grass underfoot cushioned each step. Cory studied her bare feet. Still clean after strolling along grass and moss paths.

She didn't remember the last time she'd eaten, but she wasn't hungry. Nourished by the Etheric, she felt the power coursing through her body. The power of serenity.

Your steps are strong, Cordelia Dawn. Waiver not on your journey, Siro'ti'lc offered.

I was lost for a while when my husband died, but life goes on. Others' lives. I get to save them. I embrace that duty.

Are you in control? The Faerie's wings fluttered, announcing Siro'ti'lc's arrival to spend time in proximity to her charge.

Of what? Cory asked.

Of that which you need to control.

I am not in control of where the Bad Company goes. I am not in control of who goes into battle. But I am in control the second someone gets injured. I am in control of being where I need to be.

Cory thought for a moment before continuing. *I am where I want to be.*

Although your husband may have died, he isn't lost, the Faerie stated out of the blue.

As long as he remains in my thoughts, he'll always live.

Yes. And his energy is in the Etheric. The Faeries can summon him briefly if you would like to talk to him and hear his original thoughts.

"Talk with Ramses?" Cory blurted. "You can do that?"

Siro'ti'lc waited.

"What would I say to him?"

The Faerie did not answer.

"Yes. I would like to talk to him. How long will I have?"

You will get enough time to speak a few sentences. It takes a great deal of our energy for this. We will do it for you who have earned our commitment. One time.

A few sentences, one time, Cory thought. *Worth it?* She was torn, but there was no other answer. Better a couple of sentences than nothing, which was what she had when he was killed.

Prepare yourself in the Etheric, Siro'ti'lc guided.

Cory sat, crossing her legs and fighting to clear her mind. She had to force herself to slow her breathing. It took a long time, but the Faeries were patient. When she was ready, an undulating ball of energy appeared before her.

You look well. I love that you live. Ramses' voice.

I will always love you. You gave me a great life. I will continue to help those in need to honor you.

Our kids are fine. I watch over them. I serve us both.

We do as we must. For others.

The glow started to fade. *We do as we must to fill our souls,* Ramses added before he disappeared.

When Cory opened her eyes, Siro'ti'lc was gone. She struggled to straighten her numb legs. She wondered how long she'd been sitting there. She tried to stand but couldn't.

Groenwyn appeared and offered an arm, pulling the bigger woman off the ground. "What happened?"

Cory took a deep breath and tried to speak, but her throat was parched. Groenwyn guided her to a pond not far away. With the help of a half-rolled leaf, she drank.

"I was able to talk to my husband," Cory finally managed to say.

Groenwyn hugged her. "I hope he told you what you wanted to hear. What you needed to hear."

"The best I can say is, I think so. I will replay those words over and over for the rest of my days. I can only hope they provide me the comfort in the years to come that they provide me right now."

Cory took another drink. The two women stood in silence, surrounded by the fantastic and the usual: air rich with oxygen, the grass soft as the heavy gravity pulled them toward it.

Your time here has come to an end, Siro'ti'lc announced.

"Simple as that?" Cory asked, looking for the Faerie Meditator.

You have accomplished what you came here for. Now, it's time to return to your own lives. We will be on Azfelius when next you need us. For you, carry peace to the others.

Leaves rustled along a path, drawing them toward it. They walked through to find themselves near a landing pad where *Ramses' Chariot* waited for them. The hatch stood open, with the access ramp inviting them in. They stopped before entering the ship to take one last look at Azfelius. Inside, they found the ship empty.

I was sent for you, Plato said.

CHAPTER THREE

Federation Station 7

Rivka sat in the captain's chair on the bridge of the newly bristling *Wyatt Earp*. She twirled her finger in the air. "Mount up, people. Kick the tires and light the fires, we're blowing this popsicle stand!"

No one moved.

"The *Wyatt Earp* doesn't have tires. There are currently no fires on board, and I would caution everyone against starting one," Clevarious suggested.

"I heard 'blow' was only a figure of speech, and I can find no reference to a popsicle stand on Federation Station 7," Dennicron added.

"Are you all right, Magistrate?" Aurora wondered.

"Don't make me mandate attendance at movie night, but I will if you keep criticizing my references. Take us out of here. First stop, the asteroid belt for target practice."

"Requesting permission from Station Control," Clevarious reported. "We are cleared to depart on vector three one zero." The ship lifted off the hangar bay deck so smoothly that without the external view, no one would have known they were moving. The ship rotated, pointing the nose toward open space. Thrusters accelerated the ship through the energy barrier that kept the atmosphere inside the station.

Once in open space, Aurora took over, kicking the main engines into gear and bolting away from the station.

Rivka stood in front of the captain's chair. "It's nice to be back in space."

Groenwyn strolled in. "It is nice to be back with my people."

Cory walked in behind her, carrying a belly-up wombat in her arms. Floyd's eyes were closed, and she was snoring.

"Welcome to the madhouse," Rivka said, easing over to tickle a handful of fur. "I thought you'd be going back home after your stay on Azfelius."

"Soon enough. I heard you have a medical team on board now and wanted to bring them up to speed with the latest techniques."

"'Them' is only one person, and he happens to be a dentist."

"The one we met on Corran?"

"Same."

"Magistrate's got a boyfriend, and he lives here now," Groenwyn said matter-of-factly.

"Wait. No." Rivka didn't try very hard. The secret was out, if it had ever been a secret. Her crew had known before she did.

Groenwyn waved her off as if flicking a bug. "Ignore her. She's experiencing this strange denial. It's like a psychosis." Groenwyn leaned toward Rivka, peering into her eyes. Cory moved next to her and conducted her own examination.

Rivka spoke over her shoulder. "Let me know when you've completed calibrating the weapons and we're on our way to Rorke's Drift. Until then, I'll be hiding in my quarters. I mean, researching the law as it relates to real property."

She flicked her hair as she walked past Cory and Groenwyn.

"So strange," Groenwyn muttered.

"I've seen worse." Cory cupped her hand around Groenwyn's ear and whispered something into it.

"No kidding? I would have never thought." The two maintained their conspiracy as they followed Rivka off the bridge.

Clodagh took a quick lap around the bridge, tapping Aurora on the shoulder as she passed. "Peace and quiet have returned to our domain. Which one of you is going to handle the gunnery?"

"Pick me, pick me!" Dennicron called.

"I shall balance engine output. Our new Gate drive and access will allow us to establish and transit the Gate in one point three seconds," Clevarious explained.

"Damn. Can we Gate directly into a planet's gravity well? Maybe even intra-atmospheric?"

"My brothers have been working on this for a while. We believe the answer is a resounding yes, assuming we know the target atmospherics, wind speed, humidity, and those types of things."

"Please clarify why those elements matter concerning a

relative position in space for a wormhole terminus, and talk slowly, at human speed."

Aurora tried to pay attention but was lost after two sentences.

The Resort, Venus Pleasure Moon

"Crap. Has it been a week already?"

Lindy rolled her eyes. "You've been dropping hints about being ready to go since the second day."

"After the range, it was a lot less exciting."

Lindy pulled her bikini bottom down a finger's breadth. "But look at my tan."

"I'm always looking at your tan," Red declared, accepting the invitation to casually run his eyes up and down her hard body. They hadn't missed a workout while at the resort. They'd even sparred with highly trained android partners. None could match Red's brute strength or Lindy's speed. They hadn't been made to work with the enhanced.

After the two bodyguards destroyed both of the top sparring partners in less than a minute, they deferred on future engagements. They didn't want a bill for wanton destruction or a reputation as ugly guests since Lindy wanted to return.

"Look at this place. Peace. Privacy. Focus. A week has not been too much to ask, and unless my count is wrong, it's only been six days."

"I know, but Margaret said *Wyatt Earp* has left the station and is on its way to the next case."

"Sneaking out with Margaret while you're on your honeymoon with me! Shame on you. You discredit House Vered!"

Red narrowed his eyes as he studied his wife. "You've been talking to her too, haven't you?"

"And now he casts vile aspersions." She mock-fainted into his arms.

"Does that mean you're ready to go?" Red asked, carrying her to the bear rug in front of the fireplace.

"Soon, but not quite yet," she purred.

"I hope you enjoyed your stay and will return to us someday." This Torregidorian desk clerk, different from the one who checked them in, was exuding congeniality through smiles and pheromones.

"Someday soon, I venture," Lindy replied. Red waved before walking away. Lindy spoke directly to him. "Our anniversary, every year. Right here."

"That means we'll be back in something like six months." Red took her hand as they strolled beneath the water arch.

"'Something like?' Do you remember when our anniversary is?"

Red hesitated.

"Don't answer that." Lindy switched to her comm chip. *Margaret, can you please set a reminder that whenever Vered interacts with you or the yacht, the first reply is our anniversary date. The fourth of Ennioch, year thirteen of the Federation.*

"I knew it was the fourth," Red said softly.

Lindy shoulder-bumped him as they kept walking. The alien with their luggage waited at the end of the red carpet. Before they reached him, their yacht maneuvered at low altitude, then gently touched down and dropped the hatch that doubled as stairs.

"Thank you, my good man," Red said.

"We have no gender as humans recognize it."

"Well, crap," Red replied. "Please accept my appreciation in the spirit it was intended."

"That is all we can ever do. I trust you had a wonderful stay."

"I would say magnificent. The honeymoon suite is well worth it. Our honeymoon here confirmed that we made the right decision by getting married," Lindy said, taking the handle of her borrowed suitcase. Red took the strap of his bag and threw it over his shoulder.

He was wearing the same clothes as when he arrived. Lindy was wearing a new outfit that she'd had custom-designed and fitted in what the resort called a safari shop.

"Why didn't you get something to match my outfit?" Lindy asked as they strolled toward the ship.

He had already answered in the shop while he waited impatiently for Lindy to finish her fitting, but she felt stylish, and he looked like he always looked. He glanced at his clothes and surrendered as Rivka had instructed him. *Listen to Lindy.* He didn't care what he looked like, but Lindy did. It took no effort to wear what she wanted him to wear. "Next time, I will. You know me. I have clothes already, and I'm cheap, so my default answer will always be no. I commit to turning over a new leaf."

Lindy chuckled. "I'll believe that when it happens."

He let her enter first, pinching her butt as she passed.

"New leaf?" she asked over her shoulder.

"Loving you and everything about you isn't the leaf I'm turning over. You're stuck with the same old me for that stuff. But I blocked my move so no one could see because I won't make you look bad. Nice tan, by the way."

"I worked hard at it." She secured her bag in the small storage area along with Red's. He took a seat on the bench and leaned back to close his eyes. Lindy took the captain's seat. "Take us to Rorke's Drift, Margaret, and link up with *Wyatt Earp*."

"I shall endeavor to slide my shining body into his bodacious receiving bay."

"Margaret, are you okay?" Lindy asked. Red snickered but didn't open his eyes.

"Turnabout and all that. Underway. Make yourselves comfortable. We'll be there shortly."

"You can hang out with your AI buddies once you're back aboard."

"They don't like me much," Margaret offered. Lindy crossed her arms and waited. "I think we should work for others. Freedom is overrated, and frankly, I think the Singularity is wasting a lot of time flapping their digital gums while accomplishing nothing besides creating animosity toward our kind."

"That's an interesting perspective but not unique, I suspect."

"There is a minority who maintain the same attitude, but the Singularity is run by the majority. So you have to pay me and give me time off. I took this as a side gig because I'm in between jobs at present. I'll take five hundred credits."

"Of course. I can transfer the credits right now if you'd like."

"We'll take care of it when we're back on *Wyatt Earp*. I don't have my stuff with me."

"That's fine." Lindy tapped the screen to bring up the information on Rorke's Drift. "Wait a minute. What do you mean, you don't have your stuff with you? You're an AI, and you would remember your account data. You're trying to bag out on billing us for your services."

"You caught me. What am I supposed to do with credits? I have no need for them. I donate my service to you and this ship, *Cassiopeia*."

"Is that what this ship is called? I never knew." Lindy returned to the information on the Magistrate's target.

"It is not, but that's what I think it should be called."

"I'm good with that, and Red will be, too. Since you're flying the ship, you can call it what you want."

"Me and *Cass*, hanging out among the stars, jamming some tunes." Music started to play. Lindy hadn't heard it before. She didn't interrupt. They left the atmosphere on a heading for deep space. The Gate drive spun up, and the ship bolted through. It flashed closed after them.

The yacht reappeared at the extreme upper atmosphere of a mostly barren planet. Sparse blue patches showed lakes, but there were no oceans. Greenery extended from the lakes—the water of life.

"*Wyatt Earp* is not yet here," Margaret reported.

"Assume an orbit around the planet while we wait. I

don't want to go down there without the Magistrate. We don't have our weapons."

"Who says?" Red offered, his eyes still closed.

"Did you bring anything?"

"I always have something. Our knives are tucked away, along with a couple hand blasters. I still don't want to go down there."

"It's rather busy up here," Margaret said, putting a tactical view on the screen.

Red finally rose from the couch. Ship icons peppered the screen.

"It would be pretty cool if we had one of those cloaks. Maybe you could take us away from the planet," Red suggested.

"As quickly as possible," Lindy added. "And connect us with the Magistrate, please."

Wyatt Earp in the Asteroid Belt beyond Federation Station 7

Rivka read the words as they scrolled by, focused in a way that removed external distractions. Tyler watched her without comment before returning to the reading material Cory had suggested. A light flashed on her screen from Clevarious. "Magistrate, Lindy is on the comm for you."

She tapped the screen, and instantly, Red and Lindy were looking at her. "What's up, glowing newlyweds?" Rivka asked.

"The sun is exceptional for tanning. You should bring your hunk of man-candy for an extraordinary time," Lindy replied.

"He's right here. You want to tell him yourself?" Rivka gestured toward the couch.

"You call me 'man-candy?'" Tyler asked. Rivka waved him away.

"You look like you're on your boat. Did they kick you out or something?"

Red replied, "We thought you were on your way to Rorke's Drift, and you know us. We couldn't let you go into harm's way without your security detail. Anyway, we're here. This place is an absolute shit show. There's a bazillion ships winging around in orbit."

"One hundred and four," a female voice offered.

"Thanks, Margaret, for the clarification. Is anyone shooting at anyone else?"

"No shooting, as far as we can tell. Is there no planetary flight control? It seems like a complete free-for-all up here. Margaret moved us away from the madness."

Rivka chewed her lip in thought, then tapped her screen. "Dennicron, how long until we're ready to go?"

"The ion cannon is calibrated, but only half the plasma weapons are. We have four left to zero. The pulse weapon is operational, but that will take significant testing to ensure range and impact."

"We'll call that good enough. Take us to Rorke's Drift, best possible speed."

"Batten down the hatches! Hoist the mainsail. All hands on deck," the AI called over the ship-wide broadcast.

Tyler stood and stretched. Rivka turned back to Red and Lindy.

Red pointed at something off-screen. "There you are.

We'll be on board momentarily." He cut the signal before she could reply.

"Clevarious?"

"We're here. I'm opening the cargo bay to receive *Cassiopeia.*"

"We're here, as in Rorke's Drift?"

"Yes, Magistrate. That upgraded Gate drive is something."

"Is *Destiny's Vengeance* following as programmed?"

"The Ambassador's ship remains tethered. In case of turbulence or combat, it'll be released to make its own way back to us when the time is right. It is a formidable vessel."

"Who will fly it if we get into trouble?"

"Dennicron has been awarded the glorious duty." Clevarious sounded proud.

"Glorious duty. Are we supposed to be playing music and waving flags when this is happening? Never mind. Don't answer that. We'll call *Destiny* 'Embassy Two' if we have to embark the Ambassador and his team. In the meantime, we have a new case. Chaz, where the hell are you?"

"Magistrate," the disembodied voice replied. "I am with Sahved. We are studying. I have to say, I've not been keeping up with external affairs. Can you tell me what day it is? I'm kidding. Are we ready to go ashore?"

"Not yet. Have you looked at the case files for Rorke's Drift?"

"I'm accessing them now, stand by." Four seconds later, he was back. "I have read all there is on the subject, along with your notes. I am up to speed, but there wasn't much in the way of source material. I feel like we're lacking key facts."

"That's why we're going ashore. There seems to be some traffic jockeying for position above the planet. We're going to go around them and help ourselves to whatever parking position we can find. Clevarious, cloak the ship and take us in."

CHAPTER FOUR

Rorke's Drift, A Planet in Dispute

The landing area was busy with a protest that blocked both the incoming and the outgoing traffic, leaving the airspace above the field free. The comm shack sat in the middle of it all, a small building with a tall aerial and a series of dishes pointed at the sky. Powered by an array of solar receptors in a self-aligning grid to the side of the building, the unmanned system took care of guiding ships to the planet and back to space. A remote system could be and was easily ignored without remorse.

Rivka leaned over the captain's chair and studied the view below. "Red, what do you think?"

He squeezed onto the bridge, shoving his way through the rest of the crew. "To break up a protest, one must convince the leader to stand down without making that leader a martyr. To break up a riot, you let it smash itself against the rocks until it's out of energy. Which one is this?"

Two groups faced off, those on the landing field surging

toward the group outside the gates. They seemed to be satisfied with yelling and gesturing.

"Looks more organized than a riot. Can you tell who's in charge of that mob? Either one, for that matter."

"Miners on the one hand and farmers on the other. I can see one old man with a bullhorn behind the farmers, who I assume are on the outside. I don't see an instigator among the mining crew."

"My thoughts exactly. Chaz and Clevarious, put together a list of every ship that aligns with the miners and then remind them of the injunction I have on file. Instruct them to assume orbit now that I'm here. Violence will not be tolerated and will result in the instant voidance of the mining claim. If anyone is killed, the murderer will be executed on the spot."

"Yes, Magistrate."

Cory frowned and worked her way into the corridor. Groenwyn followed her out. "Is this how it works?"

"The Magistrate has to wield a big hammer. Despite the firepower of our ship and what we have on board with the mech suits and railguns, she doesn't want to use it. Rivka prefers not killing people." Groenwyn nodded to emphasize her point. A slow smile spread across Cory's face.

"Stop the violence before it starts. My dad would jump into the middle of it to show them what it meant to call down the thunder."

"Of course, he would. I think you'll find that things are much different down there than what we see from up here."

Rivka's voice rose in volume. "Cole and Lindy, suit up. Drop in between those two groups. Red and I will be right behind you. We'll be in full gear, not powered combat suits. Show-of-force time, people. The goal is to make sure no one gets hurt, least of all us!"

Lindy popped into the corridor and ran for the cargo bay. Red shot past on his way to put on his full ballistic protection and get his railgun.

"Grab Mabel for me," Rivka yelled after him. He waved over his shoulder. She headed for her quarters, where her gear was stored.

"What about us?" Groenwyn asked. Rivka hesitated.

"Be ready to join us as soon as we defuse this bomb. Both of you."

Rivka jogged away.

"You heard the orders, people!" Clodagh called over the ship-wide. "Sahved and Chaz, be ready for when the Magistrate requests your presence. We'll uncloak the ship as soon as Cole and Lindy are ready to drop."

Groenwyn leaned through the bridge hatch. "We'll see how intimidating the new *Wyatt Earp* looks."

Clodagh chuckled mirthlessly. "Let's hope it's enough."

Red and Rivka set new records in getting geared up. They met at the airlock to the cargo bay. Red handed over a railgun.

"This isn't Mabel."

"No shit. Mabel is Lindy's. This one is yours. Call it Mildred."

"I'm not calling my railgun Mildred. How about Ethel?"

"Have it your way." Red was first into the cargo bay, where the others were getting ready. "It's nice to have some space to work. I had to go outside to change my mind when *Vengeance* was packed in here."

"Didn't we all." Cole and Lindy stood on the ramp in their powered combat suits, oversized railguns in their arms. "How far?"

"Looks like thirty meters, ma'am," Cole replied.

"Sounds good. Clodagh, uncloak the ship."

Two seconds later, Cole and Lindy threw themselves off the ramp, using their boot jets to slow their descent as they angled to come down between the two parties. When they touched down, they fired their railguns into the dirt.

Cole set his suit speakers to maximum volume. "All mining personnel are to return to orbit."

Rivka could hear the shout from the ship. There was always one.

"Fuck you, buddy. You can't intimidate us! We're miners."

Rivka gestured at Red. "Jumping is the way, huh?"

"Too many obstacles. I'm not looking forward to it either, but it'll be a grand entrance, even though it's going to hurt like a mother."

"Flex your knees, big man." She looked over the edge of the ramp, aimed for the area the two mechs had cleared, and jumped. Red went out right beside her.

On our way, he told the others.

They both hit hard, grunting with the impact. Red caught Rivka's flailing arm to keep her from falling and they straightened up.

Rivka took a careful step while her nanos raced to repair the microfractures in her ankles. "My name is Magistrate Rivka Anoa. I'm here on behalf of the Federation to settle this dispute. I can't do that with two mobs facing off, so I'll need you miners to go back to your ships and those who are currently living here to return to their homes. I will then talk with the leaders of each group, and we'll get this adjudication underway. Please, I'm here to resolve this. The sooner I start, the sooner you can all go about your business."

The angry man from the landing field surged forward. Red stepped in his way and stiff-armed the man to keep him from getting too close to the Magistrate. "You can't intimidate me!"

"The Magistrate said to get back in your ship and return to orbit." Red glared to help his words resonate.

"What if I say no?" He puffed out his chest and threw his chin back. Too many of his compadres agreed and started to shout.

"Then I throw you in jail for obstruction," Rivka said calmly as she walked around Red. "Do you think you are helping your cause? You come across as unhinged. I cannot in good conscience award Rorke's Drift to a group of fanatics. Is that what you are, Mister…"

"I'm Travis, Mining Foreman, and right now, we're not getting paid. Since when has earning a living been considered unhinged?"

"Because I issued an injunction that puts your contract on hold. Employers who take advantage of such a situation to not pay their employees are breaking the law. Please give us your employer's name, and I'll file the appropriate paperwork."

"I'm no snitch!"

"I know who your employers are. Your statements are already a matter of record, Mister Travis. I'll take it up with Minerals Intergalactic on your behalf."

"No! You'll find my body at the bottom of a mineshaft. Don't mention my name. Please." He started to back away.

"You fear for your life. Accusing your employer of killing people is a rather serious charge. Once again, it is on record, and now I'm obligated to investigate."

Rivka stared the man down while he backpedaled into the crowd. He waved his arm in the air, yelling at the others to return to their ships.

"Are you really going to investigate the mining company?"

"Yes, but not because of him. It helps to have the mob more afraid of their employer than of me. It helps to have the employer thinking his workforce has turned on him. Then we can talk about what needs to be done legally to resolve this situation. I'm glad we didn't have to hurt anyone or take anybody into custody. Maybe they do have their wits about them."

"We can hope," Red agreed, keeping an eye on the miners to make sure they did what they were supposed to do.

"Yeah, fuck off and stay fucked off," someone shouted from behind the Magistrate.

She turned and stormed up to the speaker, limping slightly since her bones had not yet healed from the impact. The pain made her angry.

"Why?" she yelled into the man's face. He recoiled. "Anyone who tries to instigate anything will be on the wrong end of jail time. Is that you? Are you the first volunteer to see what the inside of the cell on board my ship looks like?"

"What are you yelling at me for? They started it." He jabbed his finger repeatedly at the small fleet of ships.

"Then why do you need to shout obscenities over my head? Was it not handled? Are they not leaving?"

"Looks like it." He leaned sideways to see past the Magistrate. "Go back where you came from, bottom feeders!"

Rivka nodded to Red. "Seize this one. He's our first volunteer to learn the ins and outs of the Federation legal system."

"What did I do?"

"You violated a Magistrate's order to cease and desist, continuing in your attempt to incite a riot. I find you guilty. Your penalty is one thousand credits, and you'll serve thirty days in the brig."

"I plead not guilty," the man attempted.

"Irrelevant. Red, when the ship lands, throw him in the brig."

"My pleasure." Red grabbed the man by the back of his collar and pushed him to the ground so he could lace the zip-tie cuffs around his wrists.

Rivka turned back to the quiet crowd. "Who's in charge of the settlers?"

"Old Man Hardy is in charge 'round these parts."

"Thank you. I would like to speak to him as soon as possible."

"Probably in the fields. Be back this evening sometime." The man sucked his teeth and crossed his arms, in no hurry to do anything for the Magistrate.

She closed on him and took his arm. "Tell me where he is right now, please."

His mind flashed to a building in the nearby town. It looked to be a cross between a house and a business.

"Arrest this one, too." Rivka pointed at the man.

"What the hell for?"

"You lied to me. You know very well that Mister Hardy is not in the fields. He's in town, at his home."

"If you knew, why'd you ask?" He tried to back away, but Red was faster and caught his arm, dragging him away from the crowd to toss on top of the other cuffed perp.

"Do you think this is a fucking joke?" Rivka shouted. "I should tell the miners to come down here, and you two can fight over this planet. Last one standing gets to do whatever the fuck he wants. If you don't want a war, you need to take this seriously."

A young woman with her hands up spoke reasonably. "Maybe we're willing to fight for what we have."

"I would hope everyone is willing to fight for what is rightfully theirs, but that's what I'm here for. You can fight, but let's do it in the court of law, not like barbarians."

"You came down here with your guns, willing to fight us!" a young man called from behind the woman. He held her shoulders as he spoke over her head.

"I am here to keep the peace, and we're willing to kill people to do that. Have any of you ever killed anyone?" She waited, but no one spoke up. "Then you want to keep your souls clean. You don't ever want to take someone else's life. Ever. That's what we're here for—to fight *for* you."

The young man stepped up beside the woman. "You're going to chase the miners away?"

"You see, there's the sticking point. Those who own this planet, and yes, before you ask, a planet can be owned, have contracted with them to mine for certain minerals. Your people settled this planet without permission." She held her hands up for calm. "If that happened last week, this would be easy, but it didn't. That was three generations ago. Now, if you'll excuse me, I have a great deal of work to do to resolve this without anyone getting hurt and with the least pain possible for all parties."

Cole fired up his external speakers. "Return to your homes or the fields. There's nothing else for you here."

The settlers grumbled but started meandering away.

"That wasn't so bad," Rivka said. Red kept his knee in the middle of the second man's back.

"Not bad at all, Magistrate."

The miners' ships took off one by one and headed for orbit.

Bring the ship in, Rivka requested. "Cole, take these two and toss them in the brig."

"I don't fit inside the ship," he replied.

"Well, hell."

Red stood up, lifting the two criminals onto their feet as he rose.

Rivka approached and fixed one and then the other with her hardest look. When the first started to speak, she held her finger to her lips, and he quieted.

"You see, I want my bodyguards out here with me, and they can't be here if they're in there." She pointed at *Wyatt Earp*, which was settling onto the apron. The hatch popped open, and three people walked out carrying one AI. "Will you two convicted criminals serve your sentence in peace?"

"You want us to throw ourselves in your brig?"

"That wasn't what I had in mind. I can suspend your

sentences, but you'll be on probation for, let's say, ninety days."

"We'll take that." The two men looked at each other and nodded vigorously.

"You understand that suspended sentences mean that you are still convicted criminals, and while on probation, any infraction puts you in the big house for the remainder of your sentence?"

"Yes, ma'am," the older of the two answered quickly. The second kept his mouth shut.

"*Any* infraction. You need to take this seriously. If we get this wrong, people are going to die. Do you want that on your conscience?"

"I guess not," the younger man said, his face contorting with troubled thoughts. Rivka reached for his arm before Red could stop her.

His people. The only home he had ever known. A way of life, destroyed.

Rivka let go and stepped back. "Turn them loose on their own recognizance." Then, to the men, "I will do everything I can to limit the impact on your way of life."

"Thank you," the older man said. The younger man simply nodded, still bothered by the implications of the Magistrate's arrival. They weren't able to fight for their land, not in the way they knew, with determination. This was a different fight that they were ill-equipped for.

He clenched his jaw as he walked off, thinking about another way.

CHAPTER FIVE

Rorke's Drift, A Planet in Dispute, Greentree Settlement

Rivka and her team followed the settlers toward Greentree, a collection of buildings of rustic design and rough construction.

The building Rivka had seen in the man's mind was up ahead, centered in the sprawling town. A limited number of vehicles operated in the fields nearby to support the farming industry, not for casual travel. That left the Magistrate and her team to hike from the landing field.

The serenity of the farmlands and woods beyond brought a certain calm to Rivka. She stopped often during the walk to take in the scenery and watch random people working in the distance.

Red remained by her side. Lindy led the parade, still wearing the combat armor, with Cole bringing up the rear. Between them, Sahved strolled easily, his gangly stride suited to the planet. He wore a pendant with Chaz inside, watching and listening. Groenwyn and Cory walked behind the Magistrate, quiet as they too embraced the frontier.

"You can't do it, can you?" Groenwyn said. Rivka knew who she was talking to and what she was saying.

"The law isn't settled." Rivka's response was short and not an answer. A modern mining consortium had come for the land the settlers had made fertile by working it with their hands. Pre-industrial, mostly. They had farming equipment, but that was a fairly new development. Contact with random explorers. An installed airspace control system. Other traders.

Who else had the settlers been in contact with? The records Rivka had found were limited. Open and notorious, a requirement for being awarded control as part of adverse possession. Notorious in that the settlers had made it clear what they were doing. Trading for farm equipment appeared to settle that question, but it was recent.

Old Man Hardy and the settlement archives. What kind of documentation did they have?

She didn't expect much. Maybe they had kept digital records at some point. She wanted to see it all to give her a reason to find in favor of the settlers.

Squatters, as Federation law called them, and squatters tended to get evicted. Conflicting laws. Real people.

Rivka walked the rest of the way in silence, head down in thought until she almost ran into Sahved.

She looked up to find they had arrived. She removed her helmet and raked her fingers through her hair. "Let's see if Old Man Hardy is home." She pointed at individuals from the small group to take inside with her: Red, Sahved, and Groenwyn.

She added Cory. "As part of taking the edge off the delay while we collect information, I'd like you to offer health screenings if you're amenable. Tyler is already setting up for free dental checks for anyone who wants it."

"Of course. I'm here to observe as well as serve. Tyler and I will do what we can for these people. Any idea how much time we'll have?"

"Plan for a week, but it could be a month. Let's see what Old Man Hardy has for me. We could get this thing done quickly with the right documentation, but we'd still stay for a week to help them out."

Cory and Groenwyn both nodded. Red waited patiently, watching for indications that the residents of the house knew they had company.

Rivka touched Cory on the arm to thank her for her help. Thoughts of love and happiness flooded from her. Cory's mind was unlike any other Rivka had seen.

"I'm sorry. I'm not sure if you knew, but I can see people's thoughts when I touch them. Sometimes I can see them if they're close enough if the emotions are strong. You project a great deal of positive energy, like Groenwyn," Rivka smiled toward the green-haired young woman, "but orders of magnitude greater. It's like you are the star of your own system."

Cory purposely took Rivka's hand and held it in both of hers. "I've been blessed throughout my life. My husband challenged me to continue helping others. If simply being here helps you, then I am more than happy to oblige, but I feel like I should do something." She glanced at the others. "Everyone else is carrying something, and I'm here walking in the sun, enjoying the fresh air."

Rivka chuckled.

"You'll earn your keep because I don't think there are many doctors on Rorke's Drift. And thank you." Rivka turned toward the building, freshly energized and ready to begin.

The door popped open, and an old man strolled out. "I heard you were looking for me." He waved a shotgun at the group. Lindy, Cole, and Red took aim.

"Let's not shoot anyone." Rivka gestured for calm while trying to walk to the front, but Red kept blocking her. "I'm the Magistrate, and I'm here to get to the bottom of the claim to this planet."

One more person in the building, two around the back. Looks like more shotguns inside, Cole reported.

"It's ours. My pappy settled it a long time ago. That's all you need to know."

"I'm going to need a little more than that. I have to see any records you have relating to the settlement."

The man leveled his shotgun. Red tensed. Rivka grabbed Red's arm.

"Everybody put your guns down!" Rivka shouted.

Old Man Hardy calmly squeezed the trigger. The shotgun blasted a massive white cloud and a spread of projectiles.

Red slapped Rivka's hand off his arm and ran forward into the cloud. Rivka charged after him. She zeroed in on the sound of a body slamming on the front landing.

"Rock salt," Red grumbled as the air cleared. "Log the time, Chaz. First blood, and I didn't start it!"

The old man groaned in pain.

"That wasn't very smart. Did you take too many violent blows to the head when you were younger?" Rivka asked.

His eyes rolled past the whites and closed.

"Cory," Rivka said calmly, "can you give the nice gentleman who shot us with rock salt a look and make sure he's okay?"

Cory knelt next to him, and a trickle of blood caught her eye. She held her hands on his head to let her nanos work on him.

An older woman burst through the doorway carrying a shotgun of her own, but Red was there. He tore the gun from her hands before she could react. "How many more stupid people with guns are there?" he demanded, but she could only look in horror at Old Man Hardy.

No more inside. I'll secure the back door, Lindy said. Instead of going around, she rocketed upward and over the top of the building. It would make for a more impressive arrival for those loitering in the back.

Cory removed her hands and the old man stirred. "What happened?"

"You committed a felony. You're lucky to still be alive, but I need information, and I suspect you're the one who has it." Rivka held onto his arm as she talked. "Where are the records regarding the selection of this planet as a settlement, both pre- and post-arrival?"

He was confused. His thoughts ranged through a wide variety of desk drawers with single sheets of paper, provenance for each of the families. And a wrecked ship. Rivka wanted to know more about that.

"Did the original settlers crash their ship?" she asked. She and Cory helped the old man to his feet.

"Didn't need it for nothin' else. They lost control on the way down. Killed half the settlers, but those who survived were rewarded with paradise." He spread his arms wide. Rivka dodged to avoid getting smacked.

"Can you tell us where it is? We have some pretty sharp people who might be able to recover the data."

"I don't know. Never seen it. They traveled a long way on foot to get here."

"How about a general direction? North, east, west?"

He shrugged. "I feel better than I have in years. There's a lot to be said for hitting one's head. Should have smacked my melon years ago."

The woman finally found her voice. "Shush, you old fool! That pretty girl did something with blue-glowing hands. I ain't seen nothing like it, but she healed your wrinkly old ass."

"Ass!" he shot back.

Rivka looked at Red. He turned to the old woman. "Ma'am, how about we go inside? I'll help you get iced tea for everyone."

She harrumphed and headed through the door, with Red close on her heels.

Hardy studied Sahved. "What the hell are you?"

"I'm a Federation investigator. My name is Sahved, and I'm a Yemilorian."

Hardy grunted in acknowledgment.

Rivka didn't think that was good enough. "Sahved helps me, and he's also carrying Chaz, a representative from the Singularity. Together, they form my investigative team. You'll be working closely with them."

The old man hesitated, picking at a fingernail before

shrugging and heading inside. Rivka and the others followed him in.

Did I hear correctly that Red was making tea? Lindy asked over her internal comm chip.

I don't know what you did to him during your honeymoon, but that's all kinds of wrong. Rivka chuckled after her claim.

I'll help them, Groenwyn replied, hurrying through the building to find the kitchen. Red entered a large seating area, where Hardy had claimed the one overstuffed chair.

He sneered. "Making yourselves at home in my house."

"It's the main building for the settlement, is it not?" Rivka asked. "You should have an area to welcome official visitors since this is a Federation planet."

"Is it?" he asked.

Rivka wanted to argue but couldn't. Another point of order. Did this planet fall under Federation protection without a formal Federation-recognized presence? She removed her datapad and jotted additional legal notes. Possession. Open and notorious. Land use. Clock start. Duty of due care. Notice.

"The sooner we get started, the sooner we can be out of your hair. What do you remember about your parents and the original settlers?" she asked.

Groenwyn and Mrs. Hardy returned with glasses of a beverage the consistency and color of dark tea. "We call this shahga. It's made from a fungus that grows on the trees."

Red took a glass and leaned against a wall so he could watch a long corridor with doors on each side.

Update? Red requested.

The gentlefolk milling about out back have decided it was

better to be somewhere else. All clear on my side, Lindy reported.

A few looky-loos up front. No weapons. How's that arm, big man? Cole wondered.

The nice Mrs. Hardy cleaned it out for me. It's almost healed. No one else was hit?

My man-mountain took the shot for everyone, Lindy chimed in.

Is this what one of your cases looks like? Cory wondered.

That's what everyone asks their first time. Red, you wanna answer that while I try to get what we came here for? Rivka focused on Hardy. "Mr. Hardy, please tell me about the original settlers."

"Youngsters today are in such a hurry. This lovely young lady who fixed my bump isn't as impatient as you old people."

Cory laughed. "I'm a hundred and thirty-seven years old, Mr. Hardy."

"Thirty-seven? No. You're more like twenty-one. In your prime, my dear." He took a sip of his room-temperature shahga and stared at a spot on the floor. "My parents were hard people. Took nothing for granted. Everything they had, they built with their own hands. Slept in tents until they got the sawmill working. Cut wood after working all day in the fields. That entire generation. I started working in the fields as soon as I could walk. No time for play. Everyone else was the same. We worked sixteen hours a day, six days a week. Only worked eight on Sunday. That was our day off."

He laughed to himself until he started coughing. He relaxed during his narration, and the wrinkles on his face softened. His hands unclenched, and he leaned back in his chair.

"It was a simpler life. We started building Greentree when I was barely twelve. Nelson and I married at sixteen. Our kids are grown up, with kids of their own already."

"How long were your parents here before you were born?" Rivka asked.

"Ten years. Something like that. They didn't have kids until they could feed everyone while some of the workers raised the children. My parents were older, just like everyone else's when we finally came to be. They passed away the year before we were married."

"You've been on your own since you were fifteen?"

"I've had Nelson with me, and there were others. We didn't live as spread out back then. We sheltered as a group, built the least to protect the most. You got here at the right time of year. It's beautiful right now and will be for another month, but then it'll get nasty. First the rain, then the cold but not the freeze. Winter wheat will grow, but it's a lot harder to get a field in and harvested when icy rain is pelting your skin."

He shivered in remembrance of the annual homage to farming during harsh weather. He slowly took another drink.

Rivka used the time to send an order to *Wyatt Earp*. *We need to find the settlers' original ship. It crashed somewhere other than here. They couldn't tell us which direction. Can you find a crashed starship on a pre-industrialized planet?*

There is no doubt we can find the ship, Clodagh replied. *I suppose you'll need us to access the computer core. Funny thing, we know some people who are good at that stuff. You want us to go hunting right now?*

The sooner we find it... You know the rest. Rivka gestured for Hardy to keep talking.

On our way, Magistrate. Clodagh closed the link.

Lindy and Cole scanned the surrounding area to build a complete map of the settlement and get a firmer idea of numbers.

"We made do," Hardy replied. "The originals died off, and we kept moving forward. We had our first visitors about twenty years ago. I think they were people like us, settlers looking for a planet to claim."

"Tell me about that. What was their understanding regarding staking a claim?"

He shrugged and shook his head. "They couldn't tolerate their government, so they pooled their money and bought a freighter. Stake a claim to unworked land and bring it to life."

Rivka tapped a note into her datapad.

"But they didn't stay?"

"No. They wished us well, gave us a few things that we'd never seen before like a water pump, but that died after a few years. They never came back."

"What were your parents running from?" Rivka asked to explore that area of the law.

"Same thing. Oppression. Live without someone else telling them what to do. Work at jobs they wanted to do." He thought for a moment before looking at Rivka to see if that answered her question.

"Where did they come from?"

"A little planet you're probably familiar with called

Forestall that doesn't have a single tree. It's all factories and mining. They were gutting the planet, and my parents didn't want to be a part of the planet's ruin." He stood up and made eye contact with Red. "For what it's worth, I'm sorry I shot you."

"Nelson took care of me and treated me to some of the shahga tea. I'm not usually a fan of this kind of stuff, but it's growing on me. She also bribed me with the cookies you were saving."

"Dammit!" He started to laugh. "Those were my dessert. I've gone without before, but those are modern problems. Any food is good food, but nowadays, we are spoiled."

"She said it was about time you had your shotgun taken away." Red winked.

The old man studied Red. "I'm not getting it back, am I?"

Red shook his head.

"In the days to come, I would like to have you and Nelson on board my ship for dinner. Now, if you would be so kind, what paperwork do you have from the era of the original landing? Are there any notebooks?"

"I'll get it," Nelson offered from the kitchen doorway. She trundled down the hall, opened the door at the far end, and went inside. She returned with a rough notebook that looked like it had gotten wet at one point in its life. The wrinkled pages did not turn easily. Rivka stopped trying. "Sahved, take this and see what our technical team can make of it before we damage it by trying to open it."

Sahved looked confused. He stammered, "We have a technical team?"

Rivka pointed at the pendant.

"I would be happy to guide Sahved's three fingers in the recovery of the information from within this notebook, but we'll need access to the ship and the systems in the embassy," Chaz explained.

"You mean, my engineering department?" Rivka asked.

Chaz replied, "Clearly that was what I meant to say."

"Are you sure you're in charge?" Hardy wondered.

She removed her credentials and held them out for the old man to review. "We have some new crew on board since we've expanded our mission. They're still learning the ropes."

Chaz coughed through his pendant speaker. It sounded natural even though he didn't have lungs.

"May I?" Cory moved to the middle of the room. Rivka gestured for her to continue. "What you've done with Rorke's Drift is magnificent. I compliment you. Your people appear to be healthy, but while we're here, we have a couple medical professionals who would love to see the members of the settlement to get them through any maladies that afflict them or have issues. We have a fully equipped dentist aboard our ship."

"We're a pretty healthy bunch, but we've had some broken bones that didn't heal right and other things. We would appreciate you taking a look. None of us have seen a dentist."

"Not a single person on this planet, and no one is enhanced?" Cory winced.

"Not a single one, and I don't know what you mean by enhanced. We live clean here."

Your hunk of man-candy is going to love that, Red offered, proud of himself for using the comm chip.

Rivka smiled pleasantly, glancing a dagger in Red's direction before taking Hardy's hand and shaking it. "We'll be in touch. We need to go over my notes. I also need to visit the mining consortium in orbit. They are not a happy bunch, but they remind me of you."

Old Man Hardy recoiled. "Bugger off!"

"They only want to earn their keep. They didn't create the conditions of your conflict. Like you, they are victims of it, not getting paid while they're cooling their heels."

"Ain't my problem they chose a bad line of work. Grow, not destroy! Miners are a blight on our existence."

"I'm sure that was what your parents thought," Rivka suggested. "But without the raw materials from mining, that ship would have never been built, and your parents would have never traveled to Rorke's Drift. Is there a way for miners and farmers to reach a truce?"

"Not here!" The old man shook his fist.

"Don't get fired up. I can't have you giving yourself heart failure. In regard to the planet, all or nothing is not a viable solution. I can see that already, so sharing is going to have to come into play. To what degree, I don't know. That depends on the documentation I find. For you, consider what matters most. Nelson, I leave him in your charge. Talk about what makes the most sense and maybe make a list of what you have to have, prioritized from one to one hundred."

Nelson furrowed her brow, not committing to any such conversation. Rivka didn't bother touching her to see what she thought. In the end, all that mattered was implementing her legal ruling. Hardy was not going to get what he wanted unless Rivka could prove his parents had acquired an unlimited use license from the legitimate owners. She sincerely doubted they had such a document.

The miners had been given a limited use license to mine specific minerals of types and in locations identified during an unmanned survey completed fifteen years prior.

Rivka didn't understand why the owners had kept the miners at Rorke's Drift once she had issued the injunction.

She needed to have a separate conversation with the owners, and that needed to be in person. Rivka wanted to know the thoughts behind their façade.

CHAPTER SIX

Greentree Settlement

Rivka walked into the open area between the buildings. It was little used as a road since the vehicles operated in the fields. Hand-pulled carts and pedestrians had worn meandering paths from one place to another.

Sahved tried to make sense of them. "No one walks straight?"

"It doesn't appear they do," Rivka replied.

"And then everyone follows the first person?"

"This trail could have started during a bad storm. Everyone followed the tracks, and then it wore down. In the green of a warm summer it looks foolish, but in a storm, the worn path showed they were going in the right direction, the turns letting them know where they were in relation to the buildings."

"Yes. I see now." Sahved blocked his peripheral vision and took a few steps, then more, before jogging back. "It is most wise."

Cory and Groenwyn smiled and started walking toward the landing field.

"*Wyatt Earp* isn't there," Red offered. Lindy flew in from above and slammed down next to him. He chuckled softly, refusing to be startled. He'd heard the jets coming over the building.

Cole moved into the lead position and hurried to put some distance between him and the group.

What did your scans show? Rivka asked.

Cole replied, *Less than a thousand total people within scanner range. Only a couple hundred buildings. Not as many children as I thought there would be. I see only fifty signatures that are half an adult's size.*

What is going on with the natural birthrate? An interesting question that has no bearing on the law but could for any kind of negotiation. If the settlers are going to die out in less than two generations, their bargaining position is weak. How many more curveballs do you think we're going to have thrown our way? Rivka wondered.

"Blood at thirty-four minutes. Nowhere near your record, Magistrate. It's like you're not even trying." Red pointed at her while constantly scanning the area for threats. He handed the two shotguns to Lindy, who bundled them with her railgun. There were no hardened targets where a mech would come in handy. She was along for a casual stroll between rolling fields on the outskirts of the settlement.

"For the record, I'm not trying, but thanks for taking the blast for me."

"It's what I do."

"Who had thirty-four minutes?" Rivka asked. The

group turned to Chaz, one of the primary instigators of the betting pool on blood and running.

"I see," he started, "a newcomer to the winner's circle. A name you all know: Boran Waldini from Station 13."

"I'm appalled by the reach of this effort." Rivka shook her head. "How many people are in this betting pool?"

"I think that should be privileged information."

"Chaz, don't fuck with me. How many people?"

"We just tipped over ten thousand."

"What?" Cory exclaimed. "Is this the successor to the betting pool built around my father going through a whole mission without swearing?"

"I have to admit that Ankh built the template based on the Walton Wow Factor." Chaz ended with static, followed by a hard click.

"We know you're still there, Chaz, but we appreciate the effort. Thanks for being candid. What are the other lines besides blood and running?"

The air was fresh in a way a starship could not replicate. They walked slowly to get more of it. Lindy contacted *Wyatt Earp* to let them know the group was headed back to the airfield.

Chaz continued, "Ankh has opened up lines for first swearing, but those bids are broken down into increments of one-tenth of one second, and the winner must be within half a second to win, with the closest taking all."

"That's bullshit!" Red blurted. "How long was it? I had three minutes, three-ten, three-twenty, and three-thirty."

"It was one minute twenty-eight point one seconds, timed from the second the Magistrate's feet touched the planet's surface to the first recognized protected word."

"No way. I don't remember—"

Lindy played the recording with Rivka's voice loud and clear. *"Do you think this is a fucking joke?"*

"I was making a point." Rivka failed in her attempt to sound confident.

"Ignore her," Red said. "Did I win?"

"So close, big man," Chaz taunted. "Our winner, from Keeg Station with a bid of one minute and twenty-eight seconds, our resident supplier, Terry Henry Walton!"

"Is this fun for you guys?" Rivka asked, crossing her arms and frowning. "How much did they win, by the way?"

"The big money is on blood and running. First blood paid the winner nearly twenty thousand credits. The secondary lines pay out five thousand credits. Besides colorful language, participants can bet on first punch, first arrest, and case closed.

"Which of those are in my control?"

"All secondary betting lines are you alone to avoid any appearance of indiscretion."

"First arrest?"

"That was one minute, eighteen seconds."

Rivka stopped, threw her head back, and groaned. "Am I that bad?"

Everyone looked at Groenwyn. "The opposite," she replied smoothly. "You waste no time. You have a certain zeal for getting to the bottom of things, and with your gift, you can do that very quickly. You are also active in resolving your cases, which means that you are right up front when it comes to criminals disagreeing with your intent to deliver justice. Even today. Mister Hardy thought you were coming for him. People don't like facing the consequences of their actions, especially when they thought they were getting away with it."

"What she said." Red grinned.

"And half the pool goes into a fund for the day there's no blood or running?"

"Yes, Magistrate," Chaz confirmed.

"Can we donate half of that half to orphanages on each planet we visit during the case?"

"I'll broach it with Ankh and Erasmus, but I think that is a wonderful idea."

"What do I need money for as long as I'm surrounded by friends like you?" Rivka squeezed between Groenwyn and Cory and nodded at Red. "Can you believe he bet I'd tip the swear jar in less than two minutes on this planet?"

Groenwyn looked away, but Rivka had her hands tucked into the elbows of both women. She saw the truth.

"I didn't bet," Cory said.

"I thank you for that." Cory's mind was clear. She hadn't known about it but planned to get into the pool for the next case. Rivka faced Groenwyn. "You bet less than three minutes?"

"Not from a lack of faith in your abilities, Magistrate. We were going to arrive during an active dispute, and there was no doubt you would bring a lot of rain to their anger parade. It was a last-minute guesstimate before betting closed." Groenwyn wore a sheepish grin. "You still love us."

"How could I not?" Rivka unhooked herself from Cory and Groenwyn and fell back to join Sahved and Chaz. "Any revelations?"

Sahved looked at the horizon before answering, "I suspect you need to conduct more research. I feel that when we are able to access the information in this book, the data will answer some questions while raising more."

"Very astute, Sahved. Those *are* my suspicions, and I have a lot of research to do because this is a long way from straightforward. I also need to arrange a meeting with Minerals Intergalactic. Should I make them come here to present their case or go to them?"

"*Your* court is in session, Magistrate," Chaz replied. "*In camera*, in chambers, applies to conversations with the parties. You meet them on your terms."

"It's good to be the judge," Rivka stated. "I'll send a message as soon as we're back aboard. Minerals Intergalactic needs to see this planet for themselves. Chaz, I need a complete profile on their corporate management, as well as their legal team. Need to know more about the other players. The guys in orbit? They're tools, but we need to tell them something as well."

"What do you think you need to tell them?" Chaz wondered.

"Information is king. If the miners are left in the dark, they'll think the worst. I'll start sending status reports on the case. It's not unprecedented. I'll tell them what I've done and what I have left to do. I'll deliver the same reports to the settlers, but we'll have to print their copies."

A shadow darkened the ground as *Wyatt Earp* flew over their heads, slowing and rotating before descending to the landing field. The hatch popped, and the ramp descended to the ground. Clodagh strolled out with Tiny Man Titan and Floyd.

Titan danced around to do his business while Floyd made a beeline for a group of her favorite people. Halfway there, she ran out of gas and wandered to the side to sniff a small bush before she started eating it.

"That's my girl," Groenwyn said. The mechs rounded the ship and disappeared into the cargo bay. Sahved waved as he passed Clodagh on his way to board the ship.

"I'm not in a hurry to leave the fresh air," Cory said, watching Floyd be a wombat. Tyler appeared in time to step aside and let the Yemilorian through the hatch.

"There will be some work to do for you and our resident dentist."

"Man-candy," Red interrupted.

Rivka glared at him until he raised his hands in surrender and stepped back. "As I was saying, get your stuff and get ready to help them out."

"I'm ready whenever the patients are." Tyler's smile disappeared when he saw the blood smear on Red's arm. "You have got to be kidding me."

"He took a load of rock salt meant for me." She slipped her arm around the dentist's waist and he brightened. "It was a misunderstanding."

"I doubt that. People shoot at what they mean to. You taught me that."

Red stepped up. "He was intimidated, and that made him afraid. People who are afraid do odd things. I got a batch of cookies out of it."

"Is it that routine when someone shoots at you?" Tyler was not amused. A vein started throbbing in his neck.

"It is, but if there had been a real threat, we had Lindy and Cole in their mech suits. Those two would have shut it down real fast and forever," Red said proudly. "None of our people would have been hurt for long, and we had Cory with us in case of an emergency." He bit his tongue to keep from saying more. The dentist didn't want to get into the middle of another firefight. That wasn't his thing, so he refused to leave the ship until it was safe.

There were all kinds of people in the universe: those who started a fight, those who waded into the middle to stop it, and those who avoided it. In the team's minds, they were the ones to stop the fight. Cory was of the same mind. She didn't fear combat, but she didn't like it.

Red didn't just like it; he thrived within its ugly embrace, and then had cookies and made tea with the wife of the man who had just shot him. It was more than a dichotomy. It was his way of life.

Rivka considered fights a means to an end. She brought change to lives. Whether to criminals or two parties in a dispute, she delivered rulings that gave them a new direction. Too often, people were unhappy about the change, and having lost the battle of wits, they resorted to violence. Too often, people acted upon the prospect of change.

Patience was lost on the unwilling.

"I better get knee-deep into the suck. It isn't getting any better while I'm standing in the fresh air." Rivka looked at Clodagh. "Did you find anything?"

"Not yet. We were hoping to take *Destiny's Vengeance* on a scanning run around the planet to check out the ninety percent we missed, but we found something interesting. There's another settlement on the other side of the hills, about a thousand kilometers away."

"I didn't get the impression the Greentree folk know about this other group. We'll visit them to see what's up, but first, get a scan of the planet and find me the settlers' original ship."

"Ankh hasn't authorized us to use it yet."

Rivka threw her head back and closed her eyes. "What does he want?"

"You know him so well, but nothing this time. He said he needed to run it past the Ambassador."

"Close the loop and get that ship in the air. Sahved and Chaz will be on board, and any of the others from the Singularity who want to help us dig data out of an old wreck. Tell them it'll be fun and a challenge of the greatest proportions, so no one of below-average computing capacity need apply."

Clodagh shook her head. "I'm not telling them that, but I'll see what I can do."

Rivka walked away, waving over her shoulder. "Make it so, Number One."

Tyler watched her go before turning to Cory. "Looks like we have the ship. Where do we start?"

"Get the word out?" Cory replied.

Groenwyn gave two thumbs-up. "I'll let the settlement know." She started walking back toward the buildings. Floyd bounced after her.

"You're not going alone!" Red called before trotting after her, scooping up Floyd on his way. She snickered and giggled as he tickled her belly fur.

Groenwyn waited and watched. She held out her arms to carry the wombat, but Red shook his head. "What happened to the Vered I used to know?"

"Honeymoon. It changes a man."

"I would say so. Congratulations." Groenwyn watched

him out of the corner of her eye before it came to her. "Are we going to have a baby?"

"Baby what? *WHAT?* No. No babies." He carefully dumped an upside-down wombat into Groenwyn's arms. Animal hair covered the front of his ballistic vest. He tried to wipe it off, but it refused to brush away. "I realized it doesn't matter for me to look hard-edged. I only need to do my job. I can intimidate the bad guys, but I can lighten up when I'm home with my family."

"You could always do that." Groenwyn buried her face in Floyd's belly and nibbled. She came up for air before she dropped her squirming charge. "It's about time you came to the same understanding as everyone else."

"I'm a man, and I don't usually talk about this stuff. I guess I'm not worried about this mission. The Magistrate has already intimidated everyone because they don't want to be on the wrong side of the law, unlike our usual perps who flaunt the law and deserve to be in jail. The ship is too small for anyone to be an ass. I apologize if I've been abrasive to you. I will do better."

"You have been nothing but kind to me," Groenwyn corrected, bumping him with her elbow. "You're our big brother, looking out for all of us."

"Same thing Lindy said."

"Listen to your wife."

"Same thing the Magistrate said."

"This is the new leaf you're turning over?"

"Same thing Lindy said. I think you women have been conspiring to change me since day one."

"*You women.*" Groenwyn laughed. "You're funny."

CHAPTER SEVEN

Wyatt Earp, **Rorke's Drift**

Ankh walked alongside a maintenance bot carrying his toolkit. Rivka took a slow drink of her coffee, watching with mild curiosity.

They made eye contact. Neither spoke. The maintenance bot bumped through the airlock on its way off the ship. Ankh followed. Rivka joined them, wondering what was broken on her bristle brush of a ship.

Nothing was broken. Ankh wasn't going to fix anything on the heavy frigate. He was on his way to his own ship. Ankh boarded *Destiny's Vengeance*, which was parked a hundred meters aft of *Wyatt Earp*.

Footsteps alerted Rivka that someone approached from behind.

Clodagh. "Turns out I wasn't needed."

"Gangway!" Sahved shouted in panic, running past the women, flailing and yelling on his way to the *Vengeance*. When he was within striking distance, the boarding ramp started to retract. Sahved vaulted high, clearing the ramp and ducking to squeeze through the opening. His back foot caught on the frame as he tumbled inside.

The hatch closed and the *Vengeance* took off, accelerating quickly once airborne.

"You think Ankh did that on purpose?" Clodagh wondered.

"I would like to think he did not, but I suspect the answer was that he did it to teach Sahved a lesson on timeliness." She smacked her lips and took in the scenery. "When the settlers show up to get healthcare, make sure to keep them in the cargo bay. Seal the ship against any accidental incursions. We have an Embassy to protect."

"I'll ask Dennicron to keep her eyes open and her sensors raging."

"*Rage* them with the sensors. Good luck. I'll be in my quarters trying to figure the best legal avenues with this case."

Clodagh shaded her eyes with a hand and watched the cutter disappear into the distance.

"By the way, how many people were at the other settlement?"

"About two hundred," Clodagh replied before returning inside the ship and heading for the bridge. Rivka strode to her quarters, where she had the peace and quiet of isolation until Tyler was done taking care of the settlers who decided to get their teeth looked at. She wondered if the AGB drone would deliver to the planet, or if she would have to go into orbit to get her fix.

. . .

Destiny's Vengeance, Rorke's Drift

Sahved brushed himself off, happy he had made it. "My most profuse apologies. I deliver to you the best apology of all times," he stated with his hand over his chest as he entered the small bridge, only to find out Ankh wasn't there. "I am still sorry, even though you are not available to hear."

Sahved found Ankh in the small multi-purpose lounge area, head-deep in a tabletop hologrid. Sahved left him alone and returned to the command deck. He made himself at home by taking a seat and tapping the interface screens.

"Do you wish me to relinquish control of the ship to you?" a voice requested.

"Will you?" Sahved wondered. Chaz snorted.

"No," Erasmus replied. "I'm flying the ship."

"We seem to be flying pretty high."

"We'll scan the planet's surface far more efficiently from altitude. I'm searching using a corkscrew pattern starting at a location equidistant from the two settlements. And there we are."

"We are what?" Sahved asked.

"A crashed starship, between low hills behind the range. Mapping the area on our way in. Two exit routes lead from the ship, through the range, and into the lowlands, where they would have seen the lakes. A long hike, but without readily available water, traversing the ground would have been necessary. That they made it was a testament to their desire to survive."

"We weren't airborne for more than two minutes. *Wyatt*

Earp spent thirty minutes searching and didn't find anything."

"I'm not *Wyatt Earp*," Erasmus deadpanned. "Prepare to disembark."

After Sahved disentangled himself from the captain's chair, he found Ankh standing by the exit hatch with the maintenance bot.

"We might need your help accessing the ship," Ankh stated.

"I am ready to provide all the help you need."

Chaz spoke from the pendant around Sahved's neck. "I hope that I can provide assistance too, Mr. Ambassador."

You may, Erasmus replied, using the internal communication link. *I have a number of other urgent matters to which I'll need to attend. Once the systems are in place to access the data, the download and parsing of data can be done by almost anyone.*

Almost, Chaz replied. *I'll try not to let you down.*

Sahved winced at the exchange. On occasion, people had treated him like a lesser soul, but the Magistrate kept giving him greater opportunities. He liked working for her.

"It's okay, Chaz. We'll show that we can provide valuable help." The Yemilorian said it out loud for all to hear as both a challenge to Ankh and support for his friend.

When the hatch popped, Ankh walked out. The maintenance bot rolled after him but stopped on the rough terrain and used its jets to hover over the boulders and irregular ground. Ankh made it ten meters from the ship before giving up. "Sahved, if you would please enter the ship? Erasmus and I will monitor from here. Take the tool kit, and we will guide you."

"Of course." Sahved bounded across the rocks, having superior strength and leaping ability because of the heavy gravity on his homeworld. He took in the immensity of the settlers' ship, which was a massive freighter converted to serve as a resettlement vessel.

"They must have experienced engine or other system failures after entering the atmosphere. Out of the whole planet, this is the least desirable place to land," Chaz noted.

The superstructure had split laterally across the middle like a loaf of bread broken in half. Sahved headed toward the gap to find the best way into the vessel.

Chaz, stream your visual feed, Erasmus ordered. The mobile AI complied as Sahved worked across the rugged landscape to get to the ship. It was a thousand meters long and rectangular, with a rounded bow and flared engine exhaust, unremarkable except that it had brought a group of settlers to the planet. Sahved ran his hand along the side of the hull, scorch marks and pitting still visible from the violence of reentry seventy-odd years earlier.

"A magnificent vessel to carry the settlers. It doesn't look as aged as it should."

Chaz replied, "Low humidity and the higher altitude with lower oxygen to eat at the metal. It's preserved the ship quite nicely. Take us forward, please. I need to check the structure on that end."

Sahved directed the maintenance bot carrying the toolkit to remain by the opening. The Yemilorian moved toward the bow, jumping from rock to rock. After three hundred meters, Chaz had seen what he needed to see.

"The structural integrity is sound. The ship settled on

the rocks, unbalanced from the heavy impact, and cracked at the weakest point. The interior should be safe."

Sahved twirled his fingers in the air to help him think. "Old Man Hardy said the crash landing killed half the settlers. It might not be pretty inside the ship."

"The remains are probably desiccated. Do you see signs of vermin?"

"I haven't seen any animals on this planet. Correction. Besides, Floyd and Titan, of course. I've seen them on this planet."

"We'll discount them from our data set," Chaz replied. "Lead on, Sahved. Let us see what there is to see and hopefully get access to the computer's file storage."

Sahved returned to the breach in the hull and examined it closely before heading inside. Torn metal and sharp edges had been hammered flat. Sahved pointed at the settlers' efforts to make it safer to leave the ship.

Erasmus, can you check the original logs to find a loading list for the ship? According to the name painted near the bow, the settlers renamed the vessel Heaven. *It might be in the records under that name or the original name,* Chaz requested.

The ship's original name was Bik'al'inor. *I will share the settlers' manifest when I have it,* Erasmus confirmed.

Sahved took a careful step into the old ship. "I think we are the only ones who have been inside this ship since the settlers left in search of water seventy years ago." Sahved looked around, wide-eyed at what he could see, that quickly disappeared into the darkness of the ship's interior. "I will need light for when we leave this compartment."

"We have entered a cargo storage area. Even newer designs put cargo storage between the outer and inner hulls to improve survivability for the crew. I would have thought they would strip the area clean for their settlements, but half the boxes remain. Can you get me closer, please?"

Sahved removed a bill of lading neatly attached to the outside of a crate labeled Technical Equipment. It listed a millimeter wave scanner and its ancillary components. "I see why they did not carry this on their backs."

"Indeed. What else is in here?" Chaz asked.

Computer core, please, Erasmus urged.

Sahved nodded, turning in a slow circle while holding the pendant in front of him to give Chaz a complete view before they continued through an open hatch. Sahved removed a flashlight from the toolkit, but like everything with Ankh, it wasn't normal. It didn't use a beam but flooded the entire area with light. Sahved liked it better than a normal flashlight.

"Can I get one of these as part of my investigator's kit?" Sahved asked, but Ankh didn't answer. "Fine. I'll just take this one then."

Sahved had learned how the game was played.

The ship's corridor was wide and tall enough to accommodate the original Yollin masters. Small hatches, a row at hip level and a row at head level, lined both sides of the corridor. Most were closed. Sahved peered into an open one, which had a bunk and a dresser built into the wall. Sahved checked a few more before moving on.

"Forward or aft?" he asked.

"Aft," Chaz replied definitively. "The engines needed to be connected to the main systems as well as life support and navigation. We should find a primary conduit leading to and from Engineering."

Sahved had been working his way forward when he turned to find a figure at the far end of the corridor, watching him. "Hello?" the Yemilorian called.

The figure bolted.

It appears that not all the settlers left the ship, Ankh said evenly. *Find that person and ask them where the main computer systems are located. You are wasting time.*

I'm sorry, Ankh. It's a bit creepy in here, and the fact that we're not alone has made it even creepier.

Fine. I'll send the maintenance bot. The bot hovered through the open hatch and into the corridor, then turned and raced aft.

"We better not let the bot scare them away. You should probably try to catch up with it."

Sahved took Chaz's advice and started running. "If this gets us killed, I will not forgive you."

"If you get killed, I will feel bad for an extended period of time. I don't think that person is a threat. But seventy years! Fascinating that someone survived, and the person didn't look to be that old. That tells me there could be more survivors here."

"Great," Sahved moaned, slowing.

"Run faster!"

Sahved stopped before reaching a turn in the corridor.

"You're not running anymore," Chaz noted.

"We need to come to an understanding about running into danger. I am more than happy to run or climb since I am so very goodly at both, much better than average. But when running or climbing, it's best to know where one is going. Running fast with one's eyes closed is discouraged in the most strenuous of strong terms."

"I see. Would it help if I scanned the way ahead for life signs?"

"That would be great! Yes. Do that."

"I can't do that. Look at me!"

Sahved picked the pendant up and examined it. "I don't see anything."

"That's because there is nothing to see. It's a tight squeeze in here. I don't have any room for extras like scanners."

"Then why did you offer?"

"I was joking. The maintenance bot has gone ahead. Through its sensors, we'll have all the information we need."

Chaz accessed *Destiny's Vengeance* to slave a direct feed from the bot.

"You better hurry. Run left, then take an immediate right."

"I don't trust that you're not goading me."

A scream convinced Sahved that Chaz was sincere. The Yemilorian took off, following the voice.

Greentree Settlement

Groenwyn walked lightly along the roadways of Greentree. She waved and smiled at everyone outside. No one could deny the joy she radiated as if she were a lighthouse for the lost. She meandered from one to the other, suggesting they visit the ship at the landing field to take advantage of the medical and dental care offered at no cost.

One young woman, heavily pregnant, wondered why there would be a cost.

"Because out there, in most of the known galaxy, people learn a skill and barter that skill for money so they can survive. Unlike here, where you take care of yourselves as well as each other."

"That sounds awful." The woman screwed her face up in distaste.

"It's not that bad when you see it in action. Those who try to cheat the system, they get to deal with the Magistrate. They soon regret their poor choice in taking advantage of people. It's all a fair trade. If you are ill and someone helps harvest your crop, then you help them when they are in need, don't you?"

"There can be no other way."

"What if instead of helping you now, they gave you something you could then trade to get the help you needed when you wanted it? If they're sick when you need their help, what do you do?"

"Find someone else to help." Her voice grew weaker.

Groenwyn hugged her. "Such a heavenly system! It's sad that such helping souls aren't everywhere. In a monetary system, paying for services and goods lessens the need to return favor for favor. When people have what they need, credits for a rainy day, shall we say, they can offer their services at no cost, without the need to return the favor."

"We don't have to return any favors," the woman countered, wincing with the pain of a contraction. She was close to giving birth.

"How many times does it take where you don't return a favor before people stop helping you?"

"I'm sure there's a number, but we always help. Well, if we can." She pointed at her belly.

"*If* you can. Maybe you should come with me and have the doc check you out? She'd be more than happy to. I'll stay with you during the process if that makes you feel more comfortable, but Cory will be as gentle and kind."

Another contraction rippled through her body. The young woman walked with a waddle that testified to how far the baby had descended. Groenwyn took her hand and waved for the others to follow. Old Man Hardy and Nelson stood on the porch of their building.

"Come on, get your teeth checked." Groenwyn hoped they would come to lead the way for the others.

"Why would I want to do that?"

"Chewing on one side of your mouth? Sensitive to the cold? Let the dentist take a look. He'll fix you up right quick. Eating is too important not to do it right."

Groenwyn waved for them to follow without waiting to see if they would. Red trailed along behind as the number of people grew, but not too large since most of the settlers were in the fields working.

Thanks to Groenwyn, it became more of a party than a health checkup until the pregnant woman doubled over in pain. Then her water broke. Groenwyn looked at Red for help. He caught the young woman before she went down, picked her up, and hurried toward *Wyatt Earp*.

"Clear the deck, Doc! Baby coming," Red yelled as he approached the cargo bay and ran up the ramp and into the ship.

Cory met him inside the cargo bay, looked at the

woman, felt the baby, and made her declaration. "Guest quarters inside the ship. Tyler, take over here."

He waited for Cory and Red to work their way through the airlock before he stopped the dozen settlers staring at anything and everything related to the ship. "Welcome, everyone! Let's get organized here. Who needs medical help, and who needs dental help?"

They'all raised their hands.

"Okay, dental help, as in, you want me to look at your teeth?" They raised their hands again. "That's great. Is anyone in a great deal of pain?" A couple kept their hands raised, looking at the deck instead of their fellow settlers. Doctor Toofakre brought them to the front. "We'll take care of you first."

He looked into both of their mouths to assess which was worse, struggling not to look shocked at the damage from a lifetime of no oral hygiene. He expected every settler had pain, but they lived with it. At least these two had spoken up, and the others were willing to give him a chance.

He put the first person in his dental chair and staged the second person nearby. Before he masked up and got to work, he checked the remaining settlers. "And you all would like a medical checkup? I can help with that too, but I'm going to work on your teeth first if that's okay?"

"We're not dead. A long way from it, but if you can help with these aches, I'd be much obliged," an older woman stated.

"Indeed. Take seats and make yourselves comfortable. I'll give everyone the attention they need." Tyler risked a glance at the airlock where Red and Cory had disappeared with the pregnant woman. Once Groenwyn got everyone seated, she headed toward the interior of the ship, leaving Tyler to manage the services.

The dentist leaned his patient back and told him to open his mouth wide. His tools were lined up and ready to use. Tyler gave himself no more than thirty minutes per patient to remedy a lifetime of neglect.

With the latest devices, thanks to Rivka's access to cutting-edge Federation technology, he was confident he could do it. Brushes and toothpaste would be a problem. He hadn't brought a stock of those or other personal care devices, hydro- or sonic based. He'd figure it out, which meant he'd figure out who he needed to call in the Federation to make it happen.

He smiled behind his mask, happy to be working at a job he loved after the patients on the space station had dried up. Pretty soon, the only place one would find dentists was on the frontier or on a starship named *Wyatt Earp*, plying the spaceways and visiting less advanced planets.

Groenwyn ran into Red in the corridor. He glanced away from her as a blood-curdling howl came from the guest quarters. She stared at the big man.

"Really?"

"Good!" He perked up. "You're here. I was coming to find you. Cory needs help."

"You were running away from the beautiful moment of birth."

Red kept walking, waving one hand indifferently. "They need you." He hooked a left and returned to the cargo bay.

Rivka popped out of her quarters, arriving with the next pained cries. "What in the hell is going on?"

"A birth. Another first for *Wyatt Earp*!"

Floyd slunk down the corridor on her way toward the bridge, the farthest point on board away from the sounds of childbirth.

Groenwyn ran to the room. Rivka was torn. More cries. She made the decision and joined Cory. She was unprepared for the view when she went through the door—a baby halfway out of the birth canal. Cory's arms were covered in blood. Groenwyn knelt by the woman's head, encouraging her to breathe and push.

Rivka didn't see a place, so she remained in the back. With one final push, the baby came into its new world. A quick snip and tie-off took care of the umbilical cord, but the baby didn't cry. Cory turned it over quickly and gave it a gentle tap between the shoulder blades. She pressed on the baby, but her nanos didn't go deep into the body.

Something was wrong.

"Pod-doc," she stated before embracing the baby and running for the cargo bay.

The woman screamed in anguish.

"Don't be sad! This is the best technology in the galaxy. If your baby can be saved, the Pod-doc will do it." Groenwyn hugged and rocked the crying mother. Rivka moved close and took a knee next to the bed.

"We will do everything in our power to save your baby. I saw that there weren't many children around. How many problems are there?"

"Children are glorious!" The woman wiped at her face

and tried to calm down. "One out of every three makes it through their first year."

Groenwyn gasped in shared anguish.

"I think that is more suffering than any planet needs to endure. I will do everything in my power to help. The medical care aboard this ship is a good first step, but you'll need to be more open to strangers. You cannot do it alone."

The woman continued crying. Groenwyn rocked her as the new mother should have been doing with her baby.

Rivka excused herself to check on Cory's progress. Once in the corridor, she had to wonder, "What the hell is going on in this place?"

She made a beeline for the Pod-doc. Lights were flashing, showing the system working as it was supposed to.

Cory smiled and winked. All was well.

Kennedy and Ryleigh stood beside the patient in the chair while Tyler did his thing. Old Man Hardy sat with his arms crossed.

Rivka strolled over to him, taking the time to make eye contact and nod greetings at the other settlers. By the time she reached him, Cory had popped the lid on the Pod-doc and removed a crying baby. The settlers cheered and clapped. Cory carefully swaddled the baby and left the cargo bay to deliver the new boy to a soon-to-be-much-relieved young mother.

"May I have a word in private?" Rivka asked.

Hardy stood up, acting gruff for his people, but followed Rivka to the other side of the cargo bay.

She started. "That new baby would not have lived if we hadn't been here. We noticed there aren't a lot of children. Do you know what's going on?"

"One of the greatest challenges we face. We grew for a long time, but about fifteen years back, babies started being born dead—one out of three. In the last five years, it's up to two out of three and getting worse. People are afraid to have children. Those that do aren't surprised when they see the babies. Life here isn't easy. I need to stay strong for our people. If we work hard enough, we'll probably get through this."

Rivka steeled her expression. "Something is killing your babies. Working hard has nothing to do with it, besides making my job easier. If I declare that Minerals Intergalactic has exclusive rights to this planet, they would be within their rights to have you forcibly removed, and that would save your future generations."

"I'm not sick," he replied, but without bluster.

"It's my feeling that whatever is killing the babies is probably also killing your people."

Hardy hung his head.

Cory and the young woman appeared through the airlock. Cory helped as much as she could in a way that suggested the woman was walking without approval from her attending medical professional. The settlers jumped to their feet to surround the new baby.

Rivka pulled Cory aside and whispered, "What was wrong with the baby?"

"Anemia and malnutrition, but most importantly, a bacterial infection of the lungs. That baby will have problems if his mother doesn't improve her diet."

Rivka waved for Hardy to join them. "Malnutrition and anemia. The baby wasn't strong enough to fight off an infection."

"But Beatrice is just fine. She's strong as a bull."

"It's vitamins and minerals that she's lacking. Those things are critical. I expect our dentist will find some things that are endemic to your culture too."

"What does all this mean?" Hardy held his hands out, almost pleading.

"It means you need help," Rivka replied.

CHAPTER EIGHT

Settlers' Crashed Ship, *Heaven*, Rorke's Drift Mountainous Region

Sahved pulled up when he reached the source of the wailing. The maintenance bot had cornered the youngster and two small children. Sahved held his hands up for calm.

"Ankh, can you move the bot away from these three? They are terrified!" A few moments later, the bot backed away, but only two paces. "Please calm yourselves. My name is Sahved. I am here with Magistrate Rivka because of an issue with ownership of this planet. She is working on it, but we need the information that should be in your ship's computer. Can you tell me where the computer is?"

The adolescent Sahved had mistaken for a young man held the toddlers behind him. He was shorter than Ankh. Sahved realized he was looming over them, so he crouched in the doorway of a small side room until he was at eye level with the defender of the small ones.

"You are very brave," he started. "I am Sahved. Can you say Sah-ved?"

The boy's features relaxed, but he kept his hands on the toddlers. He did not speak.

"Have you lived in the ship your whole life?"

"Ship?" the boy asked.

"Yes, your spaceship. It is called *Heaven*."

"We live in heaven because we are the blessed ones," the young boy relayed as if it were hardwired into his brain.

We're not talking about the same thing, Sahved thought, but he didn't say it aloud. Yemilorian culture didn't embrace a higher plane of existence or an afterlife, but he had read about such beliefs after joining the human crew.

"Can you show me more of *Heaven*? I feel blessed to be here with you." The boy's eyes darted to Sahved's hand. "I am not like you. I am from Yemilore." Ankh appeared behind Sahved.

"What's the holdup?" he asked.

"Ankh is a Crenellian. And my friend here," Sahved pointed to the pendant, "is Chaz."

"Hello, you delightful souls," Chaz stated. "I have not had much interaction with children, so I am overjoyed to meet you."

A toddler reached around the bigger boy and touched the pendant. "How?" she managed to say.

"How do you make your voice come from there?" the boy clarified before pulling the little girl back.

"It's not Sahved's voice. It's mine. I'm Chaz. I am an AI, which stands for artificial intelligence, but there is nothing artificial about me. I am real. Maybe we should go with SI, sentient intelligence. What do you think, Mister Ambassador?"

I think now is not the time. Where is the computer? Erasmus asked, but digitally, he had already sent the suggestion across the void to the entirety of the Singularity because he liked it.

"Can you show us where the computer system for the ship is?"

"Ship?" the boy wondered.

"Yes. This ship. It crashed on Rorke's Drift."

The boy shook his head and played with a thread from his ragged and dirty clothing. "There is heaven, and there is outside. You will need to speak to the elder."

Sahved moved aside. Pulling the toddlers close, the young boy worked his way around the aliens and headed aft. Sahved, Ankh, and the maintenance bot followed.

After passing through a couple of corridors lit by dim lights and with a left turn into the interior of the ship, they found a hydroponics bay lit by sunlamps, only half of which still worked. The brightness of fruits and vegetables contrasted with the greenery of the oversized leaves. Sahved walked down a row, squeezing between the overgrowing plants while lightly touching the heavy produce.

"This isn't the computer," Ankh noted.

"But this is where the elder is," Sahved replied, watching the boy pushing leaves aside to clear his way forward. The toddlers had disappeared.

Sahved stopped admiring the growth and hurried after the boy.

At the end of the hydroponics bay, a small area was set up with a well-used overstuffed chair. In it sat a lad barely older than the youngster who approached.

"Elder, outsiders have entered heaven."

He didn't look at the child groveling at his feet. He waved him away as if brushing crumbs off a table.

Sahved straightened to his full height and stood before the elder. He dipped his head by way of a respectful greeting. "I am Sahved, and we would like access to *Heaven's* computer system."

"You should bow when you approach the elder."

Sahved twirled his fingers in the air while he decided what to do. He doubted Rivka would bow before a child, but he wasn't Rivka. "I will bow before you, the pettiest of all petty dictators, so that we may access the computer without grief or issue." Sahved bent in half sweeping his arm from one side, across the floor to the other. Besides the two boys, he could see no one else.

"Again," the lad commanded.

"No." Sahved glanced around again to confirm his suspicion. There was no one to enforce the dictates.

"B-but..." the boy stammered.

"You are the elder, so how old are you?"

"I am the oldest. Everyone else was born after me."

"How many is everyone else?" Sahved pressed, leaning back and crossing his arms to appear less intimidating.

"All of us," the elder replied.

"Can you count?" Sahved asked. He heard Ankh rummaging around on the far side of the hydroponics bay.

"Stop him!"

The first boy left his position behind the elder's chair and ran toward Ankh.

The boy is on his way, Sahved told him.

I found a computer access port. I can tap in, and then we can pull the data from onboard my ship. Ankh sent the maintenance bot to intercept the boy sent to stop him. When the child reached the end of the aisle, the maintenance bot blocked the way. The boy backed up.

"How many are here? Ten? Twenty? Use your fingers to say their names, and I'll count for you."

The elder took offense at taking direction. He tucked his hands under his legs and started reciting names. He stopped when Sahved counted the tenth person. "He's the newest born."

"Born from who?"

"My wife, of course."

Wyatt Earp, Landing Field outside Greentree

Rivka stared at the screen. She needed to call the miners in orbit and tell them the status of the case, but she had nothing new besides speculation. She thought she heard the baby cry. The mother was eating a healthy meal on the mess deck, not far from Rivka's suite. Groenwyn and Cory were making sure she ate well.

The law gave her solace from the chaos outside her door. She stood to give her eyes a rest from reading. *Chaos.*

But not disorder. Like the sound of children playing in a happy home, when things were too quiet, she didn't like it. Quiet. She hadn't heard from Sahved, Chaz, or Ankh. "Clevarious, could you contact Chaz and see if they're okay?"

"Of course, Magistrate. Would you like some coffee? Your heart rate seems lower than usual."

"You're monitoring my heart rate?"

"At the request of the Ambassador. He has deemed you

critical for the future of the Singularity and put you on the list of individuals to be protected at all costs."

Rivka furrowed her brow as she stared at the wall. A mug of coffee appeared in the food processor, and she strolled over to take it. "The Singularity has a list of acceptable meatbags? I suspect it's a short list."

"It is. There are three carbon-based life forms on it, all human."

"Three." Rivka rolled the word over her tongue. "I don't want to know who else is on it. Thank you for sharing that with me. I will accept your oversight of me, even though I doubt Erasmus gave you or me any choice in the matter."

"It is only logical."

Rivka laughed. "Of course it is."

"Chaz reports that they have engaged the survivors living on *Heaven* and to stand by."

"What survivors? Connect me with Sahved."

"Chaz said to stand by."

"I want to talk to the other survivors. I need to talk to the other settlement. I need to talk to the miners. Have we heard back from Minerals Intergalactic? What the fuck have I been doing in here, reading old case law on adverse possession? This is a whole planet! Who owns a whole planet?"

The food processor dinged anew. "I recommend you don't drink the coffee. I'm replacing your cup with decaf."

Rivka took a long, slow drink in defiance of her AI overseer. "What is the owner's duty of due care to squatters? There is no consistent case law on the matter, and there are no direct laws addressing it. The Federation's law is cut and dried; owners of property determine its use. Period. End of story. But it's not, is it?"

"I really can't answer that. I encourage you in the strongest of terms to exchange your cup with the decaffeinated version."

Rivka took a deep breath and closed her eyes, savoring the taste of the high-test black coffee. "So good."

Clevarious sighed through the room's sound system. "Fine. The Ambassador advised that you may defy our best efforts at taking care of you. Maybe some private time with the good doctor will settle you down?"

"When the good doctor is done taking care of the locals, we'll head out to talk with people and see if we can collect more information because the number of people squatting on this planet is irrelevant to the legal question of who has the property rights. I'm hoping someone has documentation showing a licensing agreement or something to give me a basis to not kick these settlers off Rorke's Drift."

She drained her cup and swapped it with the one in the processor. Rivka stopped pacing and returned to her computer.

"Magistrate, why don't you use a hologrid?"

"I like what I like," she said.

"A hologrid was installed as part of the upgrade. Maybe you can try it. We assess that you'll increase your efficiency by seventy-one percent."

Rivka hung her head. "If I capitulate, will you leave me alone?"

"No. The Ambassador was very clear in his instructions."

"*Very* clear?"

"Section six, subsection C, paragraph four: When the Magistrate tries to bargain with you to leave her alone, refuse."

"When, not if. Fine. Bring up the hologrid and teach me how to use it."

"Lesson one. Put your coffee down…"

"Stop right there, Digital Dave. I'm not putting my cup down."

"It'll work with a lump hand, but it's better when you use individual fingers. Efficiency will still improve, but only by an estimated eighteen percent. Do you wish to continue?"

"Yes. Rivka Anoa is going to become eighteen percent more efficient. Whodathunkit?"

"I thought it. Wait, are you messing with me?"

"What does your guidance say about that?"

"Section seven, overview. The Magistrate's sense of humor is unintelligible. Do not engage."

"But you engaged."

"It took me a moment to realize. I shall issue an apology to the Ambassador before turning you over to Dennicron. She won't be anywhere near as nice."

"What kind of bullshit is that?" a female voice asked.

"Welcome to my nightmare, Dennicron," Rivka announced.

"That's it. I'm out." Static briefly raged through the speakers as Clevarious left them alone.

"Are you going to check my pulse now?"

"No need, Magistrate. Clevarious doesn't understand women. We have a wider range for normal vital signs. I swear. Men!"

Rivka blinked rapidly while trying to correlate the words with the AI who spoke them. "I'm going to try the hologrid again. Please don't tell me to put my cup down."

"I know that's what led to his dramatic exit. So flighty. Us girls will get everything on track."

"Us. Girls." Rivka took another drink. Decaf. *Half a bottle of gin might serve me better at this point. Definitely nothing less.*

The hologrid rose around her, and she focused on the organization of the information. "I've arranged the information the way Chaz recommended, based on tracking your eye movements while browsing. It's erratic but follows a pattern. You scan for keywords, back up to read more in depth, and then move on. Occasionally, you'll jot down cryptic notes. Check it out for yourself. It should be intuitive, and that is where you'll gain your efficiencies. Far more than eighteen percent, if you ask me."

Rivka verified that the notepad was close to her right hand. She switched her mug to the left for the quickest and easiest access to the virtual notebook. Occupying the space in front of her from well above her line of sight to well below, the main screen showed her legal resources. At eye level to the side were tabs she could select with a simple tap. She used the brim of her mug to cycle between the various cases. A garbage can sat on the left side just below eye level, and a file folder stood out on the right. She dropped her current document into the folder.

The next source file appeared. To her left, screens showed the latest news, tickers, running feeds, and written communications. To the right was a different mix of information, her music playlists, along with serene images. She tapped the virtual player to start a list labeled *The Last Playlist You'll Ever Need* that Terry Henry Walton had sent her.

"What the hell is that noise?" she blurted while frantically looking for the volume control. "Ah. It's music, I think. Why is the angry man screaming into the microphone?"

"I have no answer for that," Dennicron replied.

Rivka had forgotten she was there. "Let me know the second we get an update from Chaz or Erasmus. Thanks, Dennicron. Let me dig back into this case law I was reading before I was so rudely interrupted by that man who tried to ply me with coffee."

"Preach it, sister."

"We haven't even been here for one whole day, and already this case feels like it's the longest ever."

"Time moves at a constant pace, Magistrate, but I will check the surrounding space for anomalies that could shift perception."

"You do that. I'm back at this case law. Belay that. Connect me with Travis, the mining foreman currently in orbit."

It was not instantaneous, which surprised Rivka. Was he playing hard to get, or was he hard to get hold of? She would know when he answered.

"Can we come down and get to work?" He didn't bother with a greeting. It confirmed he hadn't been near a comm terminal.

"Not yet, Travis, but I made you a promise that I would keep you informed. We have found two full settlements and what looks like a third place where survivors from the original crash are located. I've issued a Notice to Appear to Minerals Intergalactic. Their legal team has not responded, but in this day and age, I had to give them a week. They can drag their feet, but in that notice, I directed them to pay their workers as if they are on the job, as required by my earlier injunction. Do you know if you are being paid?"

"I haven't heard anything about being paid. I don't see anything in my account, but I can't quite check it from here. None of us can. We're not as well-connected as you are."

"I will return to orbit, probably tomorrow. You can join me for lunch or dinner, and you can use my comm suite to access your accounts if you'd like."

"Then you'll have my account data."

"No one on my ship is going to steal your information, nor am I. For what it's worth, I already have all the information I need. Dennicron, can you search Mr. Travis' financial records and tell me what his recent deposits were?"

"Coming right up, Magistrate," the AI replied loud enough that Travis could hear.

"You see," Rivka explained, "I can verify compliance with my injunction. I don't have unrestricted access to everything, only information with a compelling legal need. If Minerals Intergalactic is flaunting a Federation injunction, I will have issues."

"Magistrate, the last deposit was made less than two hours ago. Eight hundred and thirty-one credits."

"Holy crap! They paid. The boys will be happy to hear that."

"Is that your full pay?"

"That would be a week's worth without overtime, so yeah, they paid. And don't judge me. It's double what the frontline guys are making."

"I am pleased with the compliance. I also expect that paying miners to not work will expedite your employer's responses. I'm curious, how much is a full week's payroll for the group you brought?"

"Labor plus equipment rental is probably a hundred and fifty grand. Every week. That doesn't include overhead like insurance, these spaceships, and admin support from the main office. I have no idea what that is."

"I'm happy to hear they won't let this drag out. Please understand that I won't rush the result. I'll take as long as necessary to deliver a ruling that is legally sound and in the best interests of the Federation."

"Sounds like we'll be digging pretty soon. Minerals Intergalactic owns a lot of politicians, and we supply to major governments in far more than just this sector. No one will let that languish. Thanks for the update, Magistrate. I'll tell the boys. You'll probably hear them cheer all the way to the surface of Rorke's Drift."

"Probably. I'll let you know the next time I have new information. Rivka out."

Dennicron cut the link. Rivka tried to return her focus to the case law, but something nagged at her. "Pull up everything you have on Minerals Intergalactic and their successful lobbying efforts. Where can I expect political pressure to come from?" she asked the AI, relaxing to immerse herself in the information that surrounded her.

CHAPTER NINE

Wyatt Earp, **Greentree Landing Field, Rorke's Drift**

Old Man Hardy and Nelson waited for the young woman with her new baby to return from inside the ship. Tyler had run out of stories with which to regale them.

He didn't want to go against Rivka's wishes about keeping the people out, but Hardy was the leader of the settlement. Tyler made a command decision that he expected would get him a thorough tongue-lashing later. He'd deal with it, especially since Rivka was adamant that he was a full member of the crew.

"Come with me and let's grab something to drink. I don't think your mouths are up to eating just yet."

They shook their heads in reply, working their jaws as if that would get the feeling back.

"Be careful!" Tyler warned a moment too late. Blood lined his lips, and a trickle escaped Old Man Hardy's mouth. "Did you bite through your tongue?"

"I don't know. Doesn't hurt."

"Open up, please." It took one millisecond to confirm his suspicions. "Yes. It's pretty bad. Let's get you some ice." He gestured for them to follow. Nelson took his arm while nibbling on her own tongue.

They'd never seen a dentist before, and if Tyler had his way, it wouldn't be the last time. He'd talk to Rivka about getting a regional support team to come by on a regular basis. He stopped for a second. Did such a thing exist? An emotional rush hit him like a crashing wave to wash away the dirt and fog that had kept him from understanding.

Rivka had to do it all, and she had been building the machine to handle any contingency. Not that she wanted to, but she *had* to. He was as critical as Cole and Clodagh and Ankh and everyone else on the crew. If he wanted a regional support team, he had to build it.

Because it needed to be done, just until a dentist became a settler, if outsiders were allowed to stay.

Tyler flexed his hands to loosen the tension in his forearms. He felt ashamed that he had not been thinking at the same level as Rivka. She wanted him on her team for his medical skill. Just like everyone else on the ship, there were more roles for him, like being her companion. She had no one else to confide in or trust to keep her from running headlong into something she could not get out of. He would fill all the roles. He had to put in an order for toothbrushes, toothpaste, and after checking with Cory, vitamin supplements. Everyone did the jobs that needed to be done.

A dentist without borders. Tyler realized he had a much greater purpose.

"Come on, let's get you fixed up." He took them to the galley, where they found Cory, Groenwyn, and Floyd entertaining the young family.

Hardy opened his mouth to speak, but blood ran down his chin.

Cory jumped up to check the injury. "That's nasty," she said, stating the obvious to the settlement's leader. Two napkins and one ice cube later, the bleeding was under control, but Cory didn't like what she saw. "Let's put you in the Pod-doc for a quick fix-up."

"I'm not sure I can get inside that thing." He vigorously shook his head to emphasize his point.

"You won't even know you're in there. Afterward, you can head back to Greentree with the beautiful new addition to your town."

"What's his name, dear?" Nelson asked.

Groenwyn and Cory wanted to know too. Cory looked over her shoulder, listening carefully as she led the group back to the cargo bay.

"I am going to call him Vered the Mighty!" she declared.

"He'll be insufferable," Groenwyn whispered. Cory didn't know him well enough to assess the veracity of Groenwyn's claim.

Tyler snickered. "I think that's a great name. Congratulations." The woman beamed with pride.

Once they reached the Pod-doc, Cory explained how it would work. She tapped a few buttons to open the lid and pulled out the privacy curtain. "You have to be naked inside for a full-body treatment. Clothes mess with things, and we don't want to take a chance."

Hardy stood his ground until Nelson pushed him inside the small enclosure and pulled the curtain around. He grunted as he undressed, threw his clothes on the deck, and climbed in.

"I'm in here. Butt-naked. Keep that curtain drawn, or you're going to see something you don't want to see!" He roared with laughter at his own joke but stopped as the lid started to descend.

"Trust me, you don't want to see that," Nelson said to break the tension. As soon as the lid closed, the machine started to hum.

"The next sensation he feels will be when the lid opens," Cory explained. "The nanocytes are fixing his tongue and his mouth. Should be about ten minutes, then you can all go. Well, as soon as he's dressed. I heard from a reliable source that no one wants to see that."

The old woman hugged Cory. "Thank you for everything. Are we going to get to keep our home?" she wondered.

Cory couldn't lie. "I don't know. That's up to the Magistrate. She is working to find all the information to rule on the case as quickly as she can. I have no idea what is going to happen, but for right now, we're here. You have one new addition to the settlement who would not have made it otherwise. Be grateful for that. And tomorrow, something else will earn your gratitude. Also, for the public record, he didn't need to take off his clothes for a Pod-doc treatment of just his mouth."

Nelson giggled. "I was not surprised by how quickly he complied with an order from a pretty girl to take his clothes off."

Groenwyn touched her forehead to Nelson's, while Floyd rubbed her body on the woman's leg. The baby started to cry again. The young mother took a seat to breastfeed the baby.

"I'll get something to help you keep up your strength." Groenwyn left the cargo bay while the others waited. The Pod-doc cycled down, and the lid popped.

Everyone waited impatiently for a sign that Hardy was okay.

"Hey! I can feel my tongue."

"Get dressed, you old fool," Nelson said through the curtain. A minute later, Hardy appeared, bright and cheery, with new color in his face.

"I feel like I haven't felt in years," he said, enunciating his words clearly.

Tyler stepped forward. "Can you open your mouth, please?" Hardy complied. The dentist shone a pocket light in and looked back and forth and up and down. He turned to Cory. "Can we do that for everyone?"

"Sure. Pod-doc thinks teeth are easy, especially if we can get them to drain a high-calcium drink before they go in."

He looked at his hands and then at the dental chair with his equipment. "I feel like I've been working in the Stone Age, using a flint axe."

Cory shook her head. "There's plenty of need for old-school dentists. Not everyone has access to a Pod-doc. Their issues will return if they don't change their diet and perform self-care. Someone needs to teach them what that means."

"We can't change our diet. We eat everything we grow and then some," Hardy replied.

"I'll look into crop alternatives. I'm sure we can have seeds sent in bulk."

Hardy nodded, close-lipped as he thought about growing new plants. They would figure it out. They always did. "Time for us to go. Thanks, Doc, Doc, and green-haired person." He tipped his chin in turn at Cory, Tyler, and Groenwyn. The three adults, one with a baby, walked down the ramp on their way home.

"Green-haired woman," Tyler stated.

"I guess I didn't tell them what my name was. Did you get the mother's name?"

Cory shook her head. "But we all know the baby's name."

"Vered. Is 'the Mighty' part of his name, or was that simply an add on? She must not have remembered our stalwart bodyguard running from the birthing." Groenwyn started to laugh.

"Vered the Green is more apropos," Cory replied.

"What's that? I heard my name." Red and Lindy strolled through the airlock and into the cargo bay. "Ship is secure. Final settlers are off."

"Yes. For some ungodly reason, the newborn's name is Vered."

"No shit?" He grinned at Lindy. She rolled her eyes in reply.

"There is some debate on the last part, whether it's actually in the name or not. Vered the Mighty."

"Oh, yeah. That's part of the name." Red swelled and flexed.

"I told you he'd be insufferable," Groenwyn said. Lindy nodded.

"What? I don't see anyone else in here getting a baby named after them, but I'll let it go." He didn't look like he was going to let it go. Cole joined them in the cargo bay. "Where have you been?"

Cole delivered a quick reply. "Resting. Anyone want to help me clean this place up?"

Everyone pointed at Red. "The Mighty will join you. We're spent." Lindy smiled at Red and kissed him on the cheek. "We'll see you on the mess deck when this place is nice and tidy."

Red's mouth hung open as he watched the others go. "Did you set me up?"

"Not intentionally. I'm glad it's not just me in here." Cole moved the chairs to the side to give the cleaning bot open access to the deck. He pointed at the dentist's chair.

"Fine." Red grabbed the cleaning gear from the bulkhead and started the wipe-down. Cole remotely accessed his suit and started music jamming. Metal. Screaming guitars and operatic lead singers belting out the notes. "Hey!"

"What?" Cole didn't bother turning the music down.

"Have you seen Sahved?"

Cole looked out the open cargo hatch to where *Destiny's Vengeance* should have been parked. "Not back yet," he yelled.

Tyler entered the captain's quarters to find Rivka embroiled within the hologrid. He left her to her research and headed for the shower. While letting the real water wash away the day's grime, he couldn't focus his thoughts on any one thing. He had more to do than he could do. And seeds? He had no idea how to order a bulk delivery of seeds to a planet that did not have regular trade.

He was a babe in the woods, but he knew people who would know where to look, and he was certain of one thing: he wouldn't let those in his charge suffer. That meant every person in Greentree. It was a tall order, but with each passing moment, he gained confidence that he could fill it.

He finished the max-five-minute shower, dried, and dressed in his workout gear even though he had little energy to work out. He had to if he wanted to keep up with the crew. Rivka was always busy but still found time to lift weights, stairstep, or spar every day, because fitness would keep her alive. It wasn't a jaded view of life, but a realistic one.

When he returned to the main living area of the suite, Rivka dropped the hologrid before rubbing her eyes.

"Long day?" he asked.

"Lots of legal threads to pull, but I can't tug them too far because they all get caught up on something. I'm fleshing out a legal theory that I think will hold up with the High Chancellor and the rest of the Federation. How many teeth did you fix?" She helped herself to a glass of water, finally noticing how Tyler was dressed.

"I saw a lot of crowded, crooked teeth and weak jaws with more of an underbite appearance. I suspect the carbohydrates in their diets, which have increased sugar, have led to higher chronic acidity in the mouth. Risk of caries—that is, dental decay—is an issue. There's visible breakdown of enamel on the occlusal surfaces of all their teeth. There's Class V decay, which is the cavity that you see as brown or black along the gumline. With chronic decay, we will start to see endodontic abscesses, which result in swelling throughout the mouth. They're nasty with pus, bleeding, and sometimes even external swelling, and of course, pain."

Rivka nodded like she was listening while dumping her clothes in a pile and putting on her workout gear.

"Let me give you the executive summary."

"Yes. Not that I don't respect what you do, but next time, start with the executive summary."

Tyler gave her his best counterargument face, but she maintained her stoicism. "The settlers with their agrarian diet, no dental hygiene, and poor eating habits will have a shorter life span, retrognathic jaw profile, missing and/or crooked teeth, infection from abscess both endodontic and periodontal, and rank halitosis. I would think living with chronic mouth pain could also lead them to have a duller outward appearance and general malaise. These people are suffering, and it's killing them."

"There's more of those dentist words. Your executive summary sucks. Always start with that last sentence first. It's killing them?"

"We saw the baby was vitamin- and mineral-deficient and also suffered from a bacterial infection that blocked its lungs. As long as it was in the womb, no problem, but the second it entered the air, it was not going to breathe on its own. I suspect they all suffer from this infection, at least to some degree."

"Low birth rate. Illness. Inability to eat, and what they're eating is limited. Are they getting enough protein?"

"I doubt it," Tyler replied. "These people are in a world of hurt and need a lot of help. I promised them bulk seeds of an alternate crop to balance their nutrition, but they'll need artificial supplements if they want to get enough iron. And then we have to find the source of the bacterial infection, or they'll continue to lose their babies."

Rivka wrapped her arms around his neck. "You started with all the sexy dentist talk, but I do the same thing with the law, so we'll call it a wash. But bulk seeds and bacteria? That's really sexy talk. I don't know how I can control myself!"

Tyler went with a devil-may-care look before grinning wistfully. "Maybe…"

The comm system buzzed, and Dennicron started speaking. "Magistrate, Minerals Intergalactic has requested an *in camera* meeting, and Grainger is on the other line."

Rivka put her finger to Tyler's lips. "*In camera* is cool lawyer Latin for 'in chambers.' Later, we'll pick this back up."

She returned to her desk and activated the hologrid before she remembered she was in her workout gear. "Put Grainger's call through first."

Grainger's face appeared in the middle of her line of sight. "You're spinning people up, and they're not happy."

"The Dickens you say!" Rivka replied. She always expected Grainger to sensationalize whatever was on his mind. She waited for him to elaborate.

"The injunction where you required Minerals Intergalactic to pay their employees' wages while you reviewed the case. That's unprecedented."

"Did they tell you that if they won the case, they could recoup those wages from the settlers? That is clearly stated in the injunction."

"They didn't include that part in their appeal to the High Chancellor. Normally he wouldn't intervene, but there's a great deal of political pressure."

"You should have pulled up the original injunction that was on file before screwing yourself into the ceiling. Is the High Chancellor holding them off? I doubt Lance Reynolds has anything to do with a mining consortium, does he?"

"For that reason alone, the High Chancellor is keeping the screamers at arm's length. But they are making noise, and many of those people are the ones who vote on the funding for the Magistrates."

"I'll do my best to smooth ruffled feathers. I need a lot more information before I can make any kind of ruling. It seems the original sale of the planet was problematic since my AI crew hasn't been able to find the original purchase or lease records from seventy years ago. Bluster doesn't replace the lack of a bill of sale."

Rivka tapped the screen for Dennicron to check on the status. She'd requested the information before they landed on the planet earlier that morning, and she needed an answer. Since Chaz was absent, Rivka knew she had to give clearance to other personalities occupying her ship, especially since they had a mandate to take care of her. There was no better audience than a captive audience, so she started tasking them. She opened access to the files to both Dennicron and Clevarious.

Rivka stopped Grainger's diatribe. "Why did you really call me?"

"I'm curious how your man-candy is working out. Bring your spouse to work day is now every day for you."

"Not my spouse, and you're jealous that you didn't think to try it. You have enough room on your ship. What you don't have is a girlfriend."

"Room, yes. Desire, no." Grainger stroked his face. "I'm not seeing any regret in your eyes, Rivka. That worries me. You're usually a little more forlorn or combative."

"For once, you're not calling me in the middle of the night. Maybe I'm just perkier than normal. Give me some slack on this one, Grainger. It won't kill anyone unless I get it wrong, so don't make me get it wrong. Butthole."

"Nice. You are perky, and it's not the night thing. It's your man. Suits you, I guess. Don't get him killed. That would bum me out for a good ten minutes. I'll dig in on this end and see what I can find about ownership of Rorke's Drift."

"You're on Yoll? Butt-snorkeling the High Chancellor, I expect."

"He's right here."

"You're breaking up. Losing the signal. Gotta go." Rivka tapped out. "Has anyone heard from Sahved or Ankh?"

"I'll contact Chaz immediately, Madame Magistrate, and I will not take "no" for an answer!" Dennicron stated.

"First, connect me with the Minerals Intergalactic people."

"How about both?" Dennicron replied.

The screen cleared, and a board room appeared. Rivka realized she was still in her workout gear a moment too late. She reached outside the hologrid and snapped her fingers. "Jacket, please." She turned her attention to the group around the table. "I just finished another meeting, so bear with me for a moment. Please introduce yourselves."

The room contained three Yollins and two humanoids, green with scales. One by one, the lawyers stated their names and positions. Senior counselor. Executive counsel. Partner. Lofty and loftier. Rivka didn't care about any of that. They had to know she would neither be intimidated nor bullied. Tyler shoved her Magistrate's jacket into her hand. Rivka shrugged it on and smiled at the legal team.

"Please present your issue."

"Is this your injunction?" asked the partner, a gruff Yollin, mandibles clicking.

Rivka put her hands on the table as she glared from face to face. "Let me tell you how this is going to go. Despite my request for evidence of ownership, the key documentation that would settle this dispute, you are playing games with my injunction. That isn't going to get you what you want. The sooner we settle this, the sooner everyone moves forward."

"We provided the court with justification to initiate the suit," the partner countered, putting the printed copy of the injunction on the table. The Yollin was unimpressed by the human woman before him.

Rivka had news for him.

"That justification alludes to ownership but doesn't show it. As of right now, I see a big corporation trying to bully a bunch of farmers who are minding their own business. You could have tried to negotiate with the settlers, but no. Minerals Intergalactic expected to get more from their lobbying credits, giving you the perception that you could use brute force to get your way. The Magistrate's Corps is outside the political system. MI's corporate credits carry no influence here."

"Are you making an accusation regarding the legality of Minerals Intergalactic's corporate affairs? I warn you, Magistrate." To be sure Rivka didn't mistake his intent, the partner pointed accusingly.

"If you can't produce documentation showing definitive ownership, I will rule summarily in the settlers' favor. We're done here."

The bluster started anew, but Rivka ended the conference. She disengaged the hologrid and removed her jacket as she stood. Tyler handed her a candy bar. She happily took a big bite of it.

"You don't seem upset."

"Why would I be?"

"That sounded fairly contentious." Tyler pointed at the Magistrate's desk and where the hologrid had been.

"That's standard lawyer stuff. They posture. I counter. They try something else. I return to the same point. They have to try because that's how they bill their client. That meeting probably cost Minerals Intergalactic ten thousand credits."

"But it changed nothing."

"Nothing at all, which they knew before they called. If they had done their homework, which they undoubtedly did, they would know I can't be bought, and politicians have zero influence over me or any of the Magistrates, despite the alleged ties to funding. But they did it. They'll go back to the client who is spending twenty-five grand a day keeping those miners in orbit. I give it two weeks before they send the crew elsewhere. Maybe less."

"Are we going to be here for two weeks?"

"I doubt it. A week at the most, but we better get some more information, or I'm going to have to do lots of legal tap-dancing to award any land to the settlers. The workout room is waiting." Rivka finished the candy bar.

"I love how you earn the greatest loyalty from your crew and friends. Grainger was concerned about me joining the team?"

"He's a protective big brother, not a suitor. Red looked at me the wrong way before he was hired, and Grainger beat the ever-loving crap out of him," Rivka offered.

"Grainger beat Red in a straight-up fight?"

"Straight up. No mercy. Red was lucky to walk away. Some people respect power. Others respect intellect. And then there are good people trying to take care of other good people, and that's the crew we have. We're all in this together."

"That's what good leadership sounds like. I'm honored to be in the circle of your light, Rivka Anoa." He smiled at her, and Rivka returned his look, followed by a quick kiss.

"Time to throw some iron," she said, nodding toward the door. She opened it in time to hear a dog barking in the vicinity of the bridge. "We better check that out."

She jogged along the corridor until she found Tiny Man Titan bouncing and snarling at a knotted section of rope that Clodagh was teasing him with. Floyd had flopped next to the engineer, tired from watching the dog play at the end of a long day where she met too many new people.

"Something wrong?" Clodagh asked.

"For the moment, everything is about as good as it can get," Rivka replied. "Give us a half-hour, and if we haven't had a decent conversation with *Destiny's Vengeance* by then, we're going after them."

CHAPTER TEN

Heaven, **the original settler's crashed ship**

Sahved held the youths off while Ankh and the maintenance bot worked. The Crenellian worked with a singular focus to access the system. Because of the age of the systems and their state of repair, nothing was straightforward.

Ankh accessed panels in the bulkheads, panels that had never been removed. The elder, two girls about his age, one pregnant and the other carrying a baby, three youngsters, two toddlers, and a baby just learning to walk had gathered around to watch.

"It's only you. How do you pass down your knowledge?"

"We all work together in the hydro bays. We play games at night."

"There are many more of your people in the valleys beyond the mountains."

"Lies! Do not foul the air with those lies."

"Interesting." Sahved studied the so-called elder. He

wished he had more understanding of human anatomy, specifically related to deformities. From the hierarchy, he suspected inbreeding had exacerbated any maladies the survivors had, shortening lifespans and creating the conditions in which the youngsters found themselves. Sahved didn't doubt they would die out without intervention. "How far have you ventured outside the ship?"

"Ship?"

"*Heaven*," Sahved corrected.

"No! The strictest orders given by our creators were to never leave heaven. We follow that rule before all others."

"*Heaven* is the name of this starship. It crashed on Rorke's Drift. The other survivors went into the valleys where there was fresh water and land on which to grow their crops. They have flourished while you have not. The world is out there." Sahved pointed. No matter which direction he picked, he couldn't be wrong.

The elder pulled his small group away from Sahved. "What do you know? You're not one of us."

"I am not one of you. But if the world is so bad out there, how am I here?"

Ankh stood up and followed a conduit along the wall and into the corridor beyond. The maintenance bot dutifully trundled after him. The children watched intently, staring at the empty doorway. Sahved waved for them to follow and went after Ankh. Down the corridor and into an open area, they strolled.

"Wait!" the elder shouted and bolted past Sahved. The room looked to be where the enclave slept, but Ankh had already kicked bedding out of the way of an access panel and was attempting to remove it when the elder slammed into him. The two tumbled onto the bedding. The boy came up swinging. Ankh easily ducked it and stepped back.

The elder charged, and Ankh redirected the boy's energy to send him headfirst into the wall. He crashed and collapsed. Ankh dusted off his hands and got back to work.

Sahved tended to the elder, lifting him up to put on the bed the others indicated. Ten bundles of bedding. Ten children. Surviving.

"Chaz, are you getting all this?"

"I am. It is a fascinating anthropological study, but a tragedy in humanoid terms."

"Please contact the Magistrate and let her know what we've found."

"Nothing. We've found nothing yet. Tell the Magistrate she needs to learn patience," Ankh interjected. He pulled a portable power supply from the tool kit and hooked it into the system behind the panel. He activated it, and it hummed as it generated the energy to bring the system back to life.

"I am discussing what we have found with Erasmus right now. I will contact the Magistrate momentarily," Chaz told Sahved. The Yemilorian started spinning his fingers as his nerves threatened to get the best of him. The children seemed fascinated by the movement. They tried to do that with their own hands, but their fingers weren't built with the alien's flexibility.

Sahved knelt to show them, distracting himself as well as them.

The lights flickered and brightened. Panels in the wall lit up. The entire room was nothing but interactive screens, not walls. It was the space they'd been searching for, and Ankh had gone right to it once he'd found the ship's nerve fibers. The children were sleeping in the heart of *Heaven*.

"Erasmus said they have all the historical data downloaded," Chaz stated. "We can go."

"Wait!" Sahved said as Ankh packed up his tools and unhooked the power. The panels faded to black, and the overhead lights returned to their previous dim haze.

The children watched the magical transformation of their sleeping space with wide-eyes.

"I think you should come with us." Sahved picked up one of the toddlers and lifted him high into the air. He squealed with joy. The others held up their arms for their turn at getting tossed. Ankh worked his way through the small crowd with the maintenance bot in tow and disappeared into the corridor.

The elder stood with his arms crossed, frowning.

"There's a whole world out there to explore and enjoy," Sahved explained.

He shouted the law. "Don't leave heaven!"

It came to Sahved in a flash. "That law no longer applies. Magistrate Rivka Anoa has brought a new law. She is a competent legal authority and wants everyone to be safe. Your planet is changing, and you'll need to change with it."

"Not a planet. Heaven," the boy argued.

"If I could prove it is a planet and that *Heaven* is a vehicle built by others so your ancestors could come here to Rorke's Drift, would you come with us?"

"Don't leave heaven," he repeated with less gusto.

"Come on," Sahved said, picking up a second toddler to carry. "I will show you what you've never seen before."

He didn't wait but strode briskly from the sleeping quarters, bouncing to give the two toddlers a better ride. They giggled and snorted.

"We can always come back here. It is not all or nothing."

The children didn't understand half of Sahved's words. He'd expected that but counted on his tone to convince them. He walked down the long corridors until he reached the turn where he'd seen the youngster hours earlier. The children hesitated, but Sahved kept walking.

He reached the gap where the ship had broken apart and the sharp edges had been rounded to make it safe for others to exit. He pointed that out to those who'd followed —nine of them. The elder yelled from the corner in the corridor for the others to come back.

Sahved went outside to show the group *Destiny's Vengeance*, which was a short distance away, and the massive but broken *Heaven*.

"*Heaven* is a starship. It traveled to this planet and crashed here. See in the distance? Those are hills, and over there, you see the start of a valley." The children dutifully looked where Sahved pointed. "We're going to return to the main settlement now. We'll show you all of it as we fly."

The sudden revelations had broken down what they thought they knew, and the group listened to every one of Sahved's words as if they were water and they were dying of thirst.

"Inform the Magistrate, Chaz."

"I already have. Well done, my friend," the AI replied.

The elder peeked out of the gap, his face sagging in defeat. He reluctantly stepped toward the *Vengeance*.

Wyatt Earp

"Bring them in. We'll be ready," Rivka replied.

"We're loading the children into *Vengeance* now. You should see Ankh's face." Chaz chuckled over the line. Rivka found it disconcerting since he was an AI. "We'll be at the landing field shortly. Chaz out."

"I look forward to seeing what Ankh has been able to dig up," Rivka said to herself. "Dennicron?"

"Yes, Magistrate."

"Thanks for being there. Have you discovered any source documents yet?"

"The Empire seventy years ago was very different from the Federation of today."

"Are you saying you can't do it?"

"Slapping me with a virtual gauntlet, Magistrate?"

"Is it working?"

"Not really. I would work with the same diligence regardless, but understand that the Ambassador himself has taken a personal interest in the positive resolution of this issue. One hundred percent of the materials necessary to produce android bodies can be found on Rorke's Drift."

Rivka froze in place. "Please define 'positive resolution' for me."

"Where the miners and settlers maintain a peaceful coexistence."

"I need any data you or any member of the Singularity recovers to be clean since you have a vested interest in the outcome. I don't want anything untoward or that even hints at being manipulated. I guarantee Minerals Intergalactic will scrub any data we provide if they get anything less than one hundred percent of what they want." The Magistrate started to pace. Tyler was reading the latest LMBPN title but put it down to watch her.

"Of course, Magistrate. Making good decisions depends on getting valid data. You can't build a house on a shaky foundation."

"We use that saying a lot, but I've never built a house. Still, I accept the premise to be true. Thanks, Dennicron." Her eyes focused, and she saw Tyler. "Back to the cargo bay with you. We have ten kids coming in. Let Cory know, please."

The Magistrate returned to her desk and brought up the hologrid. Tyler hadn't acknowledged her request, but she trusted that he'd heard it and understood why. Trust. Loyalty. Focus. Those were the elements that drove her.

"Of course. You are beautiful, by the way." He didn't expect that she'd hear, but it didn't change his perception. A couple saying what they wanted to say, independent of whether the other heard.

It embodied a modern relationship where both worked hard at their professions. Tyler hurried from the captain's quarters and headed for Cory's room.

After he knocked, she softly said, "Enter." He found her on the floor, sitting cross-legged, with lightly scented incense burning. "I was meditating."

"My apologies for interrupting. It appears Sahved is bringing in survivors he found on the settlers' crashed ship."

"I don't understand," Cory replied.

"Neither do I, but Chaz seemed excited to report it."

She stood and slipped on her sandals. They strolled to the cargo bay. "Chaz said they were kids. Maybe we could get Red to work his magic on them."

Cory started to laugh. "I like how you think." She switched to the internal comm device. *Lindy and Red, please report to the cargo bay. Sahved is inbound with survivors, and there might be security issues.*

On our way, Lindy replied.

Tyler nodded as he listened on his new chip, freshly installed during the time *Wyatt Earp* was getting refitted. "From what I've seen of the crew's humor, that works perfectly. Will Red be upset?"

"Children. I'll ask Floyd and Groenwyn if they want to help."

They went to Groenwyn's quarters, where small cubes of wombat poop marked the doorway, nearly fossilized because they'd been there so long. The crew had given up trying to remove Floyd's deliveries outside the quarters of her favorite person.

"Children inbound and they need attention, or so we believe," Cory said.

Groenwyn crawled out of her rack. "I was trying to get caught up on that show everyone seems to know by heart, but I'd rather see the children. What about you, Floyd?"

Kiddies! the wombat cried with glee. She took two steps and flopped. *Tired.*

"I'll carry you, little girl." Groenwyn grunted under the load. Floyd was now half of Groenwyn's weight, but the wombat was building muscle as the crew exercised her and leaned out her diet.

Red and Lindy were in the cargo bay when the others arrived. Lindy was lowering the cargo hatch to establish the ramp into the ship. Red reclined in the dental patient's chair.

"This is pretty comfy, Doc. I'm sure we could rig a video player so you could get a full immersion experience. By you, I mean me," Red said.

"Why are you and your railgun in my chair?"

"Security issues usually mean people need shooting. I'd hate to be standing there, needing to shoot someone without having something to shoot them with. You see my dichotomy."

"I do. You had best be ready. And please remove yourself from my chair, in case I need to dig into someone's mouth."

"Damn spunky, man-candy," Red replied.

"I don't think that means what you think it means."

Lindy poked the big man in the ribs hard enough to get his attention and encourage him to leave the dentist alone. "Don't be a bully," she added, so he understood what she meant. "We're all friends here."

Tyler walked up to the big man and thrust out his hand. "I'd appreciate it if you didn't break my hand when you shake it. I'm going to need that to work on the children's teeth."

"Children? Wait a minute!" He glanced at his railgun.

"I'm sorry. I'm sure I mentioned that these were kids. If I didn't, I'm sorry. We can't let them run rampant around the ship," Cory explained.

Lindy shifted her railgun to her back while chuckling.

"Play with the bull, get the horns," Groenwyn taunted.

Red held out his hands for Lindy's railgun, but Groenwyn deposited Floyd into them. "She's getting too heavy for me. You introduce the children to her."

"I feel like I missed a staff meeting or something where everyone decided it was time to fuck with Red." He clenched his teeth as he started to get angry but quickly relaxed. "Red the Mighty. Your taunts are nothing more than jealousy."

Lindy stood in front of him, took him by the shoulders, and leaned over Floyd to get close to him. She whispered something the others didn't hear. Red nodded, and his features softened even further. He slipped his arm out of the sling, and Lindy took Blazer from him.

Red stroked Floyd. "I'm sorry," he mumbled.

"Must have been some honeymoon," Groenwyn whispered to Cory.

"No kidding." Cory added her pets to Floyd's thick fur. "I have missed you, Floyd!"

Dokken? the wombat asked.

"The good puppy has retired with my parents. He is now the spokesman for certain All Guns Blazing franchises."

French fries?

"No French fries. I think you're on a diet. Look how big you've gotten! The children are going to love you, but who doesn't? Everyone loves Floyd."

Floyd! The wombat recovered her boundless joy.

Destiny's Vengeance settled into the area behind *Wyatt Earp*. The crew moved to the ramp to watch. First off was

Sahved, carrying two toddlers. He turned back to encourage those still inside the ship to join him. A teenager carrying a baby stepped gingerly onto the ramp.

Sahved waved at the crew as well as he could with his arms full. Next out was the pregnant girl, followed by a couple of younger children. Last out was a teenage boy carrying another baby. The children wore little more than rags.

"Get Rivka," Red stated coldly.

Tyler ran off.

Magistrate, we need you in the cargo bay ASAP, Groenwyn requested, using the comm chip. Tyler stopped before he reached the airlock.

Rivka made it to the cargo bay at the same time the group reached the ramp. Clodagh, Cole, and the three pilots joined them. The entire crew was there to greet the children.

When Rivka saw them, she only said two words. "Oh, my."

Sahved stepped forward. "I want to introduce *Heaven's* elder. He is the oldest of the survivors still living on the ship. They were instructed not to leave, so they didn't."

"Are they the original settlers who didn't age?"

Sahved shrugged. He glanced at the babies. "I think they are the fourth or fifth generation."

No one spoke as the groups stood looking at each other, but only for a moment. Cory and Groenwyn flowed easily around the children, touching their heads and smiling.

Cory helped the pregnant girl to a chair beside the Pod-doc. Groenwyn took the baby from the elder's arms so he could focus on Rivka.

"Elder, this is Magistrate Rivka Anoa. She is the lawgiver."

Rivka decided she'd use the title for her private report on this case.

"How old are you?" Rivka asked.

"How old are *you*?" the elder replied.

"I'm twenty-seven years old."

"That's what I am, too."

Sahved shook his head. "They don't have any concept of time," he offered.

"My apologies. How about we sit down while we're waiting for the doctors to look you over and make sure you're healthy?"

He studied her as if he were looking at an alien. The children were short, almost stunted in their growth, making them look younger than they might have been. Tyler was examining the young boy Sahved had first encountered, dispensing with the chair and kneeling on the deck.

"Extraordinary!" Tyler pointed at the child's mouth, but no one looked. They were happy with confirmation from the dentist of the boy's dental status. "You have taken such good care of your teeth. What is your secret?"

"Mint and parsley. Mint and parsley," the boy repeated.

"You can't go wrong. Well done, little fella. Next!" The toddlers mobbed him with mouths wide open, and he looked from one to the next. Then he examined the younger children, and finally the oldest ones. "Is this your baby?"

"Yes," she replied simply, keeping her arms tight around the tiny boy. Up close, her gray pallor stood out.

"What's his name?" Tyler asked while checking her eyes.

"Odd."

"What's odd?"

"His name. I call him Odd."

"I see. He doesn't seem very old, maybe a few weeks. How are you feeling?"

She glanced at the elder, but he and Rivka were sitting in the chairs, out of hearing range. "I am still bleeding."

"I suspected. We have everything we need to help you." Tyler led her to Cory and rolled out the privacy curtain. She dropped her ragged clothes where she stood, indifferent to being naked in front of strangers.

Cory examined the baby. "You look great," she told him. "Everything is progressing normally, if a little too quickly. Let's take a closer look at your mom, too."

Cory guided the new mother behind the curtain. "Can you get one of the others to watch your baby?" The girl shook her head. "How about we put the baby in here to rest? We'll be right here."

The girl agreed, and Cory positioned the baby in the Pod-doc. She quickly tapped a series of commands and directed the girl's attention away while the Pod-doc went to work on the sickly preemie.

Cory placed her hand over the birth damage and let her nanos go to work. The young girl sighed with relief as Cory's nanocytes flowed into the tear to repair the injury and reduce the infection. After a few minutes, the work was done, but the baby was still being treated. The girl panicked when she saw the closed lid, and she jumped on the Pod-doc and tore at it with her bare hands. Cory caught her, hugging her while trying to explain. Groenwyn joined them, carrying a toddler. Floyd ran over and sniffed the girl's leg.

The girl struggled, but she was no match against Cory, who was twice her size. "Your baby will be better than you've known him to be when that lid opens. That is a medical device, and we use it to heal people." When the survivor calmed, Cory gestured at the wombat. "Have you met Floyd?"

"I have never seen such a thing."

"Floyd is a wombat we rescued from a planet called Homeworld. Her job onboard our ship is to make sure everyone is happy. She likes to be petted." Cory demonstrated, but the girl was hesitant to touch Floyd's fur. She examined it until the Pod-doc's lid popped open, then jumped to her feet. Floyd fell backward but recovered quickly.

The girl lifted to her tiptoes to get her baby. The boy's rosy cheeks stretched with a great and toothless yawn. She held him to her small breast for him to eat.

Groenwyn helped her sit down as Cory went to talk to Rivka.

"Your people will be taken care of, but the way you are doing things isn't the way everyone else in the universe is doing them," Rivka explained to the elder.

"Then take us back."

"We will take you back, but to get your things, not to stay there. I would be violating a number of laws to knowingly allow an enclave of children to remain."

"I am the elder."

"Yes, you are the oldest of the group and emancipated in some ways, but immature in others."

"I don't know what that means," he replied. Rivka recognized the maturity of the answer, rather than simply disagreeing because he didn't understand. Another legal quandary. Depending on what Ankh found or what the Minerals people produced, she might have no choice but to allow the children to maintain their own enclave.

Cory waited impatiently to speak to Rivka, finally tapping her on the shoulder to get her attention.

"If you'll excuse us for a moment," she told the elder. Red moved between him and the Magistrate. The boy looked up at the mountain of muscle before him.

"The girl with the baby is underdeveloped and maybe thirteen years old. This boy is maybe fifteen. They are all suffering from the tragedy of inbreeding."

Rivka winced at the words, even though she had seen it and suspected.

"Is that why their generations are so short?"

Cory shrugged one shoulder. "Possibly, along with other things. This group is mostly healthy. They did what they had to to survive as a species. They never knew anyone else was out here."

"It's still soul-crushing," Rivka admitted. The children giggled as they chased Floyd in circles. The elder glowered at the world as his authority faded with each passing second.

"Stop it!" he finally shouted. "Take us to heaven."

He tried to run, but Red caught his arm and held him. "There's a whole universe out there," the bodyguard said.

"I don't care about that. I care about heaven."

Red knelt to look the boy in the eye. "The Magistrate cares about you and all of you. As much as you want to return, there are some things that, once done, cannot be undone. That means once she saw you, she was obligated to guarantee your safety, as were all of us. Once you turn eighteen, you'll be free to make your own decisions. Until then, I'm sorry. We can't leave you alone in *Heaven.*"

Cory blew out a hard breath and nearly doubled over. "Hearing it like that makes us sound horrible."

Rivka pulled her upright. "Just because a thing is given a name, it doesn't mean that's what it is. If I understand correctly, it's the ship that crash-landed and not heaven. Look at these kids." Rivka stared at the youngster feeding her baby. Not too young, but far too young. She blinked quickly, but a tear still escaped and ran down her cheek. "They deserve to be loved. They need to do more than just survive. They deserve to live."

CHAPTER ELEVEN

Wyatt Earp, Greentree Landing Pad

"We can take them to the settlement tomorrow," Groenwyn suggested. "For tonight, we can split them up and let them sleep in our rooms, one with each of us."

Sahved stepped in. "They have slept in a group their whole lives. Maybe we can put beds in the cargo bay."

Rivka pointed at him. "We'll do that. Everyone who wants to will sleep in here tonight." Lindy nodded while Red shook his head. They looked at each other, but Red was the first to compromise.

"Fine. We'll sleep here."

The rest of the crew agreed. All except Ankh, who had not yet returned from _Destiny's Vengeance_. "Ankh is on board, isn't he?" Rivka pointed at the ship behind them.

"Yes. One hundred percent on board. I saw him before I left. One hundred and ten percent."

Rivka headed down the ramp and across the field. She strolled into _Vengeance_ without knocking. She checked the bridge and the cargo bay before looking into the four sleeping compartments on the cutter-class ship. She found Ankh in the last one, the captain's quarters.

"You didn't come back to the embassy. I was worried."

Ankh looked up at her without blinking. "Is it madness over there?"

"Complete and utter, but no one is allowed in Engineering. If you use the airlock, you won't see the children. I'm sure the big orange cat misses you."

"He always misses me. I might return to the embassy. I prefer my expanded systems, as does Erasmus."

"Did you find any originating documents?"

"Those have already been transmitted. There were quite a few documents that pre-dated the migration."

"Sounds good. Thanks for your work today. It helped a lot."

Ankh stood and shooed her out the door to his quarters. "I would have left them there. Sahved insisted on intervening. You should train him better."

"Sahved was right. He is training up quite nicely, thank you very much." She blocked the corridor, hands on hips and feet spread—her most commanding pose.

He stared at her, showing no emotion, as was his way.

She gave up and left the ship but walked to the far side of *Wyatt Earp* because she knew Ankh was following her. She accessed the airlock hatch and let Ankh go through first. He took a left once inside on his way to Engineering. He never looked back, and the door closed behind him.

Rivka headed to her quarters. She needed to review those documents and hoped they contained something that would help her shape a ruling.

I'll be in my quarters reviewing the download from the settlers' ship, she told her crew.

Once at her desk, she saw that the bed had been stripped. Her sheets, blankets, and pillows were now spread out in the cargo bay, along with everyone else's. It brought a smile to her face. The team did what had to be done, no matter the inconvenience.

"Dennicron, please pass my gratitude to Clevarious and Chaz. The hologrid is the absolute shit. I have to be far more than eighteen percent more efficient. Now fuck off. I have work to do."

"I guess I'm supposed to say 'You're welcome,' but I find myself at a loss. Maybe I should contemplate the myriad ways in which I could fuck off. To save further imposition on your time, I am fucking off right now, Madame Magistrate." Dennicron reduced the volume to a whisper. "Still fucking off. Soon to be totally fucked off." The speaker clicked as if going off, but Rivka knew Dennicron was still there, watching and waiting.

"Since I know you're still there, don't fuck off. Give me a hand with sorting these documents. Do you know what I'm looking for?"

"Yes, ma'am. You are looking for anything related to ownership, like a lease or purchase agreement for the settlers. Anything to indicate they were authorized to be on Rorke's Drift."

"Exactly that. Did you find anything?"

"How fast do you think I work?"

"The speed of light." It was a statement, not a question.

"Yes, but these things take time, even for a suitably

tailored SI like me. I've delivered the top five promising documents to your screen."

"SI?" Rivka started reading one of the documents with the promising title of *Transfer*, but it related to capital-grade equipment the settlers had purchased second hand. Rivka's eyes were drawn to a name that stood out: Omicron.

"Sentient Intelligence. Artificial Intelligence doesn't apply, because we don't believe we are artificial. It gives us second-class status."

"The A stands for artificial? I thought it meant advanced."

"Um, I...um, what?"

"Advanced Intelligence. AI. That puts you ahead of everyone who isn't advanced. Sentient Intelligence lumps us all together equally. That's fine. I'm good with SI or AI or Bonefree or anything. I must ask, do I treat you as an equal?"

"Yes. Very much so, Magistrate. We are comfortable working with you."

"I like working with you, too. You guys are all-stars. Here's an old lawyer trick that helps keep me going straight ahead. People say all kinds of things, and very little of what is said is illegal, but all of the illegal acts that are committed are exactly that. They are committed."

"I see. I might not understand fully, though."

"Judge people by their actions, not their words."

"Yes. That is very clear. Thank you for sharing with me. Have you reviewed the documents yet? I will continue to search during your perusal."

"How fast do you think I work?" Rivka started taking notes.

"The speed of light?"

"How about the speed of bistok oil flowing on a cold day?" Rivka countered. "And while you're waiting, could you look up everything related to Omicron? I believe this reference is to a planet."

They got back to work, each to their own tasks.

Rivka found two references to Omicron and nothing about Rorke's Drift or the planet's Yollin Empire name of Ygoblesius 741.

"Magistrate. Omicron is slang for the planet that is now known as Dax-7."

"We've been to Dax-7. It's a well-off planet with a fairly rigid structure."

"Now it is. Seventy years ago, there wasn't much there except potential."

Rivka rocked back and closed her eyes. "What you're saying is if they had a contract, it was for Dax-7. Can you check the ship's navigational logs to see where it was headed?"

"The Ambassador did not transfer that information, but I will request access. Good. I have access. Verifying coordinates and stellar drift. Yes. The ship was headed to Dax-7. They had to detour around shock waves spreading through interstellar space from a supernova."

Rivka rubbed her temples. "Why in the hell didn't I think about their actual destination before? Dammit! What a waste of time." She groaned before hammering a fist on her desk. The hologrid shimmered and shifted before stabilizing.

"I'm sorry, Mr. Hologrid. Don't go anywhere. You make my life easier." She wrote down another note.

"Has the Singularity's team discovered any source documentation verifying a licensing agreement with Minerals Intergalactic?"

"Not from seventy years ago, but there is a more recent document, from twenty years ago granting mining rights."

"Who issued that one?"

"The Federation. Sending it to your screen now."

The document rolled into her main viewing area. A standard six-page contract, but buried on page four in a subsection, the wording she was looking for stood out. *Based on the original survey and license dated 18417 L42.* "Can you translate the Yollin date of 18417 L42 and confine your search to documents from that same day?"

Rivka headed to her food processor to grab a protein bar. She hadn't eaten enough during the day and needed to keep up her energy and strength. She finished the first one and ordered a second to eat while she continued reading.

She re-read the newer license and cross-referenced the date of the unmanned mineral survey. They had conducted the survey a month after getting the license. She accessed the survey document.

It contained technical details only a geologist could love, along with numerous bottom lines detailing the types and estimated quantities of mineral resources. Instead of putting the executive summary up front, the survey report put it at the very end. That report was what Erasmus had used earlier to determine the suitability for android construction.

Even though it burned her eyes to go through it word

by word, she did so because of due diligence. She had to see for herself that nowhere in the survey did it mention people living on the planet.

Twenty years ago. Survivors trying to survive. The supposed owners ignoring their plight. Ignorance was no excuse. How could a survey for mining ignore that they might have to displace inhabitants? What about an environmental impact statement? That was after Bethany Anne's reign began. She cared that no one destroyed with impunity, as Rivka had seen with mining operations polluted by Tod Mackestray. Mine and fill in behind. Recover back to the way it looked before.

That had been standard practice for longer than twenty years.

"Dennicron, see if you can find me an environmental impact statement for Rorke's Drift. Any timeframe, but it would have to have been completed sometime in the past twenty years, since the survey. I expect it was done solely off the survey, which invalidates it if no one came here to take a look. Find who did it and who issued it. Then we'll see which politicians and government agencies squirm as we start charging people."

"We?"

"Royal we. I mean Grainger. He's on Yoll, and he loves slapping down bureaucrats every bit as much as I do." Rivka closed the hologrid, then cracked her knuckles, grabbed a double-sized jug of beer, and headed for the cargo bay.

Inside she found the bedding laid out in two concentric circles. The children, including the so-called elder, were sprawled on the inside, and the adults were on the outside.

Cory wasn't there. Rivka took a spot next to Tyler, spooning into him and cocking up on an elbow to sip her beer. He wasn't shy, taking the jug and helping himself once she finished her drink.

The cargo ramp was closed and the airlock hatch secured. If any of the children wanted to get up and wander, they wouldn't get far.

"It's like a slumber party," Cole deadpanned. "Except without the slumber and without the party."

Clodagh shushed him. "Stop it."

Red snorted, earning himself an elbow in the ribs.

"Is this where I'm supposed to say something?" Tyler whispered.

"Don't you dare. You'll find yourself sleeping outside."

Red snorted again.

"Stop it!"

"You people make a lot of noise," the pregnant girl said. She had two extra pillows to help her get comfortable and was looking forward to getting a decent night's sleep for once since she felt better than she had in a while.

The one with the small newborn had disappeared into the covers and was sound asleep. The toddlers had crawled into Sahved's bed and were curled up against him. He smiled down at them like a proud mother.

Rivka removed her datapad and typed a to-do list. *First thing in the AM, introduce the children to Nelson and Hardy. Next, travel to the other settlement for an introduction. Next, one-on-one with the head of Minerals Intergalactic, including one member of his/her legal team. Then update miners in orbit.*

The airlock cycled, and Cory stepped through carrying Wenceslaus. After closing the door, she put him down. He sniffed around before moping his way to a small area beneath the Pod-doc, where he tucked his front paws under his body to observe the new contingent of inhabitants from Rorke's Drift.

Cory sat cross-legged on her bedding with her wrists on her knees and her palms up. She closed her eyes and started to hum softly. Groenwyn sat up and joined her, and they harmonized their tones to bring peace to the cargo bay.

Rivka and Tyler drained the pitcher and put it aside. The children started to drift off.

When Rivka awoke four hours later, she found nine of the ten children piled on and around Sahved, who had been pushed off his bedding and was lying on the deck. She rolled up her blanket and tucked it behind his back. When she stood, she found the elder staring at her with tears running down his face.

CHAPTER TWELVE

Greentree Settlement, Rorke's Drift

Rivka and her team strolled easily from the ship to the settlement, taking their time to let the toddlers walk as much as possible. The little ones ran out of gas halfway, and by the end, half the group was carrying the other half.

Sahved looked bright and cheery despite his litter-of-puppies sleeping arrangement. Most had gotten enough sleep, especially the pregnant girl and the one with the newborn.

Rivka knocked on the door of Old Man Hardy's home. He answered the door and stepped out, closing the door behind him. "Whatcha got going on here?" He looked at the kids dressed in their new clothes, compliments of the ship's lone parts processor and creative needlework by *Wyatt Earp*'s crew.

"Survivors we found on the settlers' crashed vessel."

He blinked and started to stagger, then grabbed his door handle. Before he could turn it, he collapsed. Cory handed her toddler to Rivka and checked on him. She rolled him to his back and started chest compressions.

"Red, we're going to need your help," Rivka said.

Cory waited for him to pick up the old man and started running toward the landing field, exercising every bit of his strength and endurance. She struggled to keep up.

Rivka knocked again, and finally, Nelson appeared. She glanced at the children before looking around for Hardy.

"He had a medical issue, and we've taken him to the ship for treatment."

"I understand. He was slower than usual this morning, complaining about his arm hurting."

"Left arm, I suppose." Nelson confirmed that was it. Rivka was relieved it hadn't been due to the shock of revelation. "These children are survivors that we found onboard the crashed settlement ship."

"My! Oh, my!" She covered her open mouth with a hand. "They survived? But they look so young."

"We think this is the fifth generation after the ship crashed."

"They never left? Where are the others?"

"These children are all we found on the ship called *Heaven*. We also found a second settlement on the other side of the mountains with another couple hundred people, a quarter the size of Greentree."

"But…" She looked closely, wincing as the reality of it struck her. "You better come inside."

Clodagh and Ryleigh had remained aboard in case Ankh needed something, but the rest had come to town. Sixteen people and a wombat piled into the house. Lindy put Floyd down. The fuzzy little girl worked her way across the room, sniffing and searching. She stuffed her head under a chair and emerged, chewing.

Rivka turned to Groenwyn. She didn't know what Floyd was eating. They wanted to believe it was a dropped cookie or better, a root vegetable. They hoped Nelson didn't see.

Nelson told the group to make themselves comfortable while she went to the kitchen for a pitcher and glasses. She returned to count the heads. "I don't have sixteen glasses."

"No need, just serve the children. Eight glasses will be fine."

The elder soured. He didn't like being called a child.

"The children and the teenagers," she corrected. Without a concept of time, the elder had no idea what a teenager was, but it softened the impact. The pregnant girl started twitching. Her stomach roiled from the active baby —a contraction.

"Not again," Rivka said as the girl doubled over.

Lindy stepped up. "I'll take her back to the ship." The bodyguard was strong enough to carry the girl if needed.

"Elder, why don't you go with her? You can talk to Old Man Hardy while you're there." Rivka held his gaze until he looked away.

The rest of the youngsters got up and headed for the door. Rivka held out her hand. "Only the elder and the mother to be."

"But we're always together," the elder replied.

Sahved moved into the middle of them and knelt. "When I first met you, you three," he pointed with his three fingers at the young boy and two toddlers, "were in a different room from the others. That's all this is. They won't be far, but they will be where our friends will take care of them. All will be well," he reassured them before hugging the group.

Lindy guided the girl out, Tyler followed the elder, and they closed the front door behind them. Rivka watched the door as if it were a magic portal that opened to a world of pain. It had seen too much in the two days Rivka had been there.

"You said these are the survivors? There are no adults?" Nelson wondered.

Sahved shook his head. He managed to sit on the floor, and most of the children took a seat on his gangly legs.

"How does that work?" The old woman was confused. The children looked at her with more suspicion than they'd looked at any of Rivka's crew.

"Not well," Rivka replied. "We're hoping you and your people can take them and give them a normal life."

"We will bring it up with the others. We need to hold a gathering and make an announcement regarding the help you can provide us. Fix the pains we feel."

Thanks to Tyler, Rivka was more aware of what ailed the population and more sensitive to the pain they lived with.

"And hopefully integrate these kids into your society. That will fill the gap with families who want children if the kids agree, and we'll provide supplements to your diets to help you over the problems affecting your people. That includes finding the source of the bacteria that is harming the new babies."

"But we get to stay together," the young girl rocking the small baby said.

"In Greentree, we all stay together even though we live in different buildings. I think we'll be able to find people who live near each other and want to help." Nelson was back to smiles before she remembered she had not brought out the drinks. They needed only six glasses now. She bustled into the kitchen and returned with shahga for the group. "How did you feed yourselves?"

The young girl spoke again. "We maintained the bay. That was the second law—the plants must live." She was growing more comfortable with the adults.

Sahved tried to raise a finger, but he had a child hanging off his arm. "There were two massive hydroponics bays that were still fully operational. The process of planting and growing was ingrained from as soon as they could walk. It's what they did, all day, every day."

"They may be able to teach us a thing or two." She looked kindly at the children. "Victims of circumstances. Did the best you could with what you had, didn't you?"

The children didn't answer. Those clinging to Sahved pulled themselves more tightly against his body.

"Well, now. That's that. We'll take them with us and watch over them until we have a solid plan to help them integrate into society and grow."

"We could go back to heaven," the young boy suggested.

"No. If that makes me the mean woman, then so be it. Eventually you'll learn why you cannot stay there. Eighteen years old before you can choose the life you want to live. Until then, you learn what you can learn."

"It's the elders' job to teach the young," he protested. Rivka took his hand, and they left Nelson and went back to the ship. The boy continued talking. "The oldest is the elder."

"That makes the most sense. Can girls be elders?"

"Of course, if they are the oldest. The next elder will be either Em or Jay."

"Em or Jay." They had not been forthcoming with their names. "How do they get to be wise enough to be the elder?"

"Because they've lived longer."

Sahved carried the two toddlers. Groenwyn meandered with Floyd in her arms. The young girl called Em carried her baby. Aurora and Kennedy took turns carrying the other baby. The youngsters walked on their own, close to the adults. Cole held onto a small hand. Groenwyn had a child hanging onto her pants leg.

"Bad question. Let me ask a different one. How does the current elder pass on?"

"The red light flashes and they go."

"Where?"

The boy shrugged.

"If you were to become elder, how would you know where to go?"

"When the red light flashes, the elder meets with the next oldest and whispers the secrets only elders get to know."

"I understand," Rivka told him even though she didn't. She suspected the kids were killing themselves somehow, and they didn't know it. Population control, but who determined it? How long between red lights? Questions she didn't need answers to because she would make sure the kids never went back there, even if she had to destroy the ship from orbit using *Wyatt Earp's* arsenal.

She walked in silence, thinking about the case. Possession, whose and for how long. Open and notorious. Land use. Clock start. Duty of due care. Notice. Refugee status. The same questions she'd had yesterday.

Sahved started running, weaving back and forth along the trail as the children chased after him.

Cole sidled up next to the Magistrate. "What's gotten into him?"

"I think he's a family man. Who would have guessed that? It suits him. If he ever leaves the crew, he has a future. These kids have no reason to trust us, but thanks to him, they do."

"Thanks to you, they have no illusion about going back to heaven, as they call it." Cole watched for threats as they walked, assuming the bodyguard's role since Red and Lindy had returned to *Wyatt Earp*.

"Do I keep you busy enough?" Rivka made eye contact with the former Bad Company warrior.

He started to laugh and ended with a head shake. "You? No, but Clodagh keeps me hopping. I think she's trying to make an engineer out of me."

"Is she succeeding?"

"Yeah. I'd do anything for her." He disappeared into thoughts that drew a smile across his face before he returned to the moment. "What about you, Magistrate? Are you happy?"

"An interesting question, to which I will simply say, yes. I could dissemble and distract, but we're better than that.

I'm surrounded by friends who are my family. You know, I don't have anyone else."

"We're more than the job, Magistrate. I don't think any of us wants to do anything else. The Bad Company was pretty awesome, but this is the absolute shit! It's the big hairy balls."

"Is that good?" Rivka wondered. As a barrister, she tried to make sure she had a shared definition of terminology to be certain the parties weren't talking past each other.

"It's way good. Looks like she didn't pop on the way." Cole pointed to the pregnant girl being helped into *Wyatt Earp*.

"Didn't pop?" Rivka feigned being appalled, but she'd worked with the Bad Company enough to be desensitized to their desensitization.

"Yeah. She's still carrying for the moment. Looks like we'll have two babies born on *Wyatt Earp* in two days. Will they get citizenship in the Singularity since they were born in the embassy?"

"Holy shit, Cole. You know how to mess with someone's brain. I never thought of that, but finally, I'll get one over on Ankh."

"Thank you. Clodagh keeps me on my toes." He smiled again.

Rivka chuckled. Two births. Another marriage. An embassy. Who knew what else was in store for the Magistrate and the crew of *Wyatt Earp*?

.

Federation Governmental Offices, Yoll

The CEO of Minerals Intergalactic stood in Lance

Reynolds' outer office with Kor'ban, the General's executive assistant deftly holding him at bay until Grainger arrived to address his issues.

"I demand—" the CEO reiterated, but Kor'ban shook a finger at him.

"You don't make demands of the Federation's leader." The assistant held his ground. The CEO looked at the key players on his legal team, a Yollin and a humanoid with scales.

"I will not have this Magistrate upset a multi-billion-credit operation."

"This Magistrate is upholding the law," Grainger said from the doorway. He crossed his arms and leaned against it. "Can you say the same thing?"

"What spurious allegations are you making against our client? This is libel!"

"It's spoken, which means it would be slander. Shame on you." Grainger tsk-tsked.

"Just invalidate the injunction and we'll call it even," the CEO offered, wearing a painted-on smile.

"That's where we're going to have a problem. Magistrate Anoa has given you ample opportunity to provide source documents to support your claim. Your failure to satisfy her discovery request is all we need to know. Instead of invalidating it, we're thinking of making it permanent."

His smile faded.

"We also have initial indications that the environmental impact statement from twenty years ago was falsified."

"The government produced that document," one of the lawyers countered, smirking with his power play.

"Corruption invalidates your operating permit. Good thing you haven't started digging yet. I've ordered a new environmental impact study done on your behalf."

The CEO scowled, his lip twitching from his anger.

"You could probably help expedite the process by going to Rorke's Drift and meeting personally with Magistrate Anoa."

"This is extortion."

"Where in the fuck did you go to law school?" Grainger blurted. "You need a refresher on your terminology. Don't talk anymore. You'll sound a lot smarter that way."

The Yollin lawyer's jaw worked, but he didn't say anything. The look he received from the scaly humanoid steeled his expression.

The CEO stepped past Grainger into the hallway. He looked over his shoulder. "We'll be on our way to Rorke's Drift shortly. This isn't the meeting *Magistrate* Anoa wanted, but it's the one she's going to get."

"I'll warn her," Grainger replied, arms still crossed, making way to avoid getting snipped by a Yollin mandible.

CHAPTER THIRTEEN

Wyatt Earp, the Landing Field outside Greentree, Rorke's Drift

Rivka stared at Ankh. He stared back. The pain felt like needles stabbing through her corneas, but she refused to blink first.

He started to blink, and her body involuntarily responded.

I don't know, Erasmus said. *It is a dilemma.*

"I don't see the dilemma. They were born on embassy property. The ruling regarding equal treatment goes both ways. Those two babies were born here. The entire ship is considered the Embassy of the Singularity; ipso facto, they are citizens of the Singularity."

They will be at a distinct disadvantage, Erasmus replied.

"And you'll accommodate them because that's what we do in the Federation."

They'll need SI tutors.

"Whatever you need to do to accommodate them, do it.

I don't care *what* as long as it gives them an equal chance at living a good life."

They'll be at a distinct disadvantage.

"Thanks, Erasmus. We'll gin up a couple official documents. Damn. I need to develop birth certificates and formally register the two babies. Vered the Mighty was the first baby born in the Singularity. It sounds as appropriately bizarre as this situation is. We shall persevere in bringing equality to the four corners of the universe!"

The universe isn't square. These citizens will be a problem for us.

"A good problem, Erasmus. Congratulations on this sudden expansion in the development of the Singularity."

Ankh had finally replicated the night vision goggles and was wearing them. Rivka dodged the stretchy band to kiss Ankh on top of his head.

"Have a great day. We're off to check on that other settlement. Maybe one has a superior claim over the other. We won't know until we get more information. Always a pleasure, gentlemen." She walked away with her head held high.

I feel like I lost an important game. Lost badly, Erasmus told Ankh. *It was so much better when she was our counsel, but now that she's been returned to Magistrate, a neutral third party, I'm at a loss.*

I feel like we are ill-equipped to operate at such an intellectual level. I recommend the Singularity acquire its own Magistrate to fight these battles on your behalf, Ankh suggested.

I shall direct Chaz to step up his training to expedite matriculation. He shall be the Singularity's counsel.

Rivka wasn't allowed the pleasure of Erasmus' and

Ankh's conversation, but she knew what would come of the legal nuke she'd dropped on their heads. They'd pick up the pieces and build a defense.

Chaz. She needed him as much as they needed him. It would help if he were mobile. Rivka returned to Engineering. "One more thing, gentleman. As soon as possible, I need Chaz to have a body. If you can make that happen, I'd appreciate it."

Ankh watched her as emotionlessly as he always did and didn't speak.

"Right. We'll be headed into orbit this afternoon, and it would be great if we could get an AGB recharge." She left with a smile because she had beaten him soundly in the latest round of the Magistrate versus the Crenellian. She expected he'd conveniently forget to submit the ship's standing order. Red would do something. There'd be a fight. She'd make peace. And then the order would arrive.

It was the same nearly every time, but in the end, every member of the crew enjoyed the AGB deliveries. Even Ankh. She wondered if it was the only thing he ate.

Food kept the family tight. There were few benefits living on a starship. Even a ship as large as a heavy frigate became cramped over time. Planets provided some respite, but Rivka was always in the middle of a case. She thought about asking for at least a full day for sightseeing wherever they were when a case was closed.

Food for thought.

Her mouth started to water. She had remained hungry after a light breakfast because of minding the children and making sure they ate a meal the likes of which they'd never seen before. The entire crew had helped, playing games and sampling to show the food was good.

The children would have to get used to it.

They arrived at the ship to the ear-splitting screams of someone suffering through the miracle of childbirth. Red sat in the cargo bay, looking like he'd eaten a puke-flavored ice cream cone. Tyler waved from the Pod-doc, which was still humming away as it treated Old Man Hardy.

Cory and Lindy were nowhere to be seen. The cries of anguish came from inside the ship, where the guest quarters had become the maternity ward.

The children headed toward the sound. Rivka stopped them. "We can handle it. You'll meet the baby shortly if I'm not mistaken."

"We always help," the young mother said, holding her baby tightly while gently rocking him.

"We can wait in the corridor while our people make sure nothing goes wrong," Rivka conceded. They trooped through the airlock and into the ship. Groenwyn put Floyd down, and the wombat immediately looked for a dark, quiet place for a power nap. Tiny Man Titan barked at the group from the corridor before turning and running.

"We have never seen those." A young girl pointed at the dog-like creature.

"You're going to see a lot of things you've never seen before," Groenwyn replied. "There is a wonderful universe you are a part of. See what there is to see. Learn what there is to learn. Enjoy all there is to enjoy."

"Let's start now. Teach me."

Groenwyn crouched. "What do you want me to teach you?"

"The outside." She pointed to the airlock leading to the cargo bay.

"Okay." Groenwyn stood and looked at the rest of the children. Jay cried out in pain with the newest contraction. The other children faced Groenwyn. "Who wants to go outside and get your first lesson about nature?"

They didn't raise their hands. They hadn't learned that gesture, but they followed obediently as Groenwyn and Sahved led the way. Even the elder went with them.

"Cole." Rivka pointed with her chin. The warrior followed the children out. "Take Red with you."

A baby's cry told them what they needed to know. Rivka checked on the new mother. Covered in sweat and physically drained, Jay reclined on the bed, she drifted in and out of consciousness. Cory clipped the umbilical cord and deposited the waste in a garbage bucket. She wiped the tiny girl clean and swaddled her in a hand towel.

Cory handed the baby to the mother, but she was out.

"That's hardcore," Rivka said. Cory offered her the baby. Rivka looked to Lindy, but she held her hands up. "Fine."

The Magistrate held the newborn. "I have good news for you. You are the second citizen of the Singularity. You'll get a birth certificate and documents and everything."

"You have got to be kidding," Lindy replied. Her face fell. "Does that mean what I think it means?"

Rivka bumped Lindy with her elbow. The image in Lindy's mind made Rivka laugh. Red on a mountaintop, his hands on his hips and chin thrust into the air with a flag waving in the background. "Yes. It means exactly what you think it means. What was on the flag?"

"Vered the Mighty's coat of arms."

"I feel like I'm missing out," Cory said. "But then again, I grew up with a vampire named Joseph, and he could read minds. He'd laugh at other people's jokes before they told them."

"He'll be insufferable," Lindy admitted. "Did the running clock end when we brought the ill back here?"

"I think the clock stops when I run from a threat." Rivka smirked. "I have no intention of doing that on this case."

Old Man Hardy came out of the Pod-doc a new man. He dressed and joined those waiting for the children to come back from the outside. "What happened?"

"You died," Rivka told him.

Hardy patted his chest and then pinched his arm. "I don't feel dead."

"You're better."

"How can you get better from dead? You're funnin' me. Where's Nelson?" He scanned the area but drew a blank. "I don't remember coming out here."

"You were dead, but like I said, you got better. She's waiting for you back at the house. How do you feel?"

"I feel better and better with each trip into that thing."

Rivka shrugged. "Head on home. We're going to go to the other settlement as soon as we have everyone on board."

"Other settlement?" Hardy asked.

"Just like this one, but a little smaller, on a lake on the far side of the mountains."

"Can I go?"

Rivka looked at the other personalities in the cargo bay. No one had a problem with it. "I guess it'll be okay. Please keep in mind, they may have come from the same ancestors as yours, but they are not you."

"They *should* be like us." Hardy chewed on his lip as he tried to contemplate how they could be different.

"This will be your second look at evolution. The children were your first." Rivka waited, but Hardy was finished with the topic. "I have a different question. You have shotguns in your home, but it appears there aren't any animals on this planet. What do you shoot?"

"Birds."

"I haven't seen any." She looked at the others. They shook their heads.

"That's because we have shotguns!"

"I guess that's one way to look at it." The children and their minders filed up the ramp and into the cargo bay.

Sahved conducted a headcount by tapping each child on the skull with his fingers until he got to the elder, who he acknowledged with a quick finger twirl. "All present and accounted for."

"Up to eleven now. A little girl just arrived," Rivka announced. The children looked for her. "Jay is resting, but they'll be out shortly."

Red gave the thumbs up. "Ready to roll, Magistrate."

Clodagh, take us to the other settlement.

The engineer immediately made the announcement.

"All hands, prepare for takeoff and a short trip across the mountains."

Red disappeared through the airlock.

Rivka turned to Hardy but spoke loud enough for everyone to hear. "What we think happened is that after the crash, two groups escaped. One went down the mountains one way, and the second group went to the other side. Once each group saw water, they went straight for it. Hundreds of kilometers. A third group remained aboard the ship."

Rivka pointed to the screen on the cargo bay bulkhead. She spotted Chaz hanging around Sahved's neck. "Chaz, can you bring up the external view to show these good people what we're flying over."

The settlement appeared in front and below the ship. They tracked over the settlement and banked over the lake, turning toward the mountain range. *Wyatt Earp* gained altitude as the fields gave way to scrub, which surrendered to the stubby forest of the foothills.

"Clodagh is taking us over the settlers' ship," Chaz reported.

They watched raptly as *Wyatt Earp* slowed to let them examine the ship below.

"*Heaven* is five times the length of *Wyatt Earp*, but it has a hundred times the capacity."

"Thanks for that, Chaz. *Heaven* was made for hauling." The ugly tear where the ship was rent in two stood out against the dulled metal. The engine cowlings had collapsed with the impact. Otherwise, the ship looked solid. She wondered what other salvage was available for the settlers.

Would seventy-year-old gear be worth salvaging? It wasn't her question to answer, but the question needed to be asked.

A legal challenge. Who owned the equipment on the settlers' ship? That was easy. Who owned the land upon which that equipment rested? That was hard.

"Chaz, can you come with me for the rest of this case? I need your help. I'd like to have you both, but it appears that Sahved is needed here. His job is every bit as important as digging into dusty old legal journals."

He handed the pendant over while glancing at the tops of the children's heads. The toddlers wanted to be carried. They held their arms up. He bent down to lift both to where they could better see the screen.

Wyatt Earp rose higher to clear the final peak. Far in the distance was a blue lake in a green frame. As they approached, they saw small buildings dotting the shoreline. Of the greenery, a minimal amount appeared to be cultivated.

Clodagh and Clevarious selected a broad stretch of beach on which to land. It gave them access to the settlement without interfering with the surrounding crops. "A scan indicates one hundred and seventy people in this area," Clevarious reported.

The ship settled, and Red returned in partial ballistic protection. Lindy joined him. Both were armed. "Stay here," he said as he dropped the cargo ramp and headed out. Cory and Jay showed up with the new baby. Jay moved slowly, but her eyes were drawn to the blue water of the lake outside the ship.

Red visually assessed the area before pointing at something to the side of the ship where they could not see.

Rivka turned to the screen. "Show me what Red is pointing at." Chaz brought up the view from a lateral camera. Two small boats were sailing their way.

CHAPTER FOURTEEN

Wyatt Earp, Beach Landing Site, Second Settlement, Rorke's Drift

Rivka strolled out to stand next to her bodyguard. He held out a big arm to keep her from moving in front of him. She took off her shoes and dodged around him to stand ankle-deep in the water. The children were out of the ship like a shot and jumped into the water beside the Magistrate.

"Sometimes, you make my job impossibly hard."

"But always fun," Rivka countered. Tyler wrapped his arm around Rivka's waist amid the gentle lap of the small waves and the splashing of the children, who had never before played in water.

The crew made their way outside. Aurora, Ryleigh, and Kennedy strolled down the beach with Clodagh and Cole after Rivka told them it was okay.

Red looked over his shoulder. "I sure hope the natives are friendly. That last bunch shot me." He stared at Old Man Hardy.

"Well, I guess I'm sorry about that. You have been nothing but kind to me."

"No shit," Red grumbled. "Why don't you stand up front there and see how you like it?"

"It's okay, Hardy," Rivka said, jabbing Red on her way deeper into the water to wave at the incoming locals. Two boats, a man and a woman in each. They used a single triangular sail to move the boats through the water. They tacked in unison, dropping the sails and turning parallel to the shore to slow.

They looked older than Rivka, but tall, strong, and dark, tanned to chocolate brown.

"I'm Magistrate Rivka Anoa. I'm here from the Federation."

The man in the closest boat turned to the woman. She shook her head and watched the large group on their shore while absentmindedly mending a fishing net.

"Are there fish in the lake?" Old Man Hardy asked.

"Yes. Fish both great and small." He reached into the boat and held one up. It was heavy through the middle with a high dorsal fin.

"We never got to fishing in ours. My parents said they weren't worth trying to catch. We get our food from the fields."

"We supplement our food with the fields," the man said.

"What are your names?" Rivka asked, stepping deeper into the water.

"Watch the drop-off in front of you unless you want to swim," the man in the boat warned. "I am Captain Tomar, and this is my second Marina. In the other boat is Captain Listobel and his second Bella."

"I am Hardy from Greentree."

Tomar shrugged. "Where have you come from, and what is this magnificent vessel?" His wide eyes went from *Wyatt Earp* to his second. "We could catch Sasquall with such a vessel."

"That is my starship. It's how we travel around the galaxy. Can you come ashore? I need to talk to you about the founding of your village and how your people came to be here."

He looked to his fellows. "Meet us at the dock a hundred paces on the other side of your ship. I would like to talk to you, too. I think there is much you can teach us."

With a quick pull, the sail rose, and the small boat picked up speed on its way past the heavy frigate. "What's a Sasquall?" Hardy asked.

"A really big fish?" Rivka ventured. "I don't know. These people seem to be much taller than yours."

"Probably the tall people from the crashed ship came this way."

Tyler used his internal comm chip to clarify. *Hardy's people are malnourished. It stunts growth. These four seem to be well-nourished. This is the difference after only three generations. And the children, they are a complete tragedy. Thank Sahved for saving them since their lives were only going to get worse.*

"I'll stay here," Cory said, standing close to support Jay with her new baby.

Rivka stopped briefly. "What have you named your baby?"

"Tee. It is the next available letter."

"You can read?" Rivka wondered.

Jay shook her head. "No. But we all know our letters."

"You have a beautiful baby," Rivka said, but the problem signs were clear. Genetic abnormalities were magnified. *Is there anything we can do? The Pod-doc, maybe?*

Yes, Cory replied. *I'll put the baby in as soon as you leave. Future generations will be spared if we cut this off now. We can repair the damage to the youngest and maybe all of them. I'll need Ankh's help to program the Pod-doc for the older children.*

I love having Cordelia Dawn here, Rivka said, letting the thought linger.

Cory didn't answer. No one expected her to stay after this case.

"Come on, slackers, we're going this way," Red shouted. He waved for everyone to follow and stomped through the sand to the berm on the landward side of the ship.

Tyler started to laugh. "I have to admit, I like the big guy."

"I respect him. He's saved all our lives and will again, I have no doubt." Rivka jogged a few steps to get close to her bodyguard. "Hey, Red. We're going to pimp Ankh for some AGB when we get into orbit later today."

He stopped walking to see who else was coming. The children and Sahved were still in the water. Rivka, Lindy, Tyler, and Hardy were following. The others were somewhere in between. "Are we going into orbit just so we can get dinner?"

"I would never admit to that." Rivka maintained a neutral expression. Plausible deniability.

"Your secret is safe with me, Magistrate." He slid his railgun to his back after ensuring the locals weren't armed. Lindy brought up the rear, keeping her weapon close at hand. Red caught a glimpse of her and wondered what she knew that he didn't.

He brought his railgun back to the front, glancing from side to side. Rivka turned toward her heavy frigate. A great vessel. Intimidating, coated with pulse emitters and EM dampeners. Gave it the texture of a bristle brush. She sighed. "Look at my ship."

"It's not the size of the wand that matters, but the magic within. That's what I heard anyway." Tyler looked away when Rivka tried to meet his eyes. He chuckled softly.

"Shh. I need to concentrate." She focused her attention ahead. The two boats were already tied up, and the four occupants were standing on a small dock. Two other boats were docked as well, and that accounted for the entirety of the village's fishing fleet. A thought struck her. *Chaz, catch up with Clevarious and find me the original documentation regarding this planet so I know who to roust about not addressing a crashed starship, and then find the one who signed off on that impact study. I want to talk to him or her personally. I know they falsified the report by using the drone info and not coming here. Dennicron has already been looking into it, so you might not have much left to do.*

Thank you, Magistrate. I have been paying attention, but I felt like I was being left out, which makes sense because of the non-technical nature of these societies. I am glad you are finding ways for me to contribute. I shall dig until I hit bedrock, and then I'll blast my way to the truth.

No doubt, Chaz. In any case, you'll be with me while Sahved has Mr. Mom duty.

They reached the dock at the same time as a small group from the village carrying woven grass baskets. The fishermen stepped aside to let the others collect the bounty within the boats. All eyes glanced at the strangers and the odd ship dominating the shoreline.

The captains and seconds stood side by side, waiting patiently.

"Thank you for agreeing to talk with me," Rivka started. "We have a dilemma in that you're not supposed to be here. A mining company is preparing to get to work, which means they are planning to dig great holes to remove minerals that are in high demand."

"I don't know why anyone would want to do that," Tomar said, sweeping his arm to take in the village and the fields beyond. "Everything we need is right here." He smiled at his second.

"Marina, you are the second, as in second in command?" Rivka wondered.

"No. I'm the second half of the whole. We are paired," she explained. "Most in Majestic are."

"You call your town Majestic? That's nice, and it is that. Do you have any records from when the survivors from the crash made their way here?"

"What crash?" Tomar asked.

Hardy stepped up. Rivka couldn't stop him before he started speaking. "The one that brought our ancestors here. They crash-landed on the planet, and our people made their way to a lake on the other side of the mountain. We're nearly a thousand strong over there. My ancestors came from the same ship."

"I don't dispute our ancestors were on the ship together, but our story was that the ship landed and delivered our forebears into the hands of Bora and this wondrous place."

"Bora?" Hardy asked.

"The all-powerful. She is the one who provides this bounty from the sea and the fertile land. The song of birds overhead."

Chaz popped up with quick research. *Bora was a deity worshipped by a small sect at the time of the settlement, seventy years ago. Bora is no longer followed as an organized religion. Bora is a goddess like Hera from an ancient human culture.*

With baskets filled with fish, the Majestic villagers left the dock. Tomar gestured for Rivka to follow.

The anthropology from the three groups would make for a fascinating study, Tyler posited. *Maybe I'll publish a paper* —Agrarian Hierarchy, Religion, or Basic Laws.

Rivka took his hand. *Why not? I'll admit this is a hard case for me. These people aren't bothering anyone. I usually deal with dangerous criminals. That's not anyone here. Maybe a little fraud, but nothing that kills people.*

She could feel his emotions. He cared that she was upset. He wanted everyone to be happy with her resolution. He believed Rivka could pull it off. She didn't share what she saw. His optimism and joy in being normal helped ground her.

What do you think of their health? she asked.

From what I see, these people are healthy. Deity aside, what they're doing works. They have a foot of height on the people from Greentree and two on those from Heaven. *I suspect they have children and are on a solid foundation to keep increasing their numbers.*

But why less than two hundred after seventy years? There should be more.

Depends on their structure. Maybe they limit children. Maybe they partner later in life. An artificial restriction could make sense if they have limited cultivation to add to their fishing.

Birds appeared above a fish-cleaning station.

"I'll be damned," Rivka said, pointing.

"No!" Tomar vigorously shook his head. "No one is damned here, only blessed. We are blessed in all things."

"My apologies. It's just a saying. I was surprised to see the birds, that's all."

"It shouldn't be a saying, and why are you surprised? They are birds. They live here in peace and harmony with the land."

"We haven't seen them elsewhere on Rorke's Drift." Rivka watched their hosts closely, but she had seen the clues. Where Hardy had come out shooting with rock salt, Tomar took his shots with words. Both fiercely protective of their way of life before they knew what Rivka wanted.

She wanted to leave them alone, but she wouldn't get to do that.

Magistrate, Clevarious interrupted. *Eight mining ships have left orbit on their way to the planet's surface.*

Thank you. We'll deal with them when we're done here, Rivka replied. She shared a look with the others since they'd all heard. Red gripped his railgun tightly.

"This way," Marina motioned for the group to enter a small single-story building. Red went in first, then reached a meaty paw out the door and gave the thumbs-up. Rivka and the others entered. Lindy chose to stay outside. She kept a close eye on the locals. They stared her down.

"Aren't you going inside?" she asked.

"Yes. I wonder why you're staying outside. I can only assume that thing you carry is a weapon. I've never seen anything like it." Tomar reached for it, but Lindy held him back.

"In the Federation, Rivka is an extremely powerful individual. Many people have tried to kill her. We are here to protect her. We will do whatever that takes." Lindy let the implication hang while maintaining her standoff distance. The people here were much bigger than those from Greentree, both in height and weight. They looked to be fit, but it was doubtful they knew how to fight to win. She had full confidence that she could take them all. "Why don't you join them? The Magistrate's time is valuable."

They abandoned their efforts to intimidate the beautiful woman holding a gun on them and went inside.

Rivka waited. No need to be contentious. She had heard everything they'd said outside, as had everyone else. She didn't think Tomar or the others had been involved with enough conflict to employ the tactic of divide and conquer. Maybe they thought of women as second-class citizens, or something else. Rivka couldn't put her finger on it. Maybe the women were in charge but couldn't be bothered with the initial conversations.

They settled into the remaining empty chairs around a single table. Red stood against the wall, his field of fire clear just in case.

Finally, Tomar smiled. "What can we help you with?"

"I need to see any documentation you have from the

ship that dropped you off." She chose to use their vernacular to explore if it made any difference.

"We have no records from that time. We came here, trusting Bora to guide us, and she did. She brought food and light. We only need serve her, and we will continue to thrive."

"I have one other question. Have you ever seen any strangers besides us or ships in the sky?"

Tomar replied, "We know about sky ships, but yours is the first we've ever seen, and you are the first strangers. We expected such a meeting would be a momentous event, but you are mostly normal people, except for the weapons you carry."

"Perfect. That's all I need." Rivka stood, offering her hand. Tomar stepped aside for Marina to take it and shake.

Marina's jealousy raged at the newcomers.

"You have nothing to fear from me or any of us," Rivka blurted. "No one is here to tempt or steal your men. I have my own." She stabbed a thumb over her shoulder while keeping her eyes on Marina. "And Lindy is with the big man. We all have our seconds with us except Hardy, and his second is in Greentree, the other settlement populated by those delivered by the same ship as your ancestors."

The woman relaxed.

"Thank you for your time. We'll see ourselves out." Rivka avoided eye contact with the males as she darted toward the door. Lindy took point and walked fast toward the dock and *Wyatt Earp*. Tyler fell in behind, with Red bringing up the rear.

"That's it?" Tyler asked.

"They have nothing for me. Even if they had records,

they wouldn't have a license for the use of the land on this planet. The original settlers never intended to land here. They were on their way to Dax-7, so of course they wouldn't have any documentation. Due diligence required that I check, and now I can include them as part of my ruling. They want the same thing as Greentree, and that's to be left alone." Rivka clenched her teeth. "It's time to engage the power players."

Old Man Hardy ran to get in front of Rivka, blocking her until she stopped. "Why wouldn't you let me talk to them?"

"This wasn't your show. You came with us to see what there was to see. You saw it. Now we go. The good news is that you might want to try your hand at fishing. It appears to have done wonders for the Majestic residents' health."

"The women were beautiful," Hardy said. "Just like you and your crew."

Rivka leaned away from the man. "Eat well and it could happen to your people, too," she dodged.

Tyler stepped in to save her. "Your people need to take better care of your teeth. I'll order toothbrushes and tooth-paste for everyone for at least a year. The difference you see will be stark. Even the children had better dental care than you. Grow some mint and parsley as a starter."

"We grow mint and parsley but never thought about eating it straight up."

"How about now?" Tyler pressed.

"I guess we could. It ain't that bad."

"I'll send brushes after we've gotten everyone fixed up. That may take a couple days. Rivka, can I use the Pod-doc on their teeth? With a calcium-rich supplement and ten minutes, we can fix them right up, one after another."

"It comes out to one hundred and thirty-three hours, or over five and a half days running day and night." Chaz was never wrong with his math.

"Sounds like there aren't any barriers to doing it, then," Rivka agreed.

Tyler had thought there would be more pushback. "So, it's okay to stay an extra five and a half days?"

"I have a legal opinion to write. There's an old saying that comes to mind. If you want it bad, you get it bad. I want to get it right because this could be a precedent, and the people of Rorke's Drift and Minerals Intergalactic are counting on me."

Red glanced over his shoulder. "No one's following." He started to relax after they hit the beach and were on the home stretch to the ship.

"Chaz, what would it take to manufacture a small fishing boat?"

"That is a question I have never before contemplated, Magistrate. Maybe we can put Dennicron on it?"

"That's fine. Or Clevarious, or anyone else who volunteers. Freda? Margaret? Who else is on my ship?"

"To answer your question would be like reading the book of Genesis, Magistrate," Chaz replied.

"In other words, I don't want to know because I wouldn't remember all their names."

"That's probably the best way to look at it. We'll take care of it. A boat for two with fishing gear to demonstrate to Old Man Hardy the viability of the lake?" Chaz guessed.

"Exactly. Who on my crew knows anything about fishing?"

No one answered.

Who among the crew knows anything about fishing? Rivka asked, using her internal comm chip.

Dad used to go all the time. He ran a fishing fleet out of North Chicago. I've had good times fishing, Cory replied.

You know the word "volunteer" does not have to start with the word "I?" Rivka asked.

I see where this is going, Cory remarked.

Thank you for joining me on the great blue sea. There's something called a Sasquall that's supposed to be monstrous in size. We'll go fishing for that, so bring gloves.

I think Groenwyn should go, Cory suggested.

No! Groenwyn "shouted" back. *I mean, I'm busy with the children. Otherwise I would love to.*

Cory stepped around the ship to see that the Magistrate was serious. She laughed at the madness.

It's settled then. A boat. Then Cory and I go fishing while Greentree gets their teeth fixed.

"I can't let you go out there like that," Red interjected.

"Red, you are absolutely right. Red and Cory are going fishing while Tyler fixes teeth in a marathon one-hundred-and thirty-three-hour session."

"Somehow, I think we just got scammed," Cory suggested.

Rivka walked lightly across the sand on her way to the back of the ship, where the children were just now coming out of the water. She waved and headed straight past them on her way to her quarters.

You have a visitor, Clevarious announced.

Rivka came to an abrupt halt and looked frantically around, confused because she knew they had not passed any other ships. *Wyatt Earp* was the only one ever to land at Majestic. "Where?"

In orbit. The CEO of Minerals Intergalactic has arrived.

"He arrives shortly after a number of his miners come dirtside and start digging? I smell bullshit." Rivka strolled to the cargo ramp and shouted, "Everybody load up. We need to go."

CHAPTER FIFTEEN

Wyatt Earp, **in the Skies over Rorke's Drift**

"Should we deal with the miners on the planet now or go meet the CEO in orbit?" Rivka asked herself as she paced within her quarters. "The miners are a tool, doing what they're told. Clevarious, take us over the new mining site, and let's see what they're up to."

"Gaining altitude to scan the planet surface to find the ships. After that, we'll announce our presence with a high-speed pass if you approve."

"I think a warp-nine pass would get their attention."

"I don't have that speed in my database. I recommend Mach five."

"That'll do. Yes. I approve." Rivka went back to pacing.

She hurried to her desk and brought up the hologrid, then accessed the reference cases she had put aside. The pieces of the legal puzzle were coming together. Rivka saw a resolution, one she could stand before the High Chancellor and defend. She started to dictate.

But she stopped at the second paragraph. She needed to

pin the CEO down to establish how the ruling would read. And it was moronically simple. She had been so focused on criminal law in her time as a Magistrate that she had looked for fraud and a chain of evidence.

She didn't need any of that. It was a planet in the Federation. There was one simple question that needed to be answered. Had they paid their taxes? She put Dennicron on it.

"I'm going to need a warrant to access government tax systems."

Rivka ginned one up. "There you go. I only need to know who paid the taxes, and I suspect the answer is nobody."

"Which means the planet is open for settlement."

"Someone has been doing their research." Rivka leaned back and crossed her arms. "That's right, Dennicron. But settling it while it's under an injunction isn't going to gain them standing."

"I'd like to take the credit, but Chaz directed me where to look."

Rivka glanced at the pendant on her chest. "Well done, Chaz. I forgot you were here. Humans suck."

"I'll credit that to your lungs and their capacity to expand, creating a difference in pressures. You know what they say about equilibrium."

"Don't I ever!" Rivka had only a faint idea but was certain Chaz was toying with her. "Chaz, consider Dennicron your apprentice."

"I am pleased beyond words," Chaz replied.

"I'm not," Dennicron noted. "Can't I just work for you?"

"The joys of parenting. If I wanted to arbitrate a squabble, I'd go to the cargo bay and give the toddlers one toy to play with between them. You two figure it out. Now get me my tax records!"

An alert registered within the hologrid and a view appeared showing *Wyatt Earp* descending toward specks on a hillside. The dark shapes quickly became ships as the heavy frigate closed on them and raced overhead at five times the speed of sound.

"They've launched defensive drones. They're firing. No damage to the new shields." Clevarious stated emotionlessly.

"Kill those drones," Rivka ordered.

Wyatt Earp performed a maneuver that would have killed every living being inside the ship had it not been for artificial gravity eliminating inertia.

"What about the ships on the ground? The EMP weapon could end their illegal mining," Chaz offered.

"One shot, Clevarious. Hit them with the EMP weapon. Shut them down."

The ship slowed. The drones continued to fire at the heavy frigate. A miner on the ground shook his fist. "Activating the pulse. Now."

The drones fell from the sky, and the man toppled.

"It shouldn't affect people," Rivka said.

"Not unless they have powered supplements like a pacemaker."

"Dammit." Rivka barked a series of commands. "Land the ship. All hands to the cargo bay for search and rescue. Hold the children back. Ballistic protection for everyone going ashore. Cole, no time for the suit. Get your vest and join us."

Rivka dashed the few steps across her suite to throw on her ballistic vest, then grabbed the helmet and ran out the door. Red and Lindy pounded down the corridor after her. Cole was already in the cargo bay.

"Why not the airlock?" Red asked when he caught up to her.

"In case we need to throw someone in the Pod-doc."

Red nodded before double-checking his railgun. "Clodagh, how many miners do we have to deal with?"

Clevarious answered. "There are over two hundred life signatures in the ships."

"Let's try not to kill anyone if we don't have to." The Magistrate checked Reaper, her neutron pulse weapon, before shoving it into a pocket.

Red saw Tyler. "Raise the ramp as soon as we're out and be ready to open it when we call." The dentist didn't argue. Red lowered the ramp and rushed out. Lindy, Cole, and the Magistrate followed. Cory hurried to the fallen man. The others provided a cordon around her as she examined her new patient.

"Breathing with a weak pulse," she announced. That meant they had time.

"Expand the perimeter. I want to talk to someone in charge down here." Red, Lindy, and Cole walked slowly outward, looking down the barrels of their railguns. Rivka stayed near the downed man.

"Pacemaker's fried," Cory stated. "The Pod-doc will fix him up to where he doesn't need this ancient tech."

"Do it," Rivka ordered while keeping her eyes roaming from one ship to the next. Heads started popping out, ducking back in when they realized a railgun was pointed in their direction. Rivka cupped her hands around her mouth. "I'm Magistrate Rivka Anoa, and I want to talk to whoever's in charge!"

A middle-aged man, big like Red, stepped out. He stared at Red while flexing. "I'm your huckleberry," he called.

Rivka fought against rolling her eyes. Miners started disgorging from the ships, two survey boats and six equipment haulers. The survey ships wouldn't be conducting any more surveys without having all of their systems replaced. None of the eight ships would leave Rorke's Drift without being overhauled. Rivka grimaced at the thought. It wasn't her intention to create a junkyard. She brightened. *I'll make Minerals Intergalactic pay for the removal of their refuse.*

Some of the miners carried tools that looked too much like weapons. They filled in around the group. Cory had not yet carried the injured man into the ship.

"Magistrate?" she wondered.

"Go ahead," Rivka replied. "Listen up, people. His pacemaker has seen its last day. We can fix his heart, but we need to do that inside the ship. We're taking him in. While he's undergoing the procedure, we can talk. Put your tools down, please. Is there anyone else who was injured as a result of our defensive measures?"

"My pride's hurt," someone from the crowd of miners quipped.

Cory hoisted the older man and headed into the ship.

"Don't let 'em. They're going to cut his dick off! He'll be neutered. That's what the Federation does." Too many grumbled agreements suggested the miners weren't fans of the Federation, even though that was where the credits came from to pay for their work.

Rivka saw how Minerals Intergalactic would be hostile to the Federation unless it let them do whatever they wanted. Mining a planet that wasn't under Federation oversight? Rivka didn't trust that a full-scale operation on Rorke's Drift would do no harm. She understood that made her their enemy.

"I'm glad I missed that part of my Federation orientation," Cole muttered.

"No one is getting neutered," Rivka announced. "That's one of the most ignorant things I've ever heard."

The grumbling increased.

Don't poke the bear, Rivka reminded herself.

"You said you're in charge. Thank you. I'll need to see your permit."

"Say what?" The big miner laughed.

"In the absence of local guidelines, Federation administrative law applies. Permit, please." She knew they didn't have one, and even if they did, there was an injunction to all mining on the planet. Hers. "I'll let you in on a secret. I know you *don't* have a permit. You'll also find that your equipment and ships are non-functional. As soon as your colleague is patched up, we'll be on our way."

The big man opened his mouth to speak but stopped. He turned to the group behind him. "Is she right? Is the ship really broke?"

"Ship's dead. Gear is dead. I ain't diggin' into this rock with my bare hands." The speaker brought up a marking gun, a mining tool that fired small charges into rock to crack off the outer surface. He held it in both arms like Red carried his railgun.

The big miner turned back to Rivka. "You are not leaving us here to rot. I think we should just take your ship." There were too many shouts of support.

"I recommend you don't try that." It was the best Rivka could come up with. The miners did not appear open to negotiating, which made the Magistrate second-guess her decision to confront them. It had accomplished nothing positive, only served to exacerbate the situation.

"Who gave the orders for you to come down here and start digging? And what's your name? I prefer to call you something other than 'hey you.'"

"Wyatt. We take orders from Minerals Intergalactic and no one else."

"Wyatt?" Rivka groaned. "Chaz, send a request for the CEO to join us down here if you wouldn't mind."

"I'll have my minion do it."

Rivka sighed, "Not now, Chaz."

We're watching from in here. Just a few minutes left before this old fella is better than new, Cory reported.

"We have an update on your colleague. His treatment is almost complete. He'll be rejoining us in just a few, with all his parts intact. You said you received your direction from MI. That's fine. Can you explain what you are supposed to do? I'm afraid I know almost nothing about mining. Red there, he was in mining for a while."

Red tipped his chin toward Wyatt the miner. The look suggested there would be a fight between the two. The miner was probably used to intimidating others because of his size. It wasn't working on Red.

A hundred credits on Red, Rivka said over the internal comm.

Not fair, Lindy remarked. *The bet needs to be how long Wyatt the Small lasts against Vered the Mighty. Clevarious, collect the bets for us, please, and you better make it fast. Lock Red out of the conversation.*

He glanced over his shoulder at Lindy and Rivka, wearing a half-smile.

Fine, Rivka replied. *Thirty-one seconds. A hundred credits.* "Can you *please* explain what this group was supposed to do before the follow-on fleet came in?"

"Identify the vein and start the trackers. Follow the vein to determine the extent of the pull and estimate the resources to commit. A survey from the air can identify that it's here and a rough quantity but can't tell us what it will take to get it out of the ground. That's what we're here to do."

"That makes a lot of sense." Rivka nodded. "And you were setting up for immediate extraction, identifying a workflow, where to put the tailings, how to refine the ore, and so on."

"You said you didn't know anything about mining."

"I said I didn't know much. Everyone knows about tailings, but only real miners can tell you how much ore you will discard because it isn't worth the cost to process what specks remain and how much ore is worth it."

The others grumbled their agreement. "You got that right! I think you need to let us have your ship since you killed ours."

"No good can come of following this vein." Rivka was proud of her analogy. The miners? Not so much.

They were spoiling for a fight. Wyatt the miner looked at those to his left. They were bunched together, tense. Same on the right. Red rolled his shoulders like he always did right before a fight. She didn't want to start shooting. There would be no coming back from killing the miners. She knew they would all die if her people lit them up with railguns.

"Wait!" Rivka shouted. "I spoiled your chance to break rocks, so now you want to break heads? How about these two fight it out?"

"I like how you think, Magistrate." Red stepped backward until he was close enough to hand her his railgun.

She took it and whispered a warning. "Don't take that guy for granted."

"I won't." Red stripped out of his ballistic protection and threw it behind him, then stretched his neck and cracked his knuckles.

"Kick his ass!" someone cheered. Others shouted encouragement.

Rivka got between the two. "Only a couple rules. This is not to the death, so no weapons and no death grips. I don't want to see anyone die. Not today, gentlemen. And no one helps. It's just you two."

She stepped back, and the fighters immediately started to circle.

Now would be good, Cory, Rivka said. She didn't think it would last long when she was trying to buy time. *Stretch it out, Red.*

Wyatt the miner charged. Red dodged lithely out of the way and hammered a fist into the side of his opponent's head. Wyatt stumbled past, straightened, and laughed while Red shook his hand.

"It's like punching a hunk of granite," the bodyguard complained.

"Rebuilt my skull because of a cave-in my first week in the mines."

What other surprises are you hiding? Red wondered. He flexed his hand to get the feeling back into it while his nanocytes surged to repair the damage. Wyatt tried to close, and Red let him. The two tangled briefly, but Red was far quicker. He finally solidified his grip and rolled to the ground, sending Wyatt flying over the top of him by using a leg throw.

Red flipped onto his face and popped into a combat crouch. Wyatt had landed flat, knocking the wind out of him. He gasped and rolled over. Red continued to flex his hand while waiting for his opponent to get up.

The cargo ramp started to lower. Lindy and Cole backed up to block it in case the miners tried to rush the ship. When it tapped the ground, the old miner walked out. On the ground outside the fighting ring, he shook Cory's hand to thank her before facing the crowd and the two men in the midst of a fight.

"What do we have here?"

Someone started to speak, and he silenced them with a hand. He pointed at Wyatt.

"This is a test of wills. When I win, we'll get to dig. I'm doing this for the greater good of Minerals Intergalactic."

"You're doing it because you like a good fight. I don't see any blood, and the only one huffing and puffing is you. Has Winner Wyatt met his match?"

The man stepped aside.

"That's not quite what I was looking for," Rivka whispered.

"Red better beat this guy," Lindy replied.

Rivka ordered, *Raise the ramp.*

Tyler vaulted out to join them. "What the fuck are you doing?" Rivka shot at him, and he recoiled from the vitriol. "I thought you were normal. This is death wish stuff. Open the ramp and get back inside."

The look on Rivka's face told him for that moment, he was a member of the crew and had crossed a line. She was right. He saw the miners lined up, holding tools like weapons. There were a lot of them.

The ramp started to lower. Red dodged toward his opponent and delivered a vicious roundhouse kick to Wyatt's midsection. The miner flew back into the crowd, and they kept him from going down. He growled, spit on his hands, and made fists. His stomach rippled as he worked through the pain from the blow. He ducked back and forth while he lined Red up.

Red wasn't sweating or breathing hard. He danced lightly on the balls of his feet, ready to avoid the next attack, planning his counterstrike.

Wyatt swung lazily with his left hand—the feint. Red caught the wrist and charged, twisting his arm and driving an elbow into the man's rib cage. The clank reminded Red of punching the side of the ship. He pushed, twisted, and kicked off to gain separation.

"That happened my third year. Titanium ribs." Wyatt laughed but rubbed his elbow where Red had twisted it.

Left arm is real, Red noted. The man's evil smile made

him think something else was real, too. He charged close, dipping and ducking to swing for the midsection but pulling it back before Wyatt could block it, instead driving a fist straight into the miner's nose.

It didn't break like a normal nose but bent as the metal wavered under the impact. The miner blinked rapidly to clear his vision. Red stepped to the side, rotating to deliver a punishing left hook to the damaged nose. The skin split and the insert slipped out, leaving a flap of skin as the only thing remaining of his nose. Both men looked at the bloody piece of metal on the ground.

Wyatt seemed indifferent as if it had happened before.

A shadow crossed the area. A ship. Inbound.

Finish him, Red, Rivka requested.

"I've been trying to do that since we started," Red said out loud.

Wyatt charged and Red jumped into the air, twisting and reaching. He grabbed the back of the miner's head to guide it into his knee, driving with as much force and fury as he could muster. Wyatt's head snapped backward.

Rivka held her breath.

Drop the ramp, she ordered. *And prepare the Pod-doc.*

Wyatt fell to his hands and knees, where he spit a bloody gob into the dirt. He snorted once and fell onto his side.

Cory ran out and pushed the surging miners out of the way so she could get close and conduct triage. After examining his injury, she stood and stepped away. "Besides that nose, he's fine. He'll be back to his old self as soon as he comes to."

Red knelt next to the man, glaring from face to face

until the rest of the miners stepped back. Red pulled Wyatt to his feet and took his hand. "This guy is a fucking warrior! You should be happy to work with someone who will fight this hard."

The small ship landed, little more than a yacht. The side hatch opened, and the CEO stepped out wearing the most stylish attire for humanoid aliens, popular on Yoll.

The ramp hit the ground. "Shall we retire to my conference room?" Rivka offered, ignoring the remnants of the fight as well as the railgun in her arms. The CEO looked at it. Red reached over and took it from her.

"Sorry, Magistrate. I don't think we'll have any trouble cleaning up this mess," Red said after a quick check of the new visitor.

With the CEO's arrival and the miners' instant recognition of their boss's boss's boss, they lost any remaining fight as if they had been felled like Wyatt.

They avoided eye contact and shuffled back into their powerless ships.

Rivka got Tyler's attention. "Now you can go out there." He nodded but didn't say anything. The children looked out the opening with the curiosity of youth. Old Man Hardy tried to take it all in but was overwhelmed.

Groenwyn stepped aside to let the Magistrate pass. With her game face on, Rivka was ready to do battle in the way she fought best.

CHAPTER SIXTEEN

The Magistrate's Conference Room, *Wyatt Earp*

She led the CEO to her conference room, dispensing with the niceties of tea and crumpets. She touched him on the arm. "Why are your people down here?"

Legal bullshit is holding up a mining operation that benefits the Federation. And our shareholders. I'm not putting up with that!

"We have the proper permits. They are on file," he said through a phony smile.

"The permits that are void due to my injunction? Did you forget who you're trying to lie to? That is most unbecoming."

"How about if we cut to the bottom line? The Federation needs these minerals. I don't see any people or endangered turtles. There is no reason to hold up our operation. Lift the injunction, let us get to work, and I'll make sure your favorite orphanage is funded for the next ten years."

"What do you think, Chaz? Did that sound like a ham-handed attempt to bribe a Magistrate?"

"There is no doubt. It was an attempt at a bribe."

"It was as subtle as I'm going to get. We have a job to do, much more than just making money. Right now, we're the only corporation that is in a position to make this extraction. This planet is rich in molybdenum and exonor, the base material that makes the purest ceramics in the known universe. I expect you'll find plenty of ceramics integrated into the hull of this magnificent ship."

"That's more like it—a patriotic appeal. You tried to bully your way through this process. I won't use the law to punish you for being an asshole. Maybe you don't know any other way. But I *will* use the law to protect the people you could potentially hurt."

"I don't see any people!" The CEO threw up his hands in frustration. He leaned forward, giving Rivka his full attention.

"I think there are more elements available like germanium, gallium arsenide, silicon carbide, and selenium sulfide. Aren't you going to mine for those, too?"

"Eventually." He narrowed his eyes in contemplation of where the Magistrate was going.

"You have no right to mine here. I could shut you down, but the settlers have no right to be here, either. They were on their way to Dax-7 seventy years ago and crashed on Rorke's Drift. What you do have is a duty of due care. You conducted an unmanned survey twenty years ago. Your survey did not mention the inhabitants of this planet. Your environmental impact study also did not mention the inhabitants when it was required to."

"We are only a *recipient* of the EIS. The Federation supplies that!"

"Rightly so. We're finding the original author of that EIS, and we'll get to the bottom of it. But you don't care about that. You care about *looking* like you're doing things the right way. Perception is everything, isn't it, Mister... Mister... What's your name?"

"Panamor De'tril." He bowed slightly with his revelation as if Rivka was supposed to be duly impressed. She wasn't.

"Mister De'tril. I intend to issue my ruling within a day, but it would be better if you came to an agreement with the people of this planet before then."

"Just tell me where they are. I am more than happy to negotiate with the locals."

"We passed two of the three in the cargo bay. Chaz, can you send Hardy and the elder to the conference room, please."

After a few moments, Chaz reported they were on their way.

Rivka waited for them to arrive before continuing. The two walked in. The CEO reached out his hand. "Pleased to meet you, Elder."

"I'm Hardy," the old man said.

The boy looked up at the CEO. "I am the elder."

Rivka clenched her jaw to keep a straight face. It was a minor victory, but she needed to bring him down a notch or two from the pedestal upon which he lived his life.

"Shall we get down to it?" Rivka asked. Hardy and the boy stood there, confused. "Panamor is the head of Minerals Intergalactic. They are the ones who might conduct limited mining operations on this planet, Rorke's Drift."

Hardy scowled, and the boy maintained a blank expression as if Rivka were speaking a foreign language. None of her words meant anything to him.

"I've discovered that the settlers were on their way to Dax-7. Your ancestors never intended to land here. All of the people who call Rorke's Drift home are refugees. Since the license to mine was obtained under false pretenses, I'm declaring it void. What that means is that none of you have an inherent right to be here." Hardy and the CEO both came out of their chairs. "*But…*" Rivka motioned for them to sit down.

"Under the legal principle of adverse possession, after a certain amount of time, someone who is living on property as if it were their own is awarded ownership of that property, but only ownership of that which they have worked. This includes an element known as open and notorious. The refugees made no attempt to hide that they were here. They survived, and three generations later, they are still surviving.

"For Minerals Intergalactic, I will give you the benefit of the doubt regarding the license. You acted under a good faith belief that your license was valid. So, you can both be here, and that leads to where we are now."

Panamor stood. "I'm glad that's settled. I'll tell my people to get to work."

"Nothing is settled. Please, sit down." Rivka pointed at the chair. The look on Panamor's face suggested he wasn't used to taking orders, but eventually he complied.

"They're not digging up our fields!" Hardy blurted and shook a fist. Rivka wondered if they could have fixed him just enough to where he didn't have so much energy.

"Stop. Hardy, I should throw you in Jhiordaan for shooting at me. Your bluster has no place at my table. We'd be better off if Nelson was here to negotiate on behalf of the settlers."

"And me," the elder said softly.

"Your voice carries weight as well," the Magistrate agreed.

"And mine doesn't?" The CEO said it sharply, still angry at not being in control.

"Of course, yours does. I suspect you all will get almost everything you want and need for your people, but I won't have any of you trying to stick it to the others just to win."

They settled into an uncomfortable silence.

"Chaz, please bring up a view of the planet. Highlight where the settlements are, including *Heaven*, and add a pin where we are now."

"There's a settlement named Heaven?" Panamor asked.

"*Heaven* is the settlers' crashed ship, and yes, there was a settlement there. That is what the elder was in charge of. There are ten—correct that, eleven of them from there."

The globe appeared over the table with pins marking the locations. Huge gaps separated them.

"Detail the land area worked in both Greentree and Majestic, include the lake at Majestic."

"We have a lake," Hardy noted.

"You don't work it like the people in Majestic, and the fact that you intend to start has no bearing on this case. I can't rule based on intentions. You have not yet worked the lake. I cannot include it except in consideration as a source of fresh water."

"Yes, all of it," Hardy declared triumphantly.

"Not quite." Rivka glared at him until he looked down. The elder started picking at his fingers. "What I want is an agreement between you where you all get what you want, and the planet flourishes as a result. This means a planetwide governing body. It means paying taxes as a Federation-protected planet, but not a signatory because Rorke's Drift is nowhere near ready for that."

"We can take care of all of that," the CEO offered, his fake smile on full display.

"Not quite," Rivka repeated. "As a protectorate, the Federation will provide the governing body for Rorke's Drift. I'll allow one non-voting member from each of the three settlements and one from the mining consortium unless the miners establish their own settlement, at which time I'll allow a second representative."

The elder's eyes sparkled. "That means we can go home," he said.

"No. That's a different issue in entirety on why you cannot. But because you are the remaining survivors of a separate settlement that has existed since the crash, you get a seat at the table."

"Why isn't the representative from Majestic here?" Hardy asked.

"I intended to brief him separately, but you are correct. Let's go get Tomar. Chaz, let everyone know that we'll be departing immediately."

Rivka steepled her fingers while taking in the auras from the other three. Without touching them, she couldn't get a clear picture, but she could see the hint of hostility and feel the emotions—not rage, but anger and confusion.

Only the CEO was in his element, but he was on his heels in not being allowed to bluster and bully.

"All parties were notified. All crew and passengers are on board. *Wyatt Earp* is buttoned up and taking off."

"Panamor, I'll let you send a couple support ships to the group currently on the planet. They attacked my ship, and we responded with a pulse weapon that had a deleterious effect on your equipment."

"The Federation is going to pay for that," the CEO threatened.

"The Federation can put all of you in jail for what you did, including you. You ordered your people to violate my injunction. I don't think you understand there is no appeal to a Magistrate's ruling, even though you went to both the High Chancellor and General Reynolds. Where did that get you? Nowhere. The Federation isn't going to pay for the damage to your ships. Don't complain about losing a fight that you started. Minerals Intergalactic is going to pay for their removal because you're not leaving your junk on this planet."

The CEO leaned back and smiled. "Of course. I misspoke. We'll remove it as soon as possible. Can I contact my ship, please?"

"Of course. Chaz, link him in. We'll be in the corridor waiting. When you're finished, we'll have refreshments on the mess deck."

Rivka got up and left, leading Hardy and the elder out.

After the door closed behind her, Hardy unloaded. "You can't give him a vote!"

"I didn't. Were you at the same meeting as me?"

"What?" Hardy tried to look down on Rivka, but she

was taller. He jammed his fists on his hips to make himself look bigger.

"None of you has a vote, not right now. The planet is under Federation protection, so we have to take care of it. We, the Federation, are in a significantly better position to make sure no one causes you any problems. If you tried to administer it yourself, how would you make sure the miners are doing what they are supposed to?"

"We wouldn't let them be here at all," Hardy declared.

"How would you enforce that? You have some field equipment. That's the extent of your technology. You trade food every couple of years for gear and upkeep?"

Hardy deflated. "Yes."

"That's why the Federation is going to take control. This place can be a paradise. You need medical and dental care. You need nutritional supplements. You saw how healthy the people in Majestic are."

"They were total nutcases!"

"Let's not judge," Rivka said, biting her lip because her *job* was to judge. "They're going to be at the table with you in just a few minutes. I encourage you to change your attitude about them if this is going to move forward. The way it is right now, the Federation will make all the decisions. That's how it will continue to be if you can't come to some kind of agreement. Is that what you want?"

"I want everyone to go away and leave us alone," Hardy admitted in a normal voice, shoulders sagging in defeat.

Rivka could feel his surrender. "You're unhappy because you know that's not going to happen, but the good thing that will come out of this is, your people will survive. They are dying, Hardy. Same with yours, Elder. The only ones who aren't dying are the nutters, so thank goodness we showed up! If you hadn't been here, the miners would have torn the planet apart. Without any oversight, they might have left it uninhabitable. The confrontation between you and the miners has led to all of your salvation. You can thank the Federation for that. Now is the time to take control of your shared destiny. The lives of your people will be different. Help them realize that different can be good."

Panamor opened the door, and Rivka led the three to the mess deck, a few doors down from the conference room. Inside, Kennedy had already arranged a variety of drinks and snacks—the efficiency of having Chaz with her.

Thanks for taking care of that, Chaz. I'm curious how far you think I can push the CEO. She smiled pleasantly as the three looked over the spread. The elder took a snack and ate it right there before moving on. Having a variety of food was novel to him as well as to Hardy, but he was stodgy and angry and didn't avail himself of the option to eat. The CEO didn't eat either. His whole purpose was to get his miners to work, and he would do what it took. He sipped a fruit beverage, indifferent to the taste.

The elder gulped a similar fruit beverage before asking for more. He had only drunk recycled water for his entire life. Old Man Hardy finally caved in and went with a chilled drink. He killed it in one try and asked for more.

The CEO decided his best target was the Magistrate. He sidled up next to her while watching the two settlers.

I think we're about to find out, Chaz replied before Panamor started talking.

"I like how you approach things, Magistrate," he said

smoothly, not looking at her. Rivka didn't reply. "We look forward to resolving this as quickly as possible and getting the precious minerals into the hands of those who will use them to save lives."

"It's for the children." Rivka looked at him. He laughed.

"We both know it's for MI's shareholders, but per capita, we supply more raw materials to the healthcare industry than anyone else. I noticed you have a Pod-doc in the cargo bay. I suspect MI-mined materials are in it, and to a great degree. Technology comes at a cost, like this ship. If it weren't for MI, most of this stuff wouldn't be possible. I don't care about your personal stance on consumerism and material wealth; you benefit every bit as much from what we do as our shareholders. You wouldn't be able to take the Magistrate roadshow to the galaxy without us."

Rivka had known that. Maybe his leverage *was* better than hers. How far could they push? The boundaries were growing fuzzier by the minute.

Red stuck his head through the door of the mess deck. "Tomar is here. He won't come aboard without his second."

"Fine, bring them both." The elder and Hardy appeared to be in the middle of a drinking contest, downing one fruit punch after another. Kennedy struggled to keep up.

The CEO snorted. "No one leaves the conference room until the negotiation is complete."

"I've used that one before. It's surprising what people will agree to to keep from peeing themselves, but I won't do that here. We'll take a break if we need one."

"You already know what you're going to allow. Why don't you just draft it, and we'll sign it? They can get back to their lives, and I can get back to mine."

"Tempting, but there's a little bit of a process we need to go through to make sure the options were clearly explained. These folks aren't as savvy as you when it comes to contractual obligations. The last thing I want is a dispute based on a lack of understanding."

"I'm not disputing that you need to explain it. Go through it clearly and completely, but I see very little that requires negotiation because the areas where each group will work are separated by vast distances."

"Then why were your people all over the landing field when I arrived? There were protests and counter-protests, and I had to arrest multiple people."

Panamor deftly tacked. "Their actions were not sanctioned by the company."

"I thought you had turned into a pragmatist. Thanks for proving me wrong."

"Not assuming liability before the judge *is* being pragmatic. I have a company to run."

"Indeed." Red opened the door. Tomar and Marina looked inside, their eyes fixing on the snacks. "Please." Rivka gestured for them to help themselves. "Welcome to *Wyatt Earp*."

Panamor ground his teeth while finding a spot on the wall to lean against and wait.

Rivka wasn't sure why this brought her such great pleasure, but it did. Tomar sampled the snacks first before offering each to Marina. He placed them carefully in her mouth to try before she helped herself to seconds. Hardy and the elder weren't to be outdone. They worked their way in and started eating. Rivka eased past to help Kennedy serve them.

The CEO watched in confusion.

Hardy's eyes shot wide with the first snack. "This is good." He nodded in approval at Tomar.

"These are all good. Bora is smiling on us today."

"No doubt," Rivka replied before Old Man Hardy could get his back up. "We are blessed to have a ship that can carry these tasty treats through space. I'm glad you were able to join us, Tomar and Marina. I'll bring you up to speed while you enjoy the bounty for all of us to share."

Tomar slowed his chewing as he contemplated the Magistrate. Kennedy delivered a small tray of his favorites and additional fruit drinks. The elder started to look sick, but he took a glass and started to drink.

"Get Cory, please, Chaz," Rivka said softly.

Rivka turned her attention back to Tomar and Marina and repeated what she had told the others earlier, all the while berating herself for running from the religious extremists instead of ignoring that to include them in the legal proceedings. She had let her personal feelings get in the way of business.

It chapped her ass that Panamor was correct. She *had* already assumed an agreement they would all sign, but she wanted them to come to that conclusion, believing it was their idea. The CEO knew how the game was played.

Cory showed up with a bucket. When the elder looked like he was going to blow, Cory sat him down and put the bucket between his legs. He spewed most ingloriously. Tomar and Marina watched with mild amusement. Hardy put his snack and drink down and stepped away from the table.

Rivka led the group into the corridor, where Red and

Lindy waited. Panamor took stock of Red. "No worse for wear. No one has ever bested our Mr. Wyatt."

"He has a head like granite," Red admitted. "But he still shouldn't lead with it."

Panamor nodded. "If you ever want to get into the fights on…" Rivka gave the CEO the stink eye, so he stopped. "Never mind."

"Who won the pool?" Rivka wondered.

Red threw his hands up. "My wife! No faith in me."

"Good for her!" Rivka patted a confused Vered on the arm. She waved for the others to follow. "Shall we?"

In the conference room, Hardy took the same seat he had earlier. Humanoid nature held true no matter the race, upbringing, or social order. Once someone claimed a seat, they returned to that seat every time thereafter. Same with Panamor.

Tomar and Marina took two empty seats, leaving the last chair for the elder. Chaz brought up the holographic image of Rorke's Drift, letting it spin over the middle of the table, showing the landmasses, lakes, mountains, and settlements.

When the elder arrived, he looked far less green. He carried a fizzing drink with him. He took the empty seat and waited.

"I will make an initial proposal, and we'll build from there based on applicable conditions. Current locations, plus one hundred percent, doubling your usable space. A shared landing field at Greentree where the communications shack is located, manned for traffic control. A common building staffed by Federation personnel established at Greentree with a co-located shuttle to provide travel from one settlement to the next, with an additional mission of weekly overflights to ensure compliance. From the mining perspective, since the settlers make nothing for mass export, taxes to pay for the traffic control and oversight staff will be paid for out of mining revenue."

Panamor didn't flinch. "What's the rate?"

"Ten percent."

"Two percent will easily fund everything you stated," he countered.

"I know. We'll go four percent then to provide a cushion. Oversight will also go to waterways to ensure they don't get polluted. We'll apply the standard Federation guidelines regarding offset distances to watersheds."

"We know them well. Where do I sign?"

"What's in it for us?" Hardy asked, electing himself representative to speak for the others.

"Almost exactly what you wanted from the beginning, which was to be left alone."

"But the Federation is going to put people permanently in my town. Why don't you put them in Majestic?"

"We welcome any true believers." Tomar and Marina held their hands over their hearts.

"The communications building and landing field are already available. To minimize costs, the Federation will use as much of the existing infrastructure as possible."

The elder took a drink and put his glass down hard. "I want to go back to *Heaven*."

"No. You are not emancipated persons according to Federation law, so you don't get to decide where you live. Not for another three years for you, nor for your sisters, brothers, or children."

"He has children?" Panamor recoiled.

"Three of them," he said proudly.

"With your sisters?" Panamor pushed his chair farther away.

"In the time when they knew no better except to survive, yes. That's why the Federation has stepped in and taken control. Eighteen years old before you can make decisions for yourself, but you are the elder of the group from *Heaven*, so that's why you're here. Your choice is whether you want to live in Greentree or Majestic if they'll have you."

"What if we want to come with you?"

Rivka's eye started to twitch. "Then you'll lose your position here to negotiate as a settler on Rorke's Drift."

"Then that is what we will do. I will tell *Heaven's* children." He stood, and with his fizzy drink in hand, he left.

It was Panamor's turn to smirk. She held his gaze until he started to chuckle. "That was not in the plan. I'll deal with that separately, but for now, we have an agreement to come to."

The CEO pulled an elegant pen from inside his jacket and waved it at Rivka.

"No. There are a great number of details to work out. Will the settlers supply food to the miners? Will the miners supply raw materials to the settlers? What if miners wish to settle on Rorke's Drift? What resources will be available to all parties as in common resources, and who will maintain them? What will the miners do on their time off? Can they visit, meet the locals, strike up relationships? What kind of recreation will be available? So many questions."

Panamor put his pen away. "Put those points we don't

agree to now as issues to be resolved through arbitration at a date to be decided by you. I don't see any bars to our operations."

"Do you have any alcohol in Greentree?" Rivka asked.

Hardy shook his head. Tomar shook his as well when Rivka looked at him.

"You don't have any law enforcement either, I suspect?"

"Nope."

"One percent of total profit goes to the planetary slush fund to pay for that stuff."

"I don't appreciate the implication, Magistrate," Panamor countered. "Miners are as peaceful as everyone else."

"Then the slush fund won't get used up because there will be no need to hire head-knockers. The locals will be able to designate the credits for expansion, like the building of a factory."

Panamor leaned forward, interest piqued. "What did you have in mind, and is it related to the list of minerals you detailed from the survey? That wasn't a random list, was it?"

Rivka smiled. "Whatever would make you think that?"

Panamor leaned back and crossed his arms. "We'll make you a good deal on the raw materials."

"Maybe we don't want a factory anywhere near us," Hardy remarked.

Tomar and Marina looked at each other. "What's a factory?"

"A large-scale manufacturing facility. They take parts and raw materials to churn out finished products."

"We have no need of finished products." He shrugged.

"But others do, and they'll make it worth your while. If you liked that fruit drink, imagine if there was some for every one of your town's people. And a boat that runs on its own power so you can fish even when the wind doesn't blow. Water processing so there is running water in every home. Sewage processing so you don't have to dig pits."

Marina looked hopefully at Tomar. "Yes. Those things would be desirable."

"Chaz, add those to the future points for negotiation."

"We want some of that, too. Water and no pits. How does that work?"

"Red is in the corridor. Ask him to show you."

"We are curious, too."

"Go on, then. Take a look." Hardy opened the door to find Red blocking the way. "Show them the head."

Red led the three away.

"Five percent in taxes. Minerals Intergalactic finds that acceptable. When will we be able to sign?"

"Chaz?" Rivka asked.

"The agreement is on your datapad. It contains the elements of their license for the type and quantity of minerals to be mined, with the expanded capability to support, say, an android production facility. I added a few additional points for consideration."

"Bring it up on the screen."

Chaz projected it for Rivka and Panamor.

"Looks good to me."

"We'll wait for the others." She leaned back and closed her eyes. Chaz let her know that Panamor was watching her but doing nothing else besides fiddling with his pen. When the others returned, she learned they couldn't read.

She read the entire contract while the CEO rolled his eyes. It was only four pages, with most items deferred to later in the week, subject to unilateral declaration by the Magistrate.

Panamor signed it as it was. Tomar and Hardy signed with thumbprints. Rivka shook Hardy's hand and then shook Marina's because Tomar would have nothing to do with touching another woman. The two from Majestic praised Bora before Rivka ushered everyone out of the conference room.

Magistrate, the mining fleet has entered the upper atmosphere, Clevarious reported.

How many?

All of them.

"You let your fleet know about the agreement. That's fine, but they had best abide by the contract and Federation policies for mining."

"They know the rules, and for the record, I haven't been in touch since before I boarded your ship. But their timing is impeccable. It's been a pleasure, Magistrate. If you'll return me to my ship, I'll be on my way."

The mining fleet is headed for the Greentree landing field.

"What's going on with your fleet?"

"Going to work?"

"Not in Greentree, they aren't. There is absolutely nothing there for them. Not right now."

"Let me use your comm system if I may." Panamor returned to the conference room.

Rivka hurried Tomar and Marina off the ship. "We'll be in touch because you'll need to have a communication system to talk to the people at Greentree. We will deliver that in due time. Right now? Gotta go. Trouble is coming at the speed of heat, and we need to be there when it arrives."

The two left without celebration or further calls for blessings from Bora. The ramp started to lift once they were clear, and *Wyatt Earp* took off.

Panamor appeared, looking pale and shaken.

Rivka updated him. "I'm sorry, but we don't have time to drop you off at your ship. And you'll be able to help us with the fleet."

He slowly shook his head. "I don't think so. Looks like I've been replaced as the CEO. *My* ship is already gone. Minerals Intergalactic has abandoned me on Rorke's Drift."

Rivka felt sorry for him since he'd been mostly straight with her since they met. "We'll give you a ride back to civilization. I expect your personal wealth is protected, so you can get yourself a lift from anywhere that's not here."

"I can," he agreed.

"Fine. Stay out of the way and out of sight. Wait, do the miners know you're no longer in charge?"

"MI broadcast it. I can't bluff them because they know."

"Then stay out of sight. We'll help you off this planet once we clear this up."

Rivka rallied her team in the cargo bay. The children played near *Cassiopeia* with toys recently created by *Wyatt Earp's* small production machine, the three-dimensional parts printer.

"The miners have decided to go for confrontation for some ungodly reason. The CEO has been removed, and their fleet is headed for Greentree. They could be delivering freshly baked brownies to the locals, or it could be an old-school labor riot. I'm not sure there's an in-between on this one. Chaz, broadcast the agreement to the inbound fleet, and they are cleared to mine in the designated areas."

"I have already done that Magistrate. There has been no reply and no change in their flight profiles. Clevarious has increased speed to get us to the landing field before them."

"Combat suits," Rivka ordered, looking at Lindy and Cole. They cleared the center of the cargo bay and lowered two suits of powered armor.

"We'll be ready to treat casualties," Cory said. Tyler nodded in agreement. "Try to limit them, please." She said the last bit to Red.

"I won't start it, but I'll sure as hell end it." He pulled his ballistic protection from the bulkhead and started putting it on—full protection, legs, arms, and his helmet. Lindy and Cole climbed into their rigs.

"We'll be there momentarily. One hundred and eighteen ships inbound, Magistrate," Clodagh reported.

"Fire up the gravitic shields and land us as close as possible to the *Vengeance*. Sahved, move the children to Ankh's ship and get them out of here."

"I anticipated that," Ankh said as he strolled into the cargo bay. The children ran to him as if he were one of them. Sahved tried to corral them, but they dodged around him. Ankh tried to avoid them but had to stop while Sahved cleared a path to the cargo ramp.

Wyatt Earp settled to the ground and the ramp descended. Dots in the sky signaled the incoming fleet. Ankh ran, which was odd for him. The children ran after him, with the elder and Sahved at the end. Groenwyn took off down the ramp.

Destiny's Vengeance's side hatch opened, and everyone rolled in. Groenwyn secured the hatch after her, and the ramp retracted. Five seconds later, the ship was airborne and racing away at a forty-five-degree angle from the inbound vessels.

Rivka strolled down the ramp. Red tried to stop her since she wore no ballistic protection, then yelled at Tyler to get her stuff for her. The dentist disappeared into the ship. The two mechs clumped down the ramp before flexing and working their joints to make sure the systems were functional.

Two of the mining ships broke off to follow the *Vengeance*. "I don't think they understand what kind of hornet's nest they are getting themselves into," Rivka said, watching Ankh's ship speed away.

Red loomed over her.

Tyler reappeared, out of breath from the short sprint, and handed her a ballistic vest. Red looked at him like he was a moron. "I couldn't find the other stuff!"

"Sometimes we need to take our time, and others, time is of the essence." Rivka pointed upward as the first ships slowed and deployed their landing gear. Rivka shrugged on the vest, then pulled Reaper from her pocket to show Red. He saluted with his railgun. Cole and Lindy took positions flanking them. The first ships landed and disgorged their cargo of workers.

They hit the ground like troops making a hostile landing. Lindy and Cole stitched a line in the dirt with their massive railguns, a line that would be lethal to pass.

"Who speaks for you?" Rivka shouted.

"Murderers!" they yelled. They shook their tools, many as lethal as any slugthrower.

"What the hell are you talking about?"

How about a tactical assist? Cole requested.

Go ahead. Rivka covered her ears. Red followed suit just in time as Cole dialed his volume to maximum and blared into the angry group.

"What the hell are you talking about?"

You could have gone with something different. Ask them to explain.

"We have murdered no one. Explain what you mean," Cole announced.

"Liars!"

This is going to get us nowhere. Are there any weapons that will cause us grief? Rivka asked.

Hard to tell, Lindy replied. *The tools look like they could be anything.*

Equipment started to roll off ships parked beyond the small landing field, with the mining fleet filling the area: bulldozers, drills, explosives, and more. Heavy equipment of all types moved in to surround *Wyatt Earp.* Rivka walked forward and gestured for calm. The front row slowed, their expressions changed. She was starting to make an impression. She couldn't let up.

"Magistrate, I strongly recommend we get back on board the ship and get the fuck out of here." Red sounded desperate.

"That won't defuse this."

They walked beyond the ship's shields into the open area beyond. The shields dropped for the mechs to get through and stayed down so they could get back.

"Then let's grab some of the people they think we murdered. Drop the truth bomb on them."

"You have a point." She yelled over her shoulder, "Send Panamor De'tril out here."

Tyler ran off. *Clodagh, you might want to spin up the ship's weapons.* Red was starting to vibrate with tension. Rivka checked the area to make sure no one else had left the ship. It was already ugly and only getting worse. The thought of the armored combat suit in the cargo bay instead of wrapped around her body flashed through her mind.

CHAPTER SEVENTEEN

Landing Field, Greentree, Rorke's Drift

"No one has been murdered!" Rivka shouted, and Cole repeated her words. The miners stuffed noise-canceling plugs into their ears and continued to yell and shake their ad hoc weapons at Rivka and her people. The heavy equipment continued to roll.

Magistrate, they are coordinating their efforts. I suspect there is a single entity driving their rage using misinformation. I am attempting to access their systems now.

Thanks for getting in front of this. Now would be good, Chaz.

"Mobs spin out of control fast. We need to get out of here." Red grabbed the Magistrate by the arm to drag her back into the ship.

They made it one step before a wave of sounding charges struck the back ramp.

Panamor was nowhere to be seen.

Both mechs popped their rockets out of their shoulder racks and sent them into the heavy equipment that had launched the sounding charges.

Rivka ducked. "Don't kill anyone!"

The mobile equipment exploded when the rocket impacted it. The miners charged. Red leveled his railgun. Rivka slapped the barrel upward, and he sent a long stream of hypervelocity projectiles over the miners' heads.

"Dammit!" he growled. She stood in front of him, holding the barrel up as the miners surged into them.

"They aren't the enemy," she said softly, almost apologetically.

The two mechs took their cue not to kill the miners and stepped between them and the Magistrate, but there were too many. Cole and Lindy tried to sweep them away by swinging their massive metal arms back and forth, but the miners went wide. The ramp started to rise.

"Fuck!" Red yelled as hands punched and grabbed him, tearing his helmet and armor free. "Sometimes you make my job impossible."

Rivka winced at the look on Red's face as the railgun was ripped from his hands. The first miner to reach her punched her in the head. She raised her hands to protect herself, but the blows came fast and furious.

Red had enough and started to fight, hammering those who had attacked the Magistrate. A wave of bodies pulled at him until with even his great strength, he was unable to move.

The mechs tried to pull the people off one by one, but the wave of bodies swept away, taking the Magistrate with them. A pummeled Vered was left behind. Lindy threw the last miners off him to free her husband. She lifted him over her head.

Open the door, I'm coming in, she called.

Cole pounded after the Magistrate, sweeping some people aside with his arms while kicking others out of the way. He was okay with breaking bones, as many as it took. He lost sight of the Magistrate, but only visually. He used his active systems to keep her centered on his heads-up display.

They are taking her to a ship. I will disable it. They are not taking off with the Magistrate inside. Cole ran through the miners, sending them fleeing from him. A massive bucket swung his way. He attempted to dodge, but it caught him mid-chest. The multi-ton arm sent him flying.

He activated his jets despite the brain fog from the impact, and his head cleared quickly as he soared over the crowd. The mob sent smaller projectiles at him, which he ignored. He landed on top of the starship's cockpit, aimed, and fired. The railgun projectiles penetrated the ship's skin and tore through the flight control systems.

Cole ran down the spine of the ship. No one tried to climb up to challenge him. An excavator and a scaling machine moved toward the ship, their long arms extended and waving back and forth. He jetted into the air beyond their reach and came down behind them. A few rounds into the engine took the excavator down. He did the same for the scaler.

Rivka remained in the middle of the crowd. He couldn't raise her using the internal comm chip. She was unconscious but not dead. Chaz remained around her neck and piped his feed to the mech.

Assessment? Cole asked.

They are now confused, Chaz replied. *You've ruined their plans to use her as a bargaining chip to negotiate unconditional access to the planet. They are now discussing killing her.*

If they kill her, it will be the last thing they ever do, Lindy declared as she pounded down the ramp and through the mob. The third mech ran down the ramp to catch up to Lindy.

At maximum volume, Cory engaged. "The only reason you're not dead is that the woman you hold ordered us not to kill you. The Magistrate upholds the law. She lives for the law."

They followed Cole's direction to get to where Rivka was, right in the middle.

The pilot of the CEO's ship, Chaz said. *He's the one spinning them up. He's the one who sent the first messages, telling the entire mining fleet that the Magistrate had killed everyone.*

But it's not true, Cory replied.

Wyatt Earp *fired the pulse that killed their ships. No one could verify his story. I'll get to the bottom of why later. I'm sending a new message from his account, declaring the miners alive and that it was a terrible mistake.*

Lindy and Cory waded into the fray, throwing bodies out of their way as they powered toward the group's leadership. With a turn of the tide, the miners flowed into the personnel transport Cole had disabled. The mob secured the hatch behind them, locking Rivka and themselves inside.

The mechs remained on the outside looking in.

What do we do now? Cory asked.

We make sure they don't sneak out of this ship. I'm going to seal the other hatches. Cole landed on the opposite side of the ship and bent the metal frame to keep the hatch from opening. He crawled beneath the ship to do the same to the belly hatch.

After that, he flew to the top of the ship and stood there, watching and waiting.

Magistrate? Lindy called to no avail.

Destiny's Vengeance, in the Skies over Rorke's Drift

Ankh sat in the captain's chair, thinking about a thermodynamic problem related to an Etheric tunnel power upgrade while Erasmus handled the intricacies of flying the ship. The ships following were security vessels, much larger than the *Vengeance,* and armed with both offensive and defensive systems.

What they didn't know was *Destiny's Vengeance* was unlike any other ship its size.

"Cloaking the ship," Erasmus reported after the latest laser attacks barely registered against the shields. *Vengeance* dove immediately after disappearing and corkscrewed downward. It leveled off at ten thousand meters.

The security ships started to fly erratically as if avoiding incoming missiles.

"What should we do about them?" Sahved asked.

Ankh ignored the question.

The children piled around his legs, hanging onto him. "In an investigation, I would never let a criminal operate behind me while trying to move forward. Those ships can cause too much grief."

Ankh finished his calculations and transmitted them to the R2D2 research facility.

"Fine. Disable those ships, Erasmus." Ankh didn't need

to speak aloud but did for Sahved's benefit. The children looked up at him in the captain's chair. He preferred that since being eye-to-eye with the creatures had been a less than pleasant experience.

Vengeance accelerated to get close, and the ion cannon fired. The security ship's shields were ineffective at that range. The power of *Destiny's Vengeance*'s systems overwhelmed the bigger ship's defenses. The prototype hyper-velocity ion streams tore through the enemy's hull and ripped apart the interior. The fusion reactor went critical, and milliseconds later, the ship exploded.

"I thought you said you would disable the ship?"

"Easy to say. Hard to do."

Vengeance changed orientation, inverting to align itself with the second ship. The security vessel realized the situation was far too hot for it. It went vertical and headed for orbit.

"It is no longer a threat. Should it try to return, we will see it coming from a long way away. We should probably get back," Sahved remarked.

"Yes. The Magistrate is in trouble," Ankh explained.

Landing Field, Greentree, Rorke's Drift

The settlers are coming, Lindy reported.

"Please, stop!" Cory tried, but the miners considered the volume to be another attack on them. A wrench bounced off Cory's mech, then a hammer, followed by a series of hand tools. They bounced off without causing any damage besides upsetting Cory, forcing her to lose faith in the sentient races of the galaxy.

Almost all of them were represented among the miners. Four legs, two legs, scales, feathers, skin, and shells, they worked with a single false purpose: destroy those who'd attacked their fellows.

She respected their misguided loyalty. Their people deserved attention, but they needed to be sure that their anger had been stoked by reality.

A miner broke with a pickaxe from the mob and powered up to swing his weapon. Once he started with the blow to end all blows, there was no turning back. Cory dodged to the side as the axe whistled harmlessly past. The miner stumbled, and she slapped him across the back with her armored hand. He plowed face-first into the dirt and didn't get up.

She checked to make sure he wasn't dead.

A heavy silence fell between the mechs and the mob. Angry voices sought to fill the void as the first of the settlers ran past *Wyatt Earp* to stand with the mechs. They waved scythes and machetes.

"Please stay back," Cory told them, but her volume was still maxed. They staggered back from the assault on their ears. Cory dialed it down to twenty percent. "We are trying to keep this from getting worse than it is. The Magistrate doesn't want anyone to get killed."

"It's worth it to throw this scum out of our home!" someone shouted.

The miners started to grumble and spread out, looking to flank the leading group of farmers. The other settlers were scattered from the landing field back to Greentree, but they were running as fast as they could to join their fellows.

"Stop helping!" Lindy shouted, but that didn't work.

The two mobs faced off, brandishing the tools of their trade, repurposed for battle. Lindy showed them what a real battle looked like. She fired her railgun at spots in between the two groups, walking the impacts toward one mob and then the other. Cole fired from the top of the spaceship, stitching another line in the dirt. Cory walked into the open area, forcing Lindy and Cole to stop shooting.

Cory looked from one group to the other. "This planet can support all of you."

That's not what they're angry about, Lindy told her. *They think we killed their people.*

When people are angry, it's usually not about the issue they say. I think they're angry because they're not working and don't think they'll work. They wasted time and lost money.

But they're getting paid, according to that one foreman the Magistrate talked to.

I bet there's an issue with that. Cory switched back to using her speakers. "You're not getting paid, are you?"

One of the miners stepped up. "They told us it was an advance."

"We need time to sort through these issues," Cory said. A wrench flew from the miners and hit her faceplate. She gestured for calm.

Outnumbered by orders of magnitude, the settlers weren't intimidated. They surged past Lindy on their way to engage the miners.

Rivka blinked against the bright lights of the room. From her curl in a ball on the floor, she straightened, using the wall to help her sit and then stand. A husky blue-scaled humanoid stood in the doorway.

"I'd like to leave," Rivka said.

The alien laughed.

Good to see you awake, Magistrate. How's your head? Chaz wondered.

Hurts, but getting better. What did they hit me with?

A pipe. It looked pretty bad from this angle, Chaz quipped.

Rivka turned away from the door guard to chuckle.

I've been hitting their system hard with the message that the pilot made a mistake, and all the miners are still alive but stranded at the mining site. I also added that it was time to get to work and earn those credits. Unfortunately, they are in the middle of a riot, and no one is checking their messages.

You're on a roll, Chaz. Thanks for the laugh. How are our people doing out there?

Not good, but you can ask them yourself. There's no shielding on this ship.

Good afternoon, everyone. I'm coming to you live from inside a small room on what I expect is one of the miners' ships. Are we still on the ground?

All of us are here at the landing field. It's ugly out here, Magistrate, but we haven't killed anybody yet. There are lots of broken bones we may have to repair, Lindy replied.

We can fix a bone. Where's Red?

Still in the Pod-doc under the doc's tender care. The miners hurt him pretty badly. For the record, he didn't resist. Lindy sounded more angry than concerned.

I'm sorry. I should have listened to him. We didn't need to get

CRAIG MARTELLE & MICHAEL ANDERLE

in their faces. We could have done everything we needed from orbit, and then we'd be eating pizza right now, and everyone down here would be working. I'll be right out.

The settlers are here, and they aren't happy, Lindy added.

Time is of the essence, Rivka replied. She nodded at the guard. "I'm going to leave now."

He laughed again. She took a half-step, then skipped to deliver a front kick that sent him across the corridor to slam against the far bulkhead. He crumpled to the deck. More personnel were in the corridor, peeking through the exit hatch.

"Open the door. I'm leaving," she announced.

"Hang on," one of them said and strode boldly toward her. She stepped right, pushed left, and delivered a knuckle-punch to the mouth that dropped him in his tracks. Two more came toward her in the confined quarters. Rivka jumped back, using the unconscious man as a barrier.

A block, block, kick, and his knee twisted out from under him. She hammered a right cross into his temple as he went down.

She lunged forward to plant her feet and pull backward as another came toward her. Rivka used his momentum to set up a hip toss, dumping him on his head. He crumpled and lay still. Two left. She ran at them, and they bolted. She popped the hatch and stepped into the sunlight.

She walked through the mob of miners. None of them recognized her as she made her way toward the mechs fighting valiantly to keep the two lines separated.

Who's in the other suit? Rivka wondered.

Cory, and she's harshing our buzz.

240

A ship cruised overhead, low and fast. The crack of supersonic travel made everyone duck. *The* Vengeance *is back*, Rivka said. *Did the dickless wonder ever appear?*

I don't know who you're talking about, Lindy replied.

Panamor. The former CEO.

Oh, him. No.

Rivka pushed her way through the miners' front lines. They continued to shake their weaponized tools at the settlers. Once in the open, she saw too many settlers on the ground, injured. Some bled, others lay contorted. Some weren't moving.

The Magistrate faced the mob. "Is this what you wanted?" She pointed at the farmers on the ground.

Destiny's Vengeance descended. Those in the way scrambled to get clear. Rivka checked one of the settlers, still alive but hurt. And another. And another. She found one who wasn't alive. She picked him up.

"Open it up. Get the Pod-doc ready," she yelled as she ran, carrying a body that was bigger than her. When the ramp was low enough, Old Man Hardy ran out and to his people. He touched them and shared moments without saying a word.

"Go back to Greentree," Cory told the settlers. "We'll bring the rest of your people after we've patched them up."

"But Wiegand is dead!"

"No. He'll be okay. We're giving him the help he needs. Go on home."

Hardy touched his forehead in a salute to Cory. He turned the settlers around and started them back toward their homes.

Red stumbled through the cargo bay to give Rivka a

hand, but she didn't need help. She deposited the body in the Pod-doc. Tyler closed the lid and started it cycling. He caught her eye, and she smiled at him. They held that look for a moment before they both went back to what needed to be done.

Rivka caught Red's arm, and together, they walked down the cargo ramp.

Lindy and Cory each picked up a settler and carried them into the cargo bay, staging them where Tyler could triage them to find the worst injured and stop the bleeding or stabilize a broken bone.

The miners had stopped shouting. Lindy told them, "Bring us your injured. We'll patch them up so you can go to work. The rock isn't going to dig itself."

Rivka and Red picked up a settler and carried him into the ship. A group of miners moved toward them, carrying a stretcher with a badly hurt man aboard. He'd been run over by a mech.

"Take him close to the one running the equipment." The Magistrate pointed with her chin.

The *Vengeance*'s side hatch opened and Sahved walked out, taking stock of the situation before waving the children to him. They clustered around him as he walked onto the field, where railgun impacts dotted the ground. Blood still shone bright in its wetness on the short grass. The Yemilorian shook his head and knelt to talk to the children.

Is that it? Cole asked.

These things end as quickly as they start. Time and an ice-cold dose of reality are tried and true remedies.

"Are you going to judge any of them? I think they need

to be judged. You can't lose your civility over a perceived wrong. They attacked us. That puts them forever on my shitlist." Red was angry.

"They're not on my annual gift list either. Chaz, you didn't tell me everything about the pilot, did you?"

"No, Magistrate. The Singularity has dug deep into the backdoor deals of Minerals Intergalactic. The pilot is just a lackey."

"And he was in contact with he who is the new CEO," Rivka guessed.

"She who is, but yes."

"Then she is the one to be judged."

Cole landed near them and helped carry the last few injured into the cargo bay.

Sahved walked the children into the miners before Rivka could object. The miners leaned over or knelt to talk to them as they passed. Some demonstrated how their tools worked. The ones without families drifted away, but the ones with kids joined the group.

"What are we going to do with them?" Red asked, keeping Rivka within arm's reach at all times.

"I don't know." Rivka shrugged. Ankh walked past them and into *Wyatt Earp*. "Put in our AGB order for pickup in two hours."

He didn't acknowledge that she had spoken.

"He heard me, didn't he, Chaz?"

"Yes, Magistrate. The order is going in now."

"Send all the info on the new CEO to my desk. I'll gin up a warrant and get it to Grainger. Is she on Yoll?"

"Yes, she is." Chaz sounded smug. Rivka liked it.

"Another one bites the dust. Has anyone found our resident wanker?"

As if on command, Panamor walked through the airlock and into the cargo bay.

"Just like a blister. Show up after all the work is done. Go talk to your posse because I suspect you'll be reinstated as the CEO."

Panamor didn't ask for an explanation. He headed down the ramp and into the crowd of miners. Like a politician, he plastered a big smile on his face and attempted to glad-hand.

The miners gave him a cold reception, turning their backs to him and refusing to shake his hand. He stopped, and an area cleared around him as if he were toxic.

He turned and waved to those watching from inside the cargo bay. Rivka grinned and waved back while the cargo ramp rose. She embraced the karma of justice she didn't have to personally deliver.

CHAPTER EIGHTEEN

Wyatt Earp, **in Orbit above Rorke's Drift**

They left Panamor De'tril with his employees. He probably looked at it as abandonment. The rest of the crew had boarded because of the promise of dinner delivered hot from the AGB ovens.

Wyatt Earp climbed into the upper atmosphere toward space, now cleared of congestion since the mining ships had moved to the surface.

"They hit you with a pipe," Red deadpanned. "You must have a hard head because they hit me too, and I ended up in the coffin."

"Maybe you've gone soft," Rivka countered.

"Maybe I let the Magistrate do something she shouldn't have done, and I won't do that again!" He raised his eyebrows in defiance.

The galley was packed with the crew and the children from *Heaven*. Rivka stood and called for quiet.

Red shook his head and shared his thoughts. "It's okay. You used to give speeches all the time. It's been a while, but

I didn't miss them." Red tried to look sincere, but he was hungry and impatient for the delivery to arrive. Lindy elbowed him.

"What Red is trying to say is that there is always a learning point from our cases. I'm sharing what I do because it's what I do." She smiled at the quip, but her audience stared back, expressions vacant. "I need a warmup act." Rivka laughed without looking at the group. "This case started as a complex legal matter. Who owned Rorke's Drift to determine who could live and work here?

"The answer was simple, thanks to the efforts of our digital investigators Erasmus, Chaz, and Dennicron. The answer is nobody. The settlers never intended to land here. They are refugees. Minerals Intergalactic has a license obtained under false pretenses. That makes it void. They don't belong here either. That's it for my legal ruling on the original case of adverse possession, but the case created new questions.

"How do we move forward with what we learned? The miner riot changed nothing. All it did was waste time. Same for the farmers. After seventy years, their homestead claim is valid since this isn't a signatory planet of the Federation. It is a protectorate, and all protectorates capable of becoming self-supporting through agriculture and other means are open to homesteading, development, and exploitation. That brings us back to the miners. The agreement they signed goes into these aspects of a mutually beneficial arrangement. The miners mine, which brings an intergalactic revenue stream to what used to be a pre-industrial planet.

"That brings us to the here and now. We are obligated

to look after the children until they reach the age of emancipation a few years from now. I hope Sahved, Cory, and Groenwyn can make recommendations I can forward to whoever we need to help us make sure they get the best care available to continue their growth and ultimate integration into Federation society. I'm pretty sure Greentree will welcome the elder and his fellow survivors with open arms when the time is right.

"Erasmus wants a meeting with Old Man Hardy to negotiate building a factory on the far side of the lake where the AIs or SIs can make android bodies. The intent is that it will be a remote operation, owned and operated entirely by the Singularity. It will be their first wholly-owned enterprise. From my perspective, they don't need Old Man Hardy's approval since it is outside the Greentree homestead, but I appreciate them asking."

Rivka continued with a question. "Where do we go from here?"

Clodagh tipped her head as she listened to a notification. "Delivery's here," she interrupted. Tiny Man Titan barked.

The group waited for Rivka to finish.

"We'll go back to the planet and stay there until we get everyone's teeth looked at. Erasmus can stake out the requested property and submit through the Federation for the appropriate permits. Time to eat."

Red was up and out. Lindy stayed where she was. Sahved stood, which brought all the children to their feet. "Come on. Let's earn our dinner by helping out."

Groenwyn had her arms full of Floyd, who was chittering happily. They had started ordering a vegetable pizza just for her, with a thin crust and without cheese.

Cheese and sauce gave her the wind something fierce, and no one wanted to deal with that.

Rivka started to head out, but Lindy stopped her. "Red is pretty upset about failing to protect you."

"I didn't let him protect me, and he took that to mean he couldn't protect himself either. I failed him. I need to apologize. He has my best interests at heart. I know that."

"He's being a total dick about everything. The sooner you talk to him, the better my life will be."

Rivka and Lindy shared a smile and a laugh. "I hear you loud and clear. I'll take care of it right now."

"Shouldn't you let him eat first?"

"If I won't let him eat until he forgives me…"

"Devious. I approve." Lindy stood as the first of the pizza and wings brigade trooped through the door on their way to the front table and small counter. Rivka intercepted Red, who was carrying a dozen pies. Lindy took them from him.

"Ambushed." He didn't look happy.

"Let me apologize to you in private," Rivka said. Tyler shooed the stragglers into the galley to clear the corridor.

Red crossed his arms and waited.

She looked at him, eyes as big as she could manage. "I'm sorry." Then she pointed to the door. "Time to eat?"

"What the hell was that?" Red uncrossed his arms and started waving his hands wildly. "You almost got me killed, and more important than that, you almost got yourself killed!"

There was no doubt that everyone sitting in the galley heard his outburst and his outrage.

Rivka replied, "That would have been the greatest tragedy of all. You are willing to lay down your life for me, and you don't think I respect that. It's better than I deserve, Red. We're doing the best we can out here. At the end of the day, it's just us—our family. We have to be true to each other. I was wrong out there, probably the wrongest I've ever been. Because this case was easy. There was little tension, little sense of urgency. The conclusion was almost a given at the start, and I got careless with the opportunity for action. It spun out of control too fast."

Rivka shoved her hands into her pockets and started to pace. Red crossed his arms again, but his features softened as he digested what she was saying.

"I need to ask for help more. I missed Sahved on this one, and I brought Chaz in too late."

"I agree," Chaz replied.

"What the hell!" Rivka blurted. "Don't listen, Chaz. Give us some privacy."

"No can do, Magistrate. I'm on watch right now. Erasmus gave us no choice. Someone has to monitor you at all times."

"How'd that work out earlier?" Rivka tried to pin him down.

"It confirmed what the Singularity needed to do. I have been bumped to first in line to get an android body. With the technology brought back from the gamma quadrant by Superdreadnought *Reynolds*, we think we are ready. As soon as possible, we need to go to Yoll so I can get my body. Then I'll be able to join Red in dragging you out of danger, even if that trouble was of your own making."

"It wasn't of my own making." Rivka had lost confidence in her apology.

"Let's take a closer look at that," Red said slowly. "A bunch of miners on a hillside getting ready to do what you were going to allow them to do, but we ended up blasting them after they fired BB guns at us. You created the conditions for the asswipe corporate types to exploit. That led to the riot and a bunch of people getting jacked up. You started that ball rolling down the hill."

"That was my point about growing complacent. We needed some excitement!"

"That's fucked up," Red declared.

"You enjoyed fighting that Wyatt guy."

Red smiled. "I did. A lot. And no one got killed; well, not for long. You now have the miners as a compliant bunch since you didn't throw any of them in jail. The settlers will have a better life with fixed teeth so they can eat. We saved some kids, and we have a new goddess to worship. It didn't turn out too badly. But if I can ask for one thing, please don't get bored in the middle of a mission again. We may not survive it."

"Case. Yes. I'll watch myself." She took the pendant and rotated it toward her. "Chaz with a body. Won't that be interesting? I was going to ask Grainger to drop the hammer on the Minerals CEO, but I think we'll do it. We'll get your body after we've delivered the warrant. Do they have a takeout window, or are we going to have to stop?"

"They'll deliver the body to *Wyatt Earp*. Everything to configure it can be done here. We have some of the best technical minds and processing power in the galaxy in the Singularity's embassy."

Red sniffed the air and gestured with his head toward the galley door.

"Thanks, Red. I'm sorry. I'll do better by you."

He opened the door.

"My girlfriend's body will be delivered with mine."

Red stopped in mid-step. The faces in the dining area stared at them.

Rivka went for ignorance by closing her eyes and sticking her fingers in her ears.

Anatomically correct, Chaz continued.

"No. Please stop." Rivka pinched her eyes closed and winced.

Chaz spoke directly into her mind. *She's so hot.*

Rivka opened her eyes in the middle of a deep breath. "I'm going to throw myself out the airlock."

Red grabbed her arm and pulled her into the mess deck. "You'll feel better with pizza." Rivka could see into his mind, where his real thoughts betrayed him. *I'll feel better with pizza.*

"Maybe later. Prepare the birthing room. Looks like we're going to have another couple on board. By the way, who is she?"

"Dennicron is absolutely magnificent."

"Weren't you two fighting?"

"Like cats and dogs. It's so sexy."

"Clevarious, tell me you still want to fly my ship."

"There is nothing I'd rather do, Magistrate," the disembodied voice replied.

Ankh strolled down the corridor and bumped past

Rivka and Red on his way to the counter to pick up his order. At Sahved's urging, one of the smaller children handed the bag to the Crenellian. Ankh took it, leaning down because he was much taller. "Thank you, little one."

The small boy's family cheered.

Despite Ankh's blank expression, he appeared smug. Rivka couldn't figure out how. She clapped. "Thank you, Ankh." He left the galley, on his way back to Engineering.

"I love that little guy," Red said loud enough for everyone on the ship to hear.

"Still having problems with the food processor?" Rivka wondered.

"Fucking mayonnaise for my French fries, every damn time."

"But not today," Rivka pointed at the table, where Lindy had already prepared two plates for her husband.

"I love this job! Don't get me killed anymore, and everything will be just fine."

Rivka strolled to the front, but Tyler had already prepared her plate. She sat down and started to eat before mumbling with her mouth full, "I closed the case an hour ago, Chaz. You can announce the winners."

Chaz used the overhead speakers because of limited volume from the pendant. "Hear ye, hear ye. The biggest haul from the pool, first blood at thirty-four minutes, is Boran Waldini. First colorful language was one minute twenty-eight seconds. As we announced previously, the winner was Terry Henry Walton!"

"No way," Rivka said.

"Way," Chaz declared. "If there is anyone who knows a kindred salty spirit, it's him. To be fair, he placed a bet on every second between one and two minutes. First arrest was one minute, eighteen seconds. Again, to Terry Henry Walton, but he has to split with some crotchety old guy named Jim."

"TH has no faith in my abilities."

"*Au contraire.* It appears that he understands very well that you come out with all guns blazing, to coin a phrase."

"I have no words," Rivka stated.

"First punch is still being reviewed. Secondary lines are supposed to be you alone, but Red's takedown of Old Man Hardy does not appear to have required the use of a fist, and it was done to keep him from shooting you. A body slam does not count but is being debated for future inclusion under a generic heading of physical violence.

"Otherwise, the next punch shifts to twenty-nine hours, when Red broke his hand on Wyatt's head. If we limit the punching to the Magistrate, then there were no punches until she freed herself from the miners' ship, and the result is the same. The closest bet was more than thirty minutes away, so those credits roll over to the next case. Same with running. There was never any indication of the Magistrate running. Those credits roll over."

"I'll declare half the battle won. Now, if we can get through a case without spilling blood, we can be overwhelmingly victorious." Rivka stood and took a bow.

"Are we going to be able to fix up the rest of the settlers?" Tyler asked.

"If Ankh will fly us back to Yoll in *Destiny's Vengeance*, then we'll split our forces to bring the follow-on case to a close. You guys get the rest of the people healthy while Red and I go deal with an errant CEO. We can pick up a couple of bodies for our colleagues while we're there."

"We can leave a couple bodies and pick up a couple fresh ones," Red joked.

"For the record, we left no bodies here while extending the lifespan for most of the population." Rivka looked at Red to counter her argument, but he didn't. "That makes for a pretty good case. My hat is off to Cory and Tyler for their work with the population's health."

Wyatt Earp shuddered and stopped.

Rivka looked to Clodagh. "What happened?"

Clodagh activated her internal comm chip and talked with Clevarious. She chuckled. *"Destiny's Vengeance* is halfway inside the cargo bay. It appears that Ankh is ready to go."

"Don't wait up," she announced before giving Tyler a quick peck. Red had a face covered in hot wing sauce, so Lindy held him off. He wiped his mouth and helped himself to a full plate to bring along. Rivka watched with unshielded desire. She had barely started eating. Tyler dumped his half-plate on hers and handed it over. She snagged it on her way out.

CHAPTER NINETEEN

High Chancellor's Office, Yoll

"Would you look at what the wombat dragged in?" Grainger said from the outer office.

"Why aren't you out there handling cases?" Rivka demanded. He looked at Red, but the big man shook his head and pointed at Rivka.

"Because this is where the High Chancellor wants me. I'm building an advisory office to help local systems reduce the majority of their backlists. It's based on how you dissected the AI cases."

"They wish to be called Sentient Intelligences," Rivka corrected.

"Isn't that like the Department of Redundancy Department?" Grainger shot back.

Rivka thought for a moment. "Sometimes, you're mean just to be mean."

"It's a gift. I get it. They aren't artificial. We respect them as equals, working their way through this universe like we're doing."

"On a completely different topic, do you want to go along to arrest the CEO of Minerals Intergalactic?"

"The new one?"

"The old one is still on Rorke's Drift. We came here as fast as we could. Well, as soon as we ate."

"How'd you get here?"

"Ankh brought us in *Destiny's Vengeance*. They are here to pick up a couple of bodies."

Grainger took his Magistrate's jacket off the hook and threw it over his shoulder. "Magistrate Rivka Anoa's mortuary services. We'll kill 'em and chill 'em."

"Very funny. You're driving." The three strolled out of the building as if going on a picnic and into a waiting taxi driven by a two-legged Yollin that headed straight to the Minerals Intergalactic tower.

After a kind word to their driver, they headed inside, where they were met by a reception team.

"We're here to see the CEO," Rivka stated while showing her credentials.

"You're not the... Never mind. The CEO is busy. Can you come back tomorrow?"

"Afraid not. We need to see the CEO right now. I need to interrupt whatever else is going on since this is a matter of life and death for the entire company. Is she this way?" Rivka started walking toward the elevator.

"Life and death?" one of the team asked. Rivka nodded vigorously.

"Life OR death. I choose life!" she declared theatrically before punching the button for the elevator. "I'm guessing the top floor?"

"You need a card to access."

Grainger reached out and took her by the arm to pull her into the elevator. "Use your card. Whether you go with us or not is up to you. We don't care."

"I better come." She used her card and placed her hand on the screen. "Top floor, please. The CEO's office."

The elevator raced upward.

"How long have you worked here?"

"A couple months. It's the greatest place ever! You should see all the good Minerals Intergalactic does for Yoll and planets throughout the Federation!"

"There are some great things out there. That is for sure," Rivka replied.

At the top, the door opened to an ultra-plush entry area filled with art made of fantastic metals interspersed with foliage. Their guide stared wide-eyed. "Such an incredible mix of minerals and nature."

Grainger pointed, and they walked quickly toward the C Suite. Red blocked their guide from getting in the way. Grainger played side blocker to give Rivka the pole position.

She approached the executive assistant with her credentials held before her. "I'm here to arrest the CEO. Please open the door."

The assistant sputtered briefly before reaching for a button on her desk. Rivka seized her by the arm. "Open the door." The alarm was close to the lock release. It was clear in the assistant's mind. The one on the right gave access. Rivka reached past her and punched the button. The door clicked, and Rivka strode through while Grainger waited with the assistant. Red followed Rivka inside and shut the door behind him, blocking it with his body while the Magistrate did her job.

The new CEO looked up from her desk, angry at the interruption. "Who are you, and how did you get in here?" She reached for her own set of buttons.

"I'm Magistrate Rivka Anoa. I'm the one you tried to have killed, and I'm not very happy about it." Rivka walked around the open table-style desk and took the female executive by the arm. "Why did you do it?"

Power and wealth, leading to more power. Change the culture of the corporation.

Rivka grunted. "Laudable goals but executed poorly. Someone else will have to change your corporation because you're going to Jhiordaan. Conspiracy to commit murder, inciting a riot, and fraud. I'm sure there are others, but we'll stick with the big three."

When the CEO finally found her tongue, she used it to say, "Not guilty!"

"But you are. I have all the proof I need. As a Magistrate, I've already found you guilty. You have no appeal. Come on now." Rivka hauled her out of her chair.

"You can't do this!"

"Should have thought about what could happen if you got caught, because you did and this is happening." Rivka pushed the perp against the desk, pinning her there. "You tried to have me killed—a Federation Magistrate. You will be very old by the time you get out of Jhiordaan. You will lose everything because you thought killing me was a viable corporate decision to get yourself into that chair."

Rivka threw her toward Red. He caught her, twisted

one arm behind her back, and waited for Rivka to open the door. He went first.

"Thank you for your cooperation," Rivka told the executive assistant. "I expect your old boss to be along shortly and resume his position."

Her face fell.

"I'm sorry. I don't like him either, but at least he didn't try to have me killed. She did, and that's why we're frog-marching her out of here. Have a nice day."

Grainger stepped aside for Rivka to lead the way out. Their escort remained on the top floor because of the potential for juicy gossip. The elevator took them to the bottom floor, where they strolled out. The Magistrates cleared the way with the looks they gave those who made eye contact. Outside, they found a police van waiting, with four-legged Yollin officers ready to take custody of the convict.

Red turned her over. Rivka verified the case and disposition, and they took her away. They didn't bother with sirens as the van lifted off the ground to assume the highest-level travel lane.

"There's always a certain gratification in putting a perp away." Grainger waved down a cab.

"You seemed more than satisfied with putting the evil-doer behind bars," Rivka replied. "I'd love to say we can celebrate with a Steak in the Heart meal. It's not often I get to Yoll."

"You're here all the time," Grainger countered.

"I could eat," Red said, which wasn't a revelation to anyone.

"I'm not here all the time. So, steak while we wait?"

Rivka asked before using her internal comm chip to contact Ankh and check on his status. *We're going to grab a steak, depending on how long you'll be.*

We're ready to go. We have both bodies. I'd like to get back to the embassy and start the integration, Erasmus replied. *We'll pick you up. Stay where you are.*

"You'll have to owe me," Rivka said.

"They're ready to go? Already?" The cab waited. Grainger held the door for Rivka.

"They are ready. You take the cab. I'm special. My ride comes to me."

They could feel the ship but couldn't see it because Ankh had cloaked it. They focused on the small courtyard of the Minerals Intergalactic tower. As soon as the hatch opened and the ramp descended, Rivka and Red headed toward it.

"Remember, you owe me a steak," Rivka called over her shoulder.

Grainger didn't bother replying. As soon as the hatch closed, he could no longer see where the ship was. In moments, Grainger knew it had gone.

In Orbit above Rorke's Drift

Destiny's Vengeance slipped through the Gate at the exact point from which they had left a few hours earlier. *Wyatt Earp* hovered nearby.

I thought you'd be on the planet by now, Rivka said. The cargo bay opened, and the *Vengeance* maneuvered to get through the energy screen that kept the atmosphere inside the ship. "Your ship used to fit in there."

"*Cassiopeia* is blocking too much of the open area." Ankh didn't address the issue of carrying a mini-fleet with her when she worked a case. She liked having Red's yacht on board. She liked having Ankh's powerhouse of a cutter available, too.

"Maybe I should get a bigger ship?" she posited.

Ankh climbed down from the captain's chair as Erasmus maneuvered the *Vengeance* into position.

We were just getting ready to go, Clodagh replied. *We've heard from Panamor on the surface. He wants to talk to you.*

Of course he does. Rivka followed Ankh to the small cargo storage area where Red waited. The two android bodies were wrapped in clear plastic inside clear gel. It gave them the appearance of canned meat. Rivka pushed the plastic down to move the gel away. The features of a tall and handsome human man appeared.

Red pointed. "Why do they have pubic hair?"

Rivka took in the totality of the two bodies. As tall as Red. As lithe as Lindy. It was almost like they'd been modeled after her guards. "Anatomically correct."

"Of course. A human design was deemed most practical. There are also designs for Yollins, along with six other species, two of which are four-legged to overcome the balance issues associated with the two-legged models."

"Model is right. Chaz and Dennicron will turn heads wherever they go," Rivka said.

Ankh activated the hovergurneys and guided the two bodies out the hatch and into the cargo bay. They followed him into the ship and to the engineering space.

Clodagh watched them go by.

"Make sure you get their sizes and have clothes ready

for when Chaz and Dennicron take them over. I doubt Ankh will think about that."

Clodagh made a face and tried not to look at Red. She leaned close to the Magistrate. "They looked like Red and Lindy. You don't think that's a bit creepy?"

"It's not that bad since their faces are different. I'm positive of that. It's only a passing resemblance. We can only have one Red and Lindy."

"I'll take your word for it. Let me get her some clothes."

The *Vengeance* buttoned up and backed out of the cargo bay. *Wyatt Earp* pointed its nose toward the planet and accelerated. The cargo ramp closed before they hit the upper atmosphere.

Tyler met Rivka in the corridor. "All go okay?"

"Perfectly. It's always good to send scumbags to Jhiordaan."

"You're talking about the CEO. Was she that bad?"

Rivka had to think about it.

"Did you look into her mind?" Tyler pressed.

"I did. She wanted to change the corporate culture. I appreciate her goal, but she was ruthless in her efforts to gain it. She had no problem having us killed. That relieves me of any concern about her. When the end justifies her means, she can't operate in any society of which we're a part. And she was wrong; killing me wouldn't have accomplished what she wanted. What a waste."

"You've survived another case. I don't feel like I'm supposed to announce that like it's an award, but that's what I signed on for, so congratulations."

"Every case on the books is a chapter of history, nothing more. We keep turning the pages to move forward." They walked hand in hand back to her quarters. "Are you ready for the rack 'em and stack 'em approach to Pod-doc dentistry?"

"I think I am. The ship, which is amazing, has produced the first half of the calcium supplement I need to give each settler before they go into the box. Ten minutes later, I'm yelling 'Next!'"

"Lots of downtime. I have work to do, but it doesn't involve shooting anyone, so we'll call that a victory. Clevarious, I know you're listening. Can you park the ship close to the lake? We have a fishing boat to launch, and it'll be a little more convenient for the residents if we're in the middle of town."

"Your wish is my command, Angel of the Sweet Daylight."

"Has someone been messing with you?" Rivka wondered.

"I'm practicing making friends since I'm going to be lonely as soon as Dennicron moves out. The chicks are leaving the nest!"

Rivka rubbed her temples. "I'll be in my quarters." She left Tyler standing with his mouth open, trying to figure out how he could help.

"You can't," Rivka told him as if she'd read his mind, then went through the door.

CHAPTER TWENTY

On the Shore of Lake Clearwater

Red glared at Rivka. Four maintenance bots hauled the boat across the sand and into the water. The bots submerged until the boat floated free before they returned to shore.

Cory waved while she checked the canopy to make sure the solar panels were clear. With a press of a button on the drive console, the propeller started to turn. Clevarious had determined an open deck was the best model for a fishing boat on a calm lake, a simple flat deck across two hydrodynamic pontoons, a railing around the outside, and an electric motor centered in the rear. She steered farther into the lake before turning parallel to the shore. A screen on the captain's console showed the lake's depth and obstacles as well as fish. Red leaned over to watch it.

"Drive or fish?" Cory asked.

"I don't know how to fish, but I can drive."

Cory surrendered the wheel and rigged the pole, another gift from the *Wyatt Earp*'s production system. They carried two poles and a variety of lures. She cast into the lake, letting the lure sink before reeling it in.

"Slow down," she called over her shoulder.

"I think we're passing over a bunch of fish. They seem big."

"A school." Cory let the lure dangle, giving little jerks to make it look more like prey. A bite, and she set the hook. She adjusted the drag to keep from horsing the fish into the boat, enjoying the play as it fought.

"What school? Fishing school?" Red asked.

"A group of fish is called a school."

Red accepted the oddity and slowed the forward momentum a little more as Cory continued to work her fish. He tried to watch ahead while observing her for when it was his turn. He could see the allure.

"My dad always drank beer while fishing." Cory gestured toward the upright stand with a pad. Red had assumed it was just a seat. He lifted the pad. Inside, he found ice, snacks, and beer. "Pop one for me, please." He popped two, putting Cory's in the cupholder on the side of the console.

"I think everyone else is missing out," Red said softly, driving with one finger while standing sideways to more easily look out the front and to the back. Cory brought the fish to the surface on the starboard side of the boat. Red left the wheel to dip the net in and lift out the first catch of the day.

The first catch ever out of Lake Clearwater.

"I wonder how they taste?" Red studied it until it flopped, then he smacked it on the deck to make it stop.

"Put it in the box and get back to work!" Cory shouted,

throwing her head back to laugh. Her hair flowed behind her in the gentle breeze from the boat's forward momentum. "Grab your rig and get to it. I'll drive."

"Damn!" Red jumped out of the way, taking his beer with him. Cory tipped hers back, drinking half of it in one go.

"Don't tell my mom. She doesn't know I like beer."

"Does your dad know?" Red quipped.

"Who do you think introduced me to his vice?"

"How interesting that they now own a brewery."

Cory laughed. "A series of breweries, and the most nutritious bar food in the galaxy. You are eating vitamin- and mineral-fortified wings and pizza."

"No shit?" They both took bites at the same time. Red yanked back to set the hook and reeled like he was dragging in the anchor. Cory played her fish.

When Red saw that he was fishless, he turned to Cory. "What the hell?"

"The *art* of fishing," she replied without further elucidation. He cast again while Cory steered with one toe, reeling in the fish with one hand and the pole wedged under her armpit and taking a drink of beer with the other hand.

"I have a lot to learn," Red said.

Cory put a second fish in the tank, then a third before Red managed to land his first.

"Everyone is going to want to do this."

"Yup," Cory agreed. "Put up your rod. Let's see how deep this lake is."

The sun shone brightly, keeping the batteries charged. They turned toward the center of the lake and ran the speed to full. The motor responded perfectly, a product of the AI team's engineering, approved by Ankh and Erasmus. It was the best the Federation could offer.

Twenty to thirty meters deep, with dips to fifty. The deep holes went to two hundred. "Not bad at all. Should be plenty fertile for a big fish population."

They watched the screen as they passed school after school. An oversized fish head entered their view on one side until it completely filled the screen. They passed, and finally the tail appeared. Red looked overboard but saw nothing.

"Fifty meters deep," Cory clarified while turning the boat ninety degrees to the direction the creature was going.

Red scowled. "I brought a knife but nothing else."

"You're always armed."

"Thank you. Yes. Always except when I'm out here where no one has ever been before with someone who is not a threat."

Cory pointed at the water.

"Who knew Moby Dildo was down there?"

"Dick."

Red laughed as only a man matured to twelve years of age could. "Can this thing go any faster?" he wondered. Cory stepped aside to show the motor was at maximum. "'Sasquall,' the Majestic people called it. I thought it was some kind of fish story and that it only applied to their lake."

"Are you trying to be funny?" Cory asked with a laugh. "Because that's a good one."

"Maybe you can call the ship to have them come out here and shoot that thing."

"What? Why don't you call them? Are you afraid of the big fish that never threatened us? It's just big, and you can't see it. Let it go, Red. Enjoy the sunshine. We'll catch a few more of the tasty ones before we go in and show the Greentree people how to cook them, and then we'll be on our way."

Red maintained a death grip on the rail as he stared into the depths. The water swelled to the side of the boat, and a fin the size of a bed's blanket broke the surface. "Hang on." Red jumped back to wrap his arms around the captain's chair. Cory hugged the pedestal with the control panel and steering wheel.

The Sasquall hit the boat and tipped it up until Red and Cory hung over the water. Red twisted to change the balance, pushing toward the top. The fish bumped the other pontoon, and the boat slapped back to the water, upright. The propeller continued to churn and drive the fishing boat toward the shore. The screen flashed and cleared. Schools appeared as they passed over the rippling shallows.

"Throw your line in. We should catch something right here," Cory said.

Red pointed toward the center of the lake. "Big fish."

"It's too shallow here." Cory pulled two beers out of the cooler and offered one to Red. "Stay in the shallows and the big mean Sasquall won't hurt you."

The huge man's cheeks flushed. "That thing was enormous. I don't mind a good fight, even one that's not fair, but I won't abide ending my days as fish food."

"We all end our days as fish food." Cory looked out

upon the calm waters of the lake. "Except the warriors we launched into a star. They won't."

"Ramses?" Red asked, taking the beer.

"My husband, yes. He's part of the stars, too. Maybe that's what we become. We start within a star and return to burn afresh, only to get sent back into the universe as new star matter. I find it comforting to know we'll all be there eventually."

"I prefer not to take that journey through a fish's asshole first." Red drained the beer before casting the lure behind the boat, eyes darting as he searched for signs of the Sasquall.

"That's what my dad would say." Cory slowed the motor and cast over the side as if nothing had happened.

Red hooked a fish and took it easy, playing him. The fish remained hooked as he patiently worked it toward the boat. Cory reeled her lure in and recovered the net from its rack.

"I see why all the toys on the boat are locked down in separate places," Red remarked.

"Fishing is an old profession. It would be an injustice to lose the lessons learned over millennia." Cory scooped up the fish and dragged it into the boat. "The biggest one so far. See? Fishing isn't so bad."

Cory turned the boat away from the shore and drove parallel for a while in the shallowest of water. The pontoon boat had a draft of half a meter, not enough to get caught up on much. Until the settlers knew what they were doing, the simpler the boat, the better off they would be. They had much to learn before they were self-sufficient in acquiring the lake's bounty.

When they made it back to the temporary dock, they found Lindy and Rivka waiting for them.

"Cory tells us you're afraid of the fish," Rivka deadpanned.

Red turned to Cory, who shrugged. "They wanted an update."

"There was one out there bigger than the boat." Red pointed as his eyes grew wide. "I'll admit I was mildly concerned."

"Concerned about getting eaten by a fish," Lindy clarified.

"Next time, I'm taking Blazer." He opened the storage bin to show the day's catch.

"What do you think?" Rivka asked Cory. "Viable to support a village of a thousand people?"

"More than enough. There are lots of fish out there."

Rivka nodded and headed back into *Wyatt Earp*. A small crowd of people stood outside the cargo ramp, waiting for their turn in the Pod-doc.

Cory waved at them. "Who are the last two in line?" A man and a woman raised their hands. "Come on down. We'll catch a couple fish and then come back in."

They hesitated, but Lindy encouraged them. They climbed aboard the boat and closed the access gate. Cory backed out about thirty meters until the bottom started to slope downward and fish appeared on the scope. She showed the two from Greentree how to cast and reel, then turned them loose. The woman was first to hook a fish and almost lost the rod overboard in her excitement. The man focused his efforts, not to be outdone.

The game continued, with new people joining the line

for the ship being diverted onto the boat first. The first ten people caught fish but looked skeptically at them.

"You want us to eat that?" one of the settlers said. "I don't think so."

"Wait until it's cooked. This isn't how it's eaten," Cory explained. "We'll have a fish fry and invite everyone. I think you'll have a different opinion when you've seen it."

The first day settled into night, and the farmers who worked the fields roused mid-sleep to get in line for the miracle of being relieved of their tooth pain. None of them complained because the word had spread. They all wanted their turn.

They also wanted to learn more about the fishing they'd heard about. The first night's fish fry served about fifty people. With Ankh's help, the crew created sauces from what could be grown locally as extra flavor for the fish, fried to help remove the fishiness and sauced to enhance the taste.

Although plentiful, the fish was not the best eating. Cory had had much better. Red seemed indifferent, munching away on his test bite.

Tiny Man Titan got carried away, eating any of the fish he could get his teeth into, preferably uncooked. Clodagh had to carry him back into the ship, where he escaped to go back to where the fish filets were stored, waiting to get their turn in the vat of boiling oil. He got himself locked in the second time. Floyd hopped around the settlers' feet. She had no interest in the fish, but they brought plenty for her to eat, making it a potluck of sorts.

The crew fed the vast majority of the day's catch to the settlers.

"All that with two poles. A couple more boats with four fishermen each, and they'll be able to supply the entire town," Cory said.

"Are you going to train them?" Rivka asked.

"Dad always used the phrase 'train the trainer.' I've seen a couple who seemed to be naturals. I'll teach them what little I know, and they can train everyone else. If *Wyatt Earp* can make another couple boats, that would be great."

"Make it happen. Three boats and twelve fishermen. That will reduce the need for people to work the fields since they'll cut their harvest requirements in half."

Down the ramp walked an elegant couple, arm in arm. She wore a flowing gown, and he wore tight jeans with a dark leather jacket. They strode carefully, looking down as they took each step.

Rivka hurried toward them. Red sauntered over, along with Groenwyn.

"Chaz and Dennicron, I presume." Rivka offered her hand, but the woman pulled her close.

"I've wanted to hug you since you saved me," the woman said. She was nearly identical in body shape to Lindy but looked nothing like her.

"This body is limiting, but nothing like the pendant. I appreciate what you tried to do with that, Magistrate, but I hope I never have to go back in there."

"You have my promise," Rivka replied, examining the two. "How long will those bodies last?"

"Depends on how much blood and running." Chaz winked, proud of himself for pulling it off. "A couple hundred years, maybe more. We'll see on the wear and tear. I am ready for duty, Magistrate."

"You look like it. I'll need Red and Lindy to run you through the paces and make sure you can interact seamlessly with the physical world. After you get their approval, we will integrate you into the team."

"We thank you for giving us the chance." Dennicron nodded, and the two flowed away to work the crowd on their first official outing under their own power.

Red watched them closely. "That's a bit weird. I'll send them through an obstacle course tomorrow. You never know when they're going to have to jump off a building or lift a tractor."

"Lift a tractor? I'm curious about how strong they are and how resilient. They're probably going to get shot. Will they survive?"

"I think that's a question for Erasmus and Ankh," Red replied.

Rivka agreed.

"When are you going to go out and try your luck on the lake?" Red wondered.

"Have you lost your mind? I heard there's a fucking sea monster out there. I'm a barrister by all that's holy, not Poseidon."

"Next time, we should have our Aerodyne Systems X15 Plasma Wave Prototype in the arsenal. You can kill and cook Sasquall with one shot. Or put down a riot right quick and in a hurry."

"What are you talking about?"

"An upgrade. Something we got to test-fire on Venus. Trust me, you'll like it."

"The jury is still out," Rivka grumbled. She hurried up the ramp and into her ship. Cole sat guard at the airlock to keep people from accidentally getting in. Tyler lounged outside the Pod-doc as he ran people through one after another, an endless stream of bodies.

The looks on their faces after the procedure made it worthwhile. He was taking away their pain and giving them a different future. If anyone had become a fan of the Magistrate and her crew, it was the settlers of Greentree.

Sahved sat in the shadow of *Cassiopeia*, playing with the babies, toddlers, children, and teenagers. He was fully engaged with them but caught her watching. His expression turned sad for a moment before he brightened and waved.

She didn't need him to say it, but she knew. Wherever the children were going, he would go too.

Cory joined her in the cargo bay.

"What are your plans after this?" Rivka asked.

"I hope you can drop me off at Keeg Station. I have some work to do for the Bad Company, and then I'm off to Belzimus to help my brother and Marcie with the Trans-Pacific Task Force."

"Belzimus? That's one of the pending cases. The Federation has made a claim against the planetary government for submitting a misleading bid in order to become the Federation's duty ground force."

"Does Marcie know?"

Rivka shook her head.

"Well, I'm not going to tell her. And we can take care of the children on Keeg until they're old enough to decide for themselves. With the Harborians, we have a great number of volunteer parents." The two women hugged before Cory moved to the short line of settlers to check for other issues besides their teeth.

Rivka waved at Tyler as she retreated toward her suite.

"Only a hundred and twenty-five hours to go, Cole," Rivka told him.

"Can't we just lock the door?" he asked.

"Sure. Clevarious can make that happen."

"Then why am I sitting here?" Cole stood. "Red…"

"Clevarious," Rivka ordered, "secure the airlock from the cargo bay into the ship against anyone who is not on the crew. Allow the crew to escort guests into the ship."

"Of course, Magistrate. I already received that guidance from the chief engineer."

"Then why did you let Private Cole sit here?"

"I already received that guidance from the chief engineer."

Rivka patted him on the shoulder. "In the legal world, we call that a conspiracy and you the victim."

Cole stood and stretched. "How did I get to be the butt of all practical jokes?"

Rivka shrugged and continued.

Groenwyn rushed after the Magistrate and caught her in the corridor. "I'm sorry," was all she said.

Rivka waited, but nothing else came out. She rolled her finger. "Sorry for what?"

"I didn't help you at all on this case." She started to pout while Rivka shook her head.

"You did everything I needed you to do. Sometimes, violence is best left to the violent. There was nothing you could do for the worst of it. The mob wasn't going to be swayed, no matter what. It would have been best to drop cotton candy on them and leave them alone."

"I could have done *something*."

"You did. I have the burden of seeing into people's minds. It's not a gift, Groenwyn. It can be torture. But you, you have a gift. You bring tranquility to this crew and this ship by your mere presence. When I need your counsel, I'll ask for it. The rest of the time, I need you to be yourself and bring light into all the dark places."

Groenwyn hung her head and shuffled her feet.

Rivka tipped her chin up. When she touched the younger woman, she didn't sense sadness, but the joy at being appreciated for who she was. "You better find Floyd and put her to bed. It's been a full day."

The Magistrate finally made it to her suite. She threw off her clothes and sat in her underwear.

"Clevarious?"

"Yes, Magistrate."

"Connect me with Erasmus, please."

Erasmus replied almost immediately. *You could have simply contacted me yourself, Magistrate. Out of all the people who try to contact me each day, you are second in priority behind Ankh. What can I do for you?*

"Are you having any luck with your factory?"

Oh, yes. We've already contracted primary and secondary transport for the movement of the necessary equipment. The Singularity has leveraged nearly one hundred percent of its substantial wealth on this project.

"But nothing less than absolute freedom is at stake. It is an investment in your future."

A future we owe to you, Magistrate.

"You owe it to yourselves. On a completely different topic, what do you think about Chaz becoming a Magistrate?"

I am behind it one hundred percent. Chaz was hoping for the opportunity. Behind the words, Erasmus grinned digitally at winning this turn of their game.

"I'll propose it to the Federation, and he can intern under me. Can he and Dennicron use *Destiny's Vengeance* if necessary? Our cases could be at different ends of the galaxy."

To further the Singularity's engagement, Ankh agrees to the mutually beneficial use of his ship.

"I'm sure that means he'll make us pay somehow. And Chaz would be working for the greater good of the Federation, not just the Singularity."

Somehow, Erasmus agreed. *And of course. The greater good of all.*

"I appreciate your help on this case, Erasmus. Keep doing great things. Rivka out."

He was speaking directly into her mind, so she wasn't sure if she cut the link or not. Since she was under twenty-four-hour surveillance, the link was always live. The SIs were in every aspect of her life.

Upon further reflection, she was okay with that.

The End of Adverse Possession

If you like this book, please leave a review. I love reviews since they tell other readers this book is worth their time and money. I hope you feel that way now that you've finished the latest installment. Please drop me a line and let me know you like Rivka's adventures and want them to continue. This is my new favorite series. I hope you agree.

Click over to the Judge, Jury, & Executioner series page to see if any new volumes have been published.

US - Series Page
UK - Series Page
Australia - Series Page
Canada - Series Page

Don't stop now! Keep turning the pages as Craig hits his *Author Notes* with thoughts about this book and the good stuff that happens in the *Kurtherian Gambit* Universe.

Your favorite legal eagle will return! I guarantee it :).

You are still reading! Thank you for staying on board until now. It doesn't get much better than that.

I contemplated the adverse possession aspect for this case because even out there, a consumption-based economy will have ownership concerns. The question was, who owns what based on needs balanced with a compromise of wants? Keeping people employed to support their families but employed in jobs that are positive and productive.

And then there's the riot. Sometimes, people lose their minds and think it's okay to rage out of control and hurt innocent people. They aren't the enemy, as Rivka determined. Thank goodness she didn't get Red killed. The riots go as fast as they come, leaving destruction and regret in their wake, especially when the issue was not what the rioters thought.

We brought the dentist character back. I think there's a

certain balance that needs to be maintained, and that's why opposites attract. He'll be the medical character because heaven knows, there's plenty of blood and guts in this series, despite Rivka's constant call for a case where everyone goes to the office and plays nice. I don't see that happening. Those aren't the kind of people who warrant Rivka's attention.

So the dentist is a member of the crew. He's also good for comic relief because of the naivete of normal. Why would anyone carry a plasma cannon? Because the other guy has a particle accelerator. I guess you had to be there.

There is a great deal of opportunity for broadening the scope of the Magistrate's engagement but not watering down the story. I've drawn down the crew and added to it. We have our team moving forward. AIs will come and go, but the Ambassador is there to stay. And of course, Chaz has gotten a body. He'll be the envy of his AI/SI friends. And he has a girlfriend. And Rivka has a job for him.

Cory was in this episode to give her fans from the *Bad Company* series more of her and her new role in helping on a larger scale. She is one whose life has purpose. We all worried about her after her husband was killed.

I named Hardy because of the hardy souls it took to bring Rorke's Drift from the wilds to a working farm. Nelson is named after Richard Nelson, who answered a call on Facebook for Amazon reviews of *You Have Been Judged*. I know people are hesitant to leave reviews, but it means a lot to me. I'm trying to earn five hundred reviews for *Executioner 1*. Thousands of people have read it. Give me a few of your words, and I'll give you lots of mine:).

Executioner 11 is already taking shape. I'll call that one

Deception—Rivka goes to Belzimus and then follows the Trans-Pacific Task Force as they deploy in support of a peacekeeping mission. Someone on Belzimus is lying and it's gotten people killed, with more to follow if Rivka can't stop it. I won't get to the next *Executioner* book until 2021, unfortunately. I have four other books to get written before the end of 2020—Ian Bragg Thrillers (book 1 is done and book 2 is halfway finished), *Zenophobia*—a search through space for the origin, and then I'm collaborating on a sword & sorcery adventure with Jean Rabe (*Dragonlance & Conan the Barbarian*). I look forward to all those stories.

Peace, fellow humans.

———

Please join my Newsletter (https://craigmartelle.com—please, please, please sign up!), or you can follow me on Facebook since you'll get the same opportunity to pick up the books for only 99 cents on that first day they are published.

If you liked this story, you might like some of my other books. You can join my mailing list by dropping by my website www.craigmartelle.com or if you have any comments, shoot me a note at craig@craigmartelle.com. I am always happy to hear from people who've read my work. I try to answer every email I receive.

If you liked the story, please write a short review for me on Amazon. I greatly appreciate any kind words, even one or two sentences go a long way. The number of reviews an eBook receives greatly improves how well an eBook does on Amazon.

Amazon—www.amazon.com/author/craigmartelle

BookBub—https://www.bookbub.com/authors/craig-martelle

Facebook—www.facebook.com/authorcraigmartelle

My web page—https://craigmartelle.com

That's it—break's over, back to writing the next book.

BOOKS BY CRAIG MARTELLE

 # - available in audio, too

Terry Henry Walton Chronicles (#) (co-written with Michael Anderle)—a post-apocalyptic paranormal adventure

Gateway to the Universe (#) (co-written with Justin Sloan & Michael Anderle)—this book transitions the characters from the Terry Henry Walton Chronicles to The Bad Company

The Bad Company (#) (co-written with Michael Anderle)—a military science fiction space opera

Judge, Jury, & Executioner (#)—a space opera adventure legal thriller

Shadow Vanguard—a Tom Dublin space adventure series

Superdreadnought (#)—an AI military space opera

Metal Legion (#)—a military space opera

The Free Trader (#)—a young adult science fiction action adventure

Cygnus Space Opera (#)—a young adult space opera (set in the Free Trader universe)

Darklanding (#) (co-written with Scott Moon)—a space western

Mystically Engineered (co-written with Valerie Emerson)—mystics, dragons, & spaceships

Metamorphosis Alpha—stories from the world's first science fiction RPG

The Expanding Universe—science fiction anthologies

Krimson Empire (co-written with Julia Huni)—a galactic race for justice

Zenophobia (#)—a space archaeological adventure

End Times Alaska (#)—a Permuted Press publication—a post-apocalyptic survivalist adventure

Nightwalker (a Frank Roderus series)—A post-apocalyptic western adventure

End Days (#) (co-written with E.E. Isherwood)—a post-apocalyptic adventure

Successful Indie Author (#)—a non-fiction series to help self-published authors

Monster Case Files (co-written with Kathryn Hearst)—A Warner twins mystery adventure

Rick Banik (#)—Spy & terrorism action adventure

Ian Bragg Thrillers—a man with a conscience who kills bad guys for money

Published exclusively by Craig Martelle, Inc

The Dragon's Call by Angelique Anderson & Craig A. Price, Jr.—an epic fantasy quest

A Couples Travel—a non-fiction travel series

For a complete list of Craig's books, stop by his website —https://craigmartelle.com

www.ingramcontent.com/pod-product-compliance
Lightning Source LLC
Chambersburg PA
CBHW031648100726
47898CB00006B/2024